REBEC

Cicily Isabel Fairfield was born in London in 1892. Her father had come from County Kerry, Ireland, and she acquired her early education in Edinburgh. She adopted her pen name, Rebecca West from the strong-willed character of that name in Ibsen's social drama, Rosmersholm, in which she once acted in her late teens. She began to appear in print as a journalist and political writer in London as early as 1911, in *The Freewoman,* and was soon deeply involved in the causes of feminism and social reform. Some of her early writings (1911-1917) have been collected into one volume, *The Young Rebecca,* published by Macmillan in association with Virago, to be published in paperback in 1983.

Rebecca West's first book, *Henry James,* was published in 1916. Since then she has written novels, criticism, satire, biography, travel and history. Her works of fiction include *The Return of the Soldier* (1918 – now a major British film), *The Judge* (1922), *Harriet Hume: A London Fantasy* (1929), *The Harsh Voice* (1935) – all four published by Virago; *The Thinking Reed* (1936), *The Fountain Overflows* (1956) and *The Birds Fall Down* (1966). Other notable works include her biography of St Augustine (1933), her two-volume magnum opus, *Black Lamb and Grey Falcon* (1937), her study of traitors, *The Meaning of Treason* (1949 – also published by Virago), and her critical work, *The Court and the Castle* (1957).

Her only child, Anthony West (b. 1914), is the son of the novelist H. G. Wells. In 1930 she married Henry Maxwell Andrews, the banker, and began a lifelong companionship at their country house, Ibston, in Buckinghamshire, with visits to London and many travels together, including her journey to Yugoslavia that inspired *Black Lamb and Grey Falcon.* Rebecca West was created a Dame Commander of the British Empire in 1959. After her husband's death in 1968 she returned to London where she now lives.

REBECCA WEST

THE HARSH VOICE

Four Short Novels

*With a New Introduction
by Alexandra Pringle*

TO

GEORGE T. BYE

Published by VIRAGO PRESS Limited 1982
Ely House, 37 Dover Street, London W1X 4HS

First published by Jonathan Cape Ltd 1935

Printed in Great Britain by litho
at the Anchor Press, Tiptree, Essex.

British Library Cataloguing in Publication Data
West, Rebecca
The harsh voice.
I. Title
823′.912[F]   PR6045.E8
ISBN 0-86068-249-8

CONTENTS

Speaks the harsh voice
We hear when money talks, or hate,
Then comes the softest answer.

RICHARD WYNNE ERRINGTON

INTRODUCTION

'THE two chief ills of life . . . are the loss of love or the approach of death;' wrote Rebecca West in 1934, sounding a darker note in her generally lighthearted commentary to Low's illustrations of *The Modern 'Rake's Progress'*. In the next year she published *The Harsh Voice*, a collection of four short novels (or long short stories) which deal, in different ways, with these 'ills', and with the corrupting power of money and hate.

Three of these stories had already appeared in American magazines, the first two in the *Saturday Evening Post* and the third in *Woman's Home Companion*. 'The Abiding Vision' was published for the first time in this collection. Rebecca West's previous works of fiction were *The Return of the Soldier* (1918), *The Judge* (1922) and *Harriet Hume* (1929). They had been exclusively English in their background and flavour. The present stories, set in America and Paris as well as in England, announce that international outlook in Rebecca West's writing that would shape her masterpiece of travel *Black Lamb and Grey Falcon* (1937) and her political thriller *The Birds Fall Down* (1966). Both the short stories and the next novel, *The Thinking Reed* (1936), deal with personal antagonisms in often vulgar milieux. For while her female contemporaries, in particular Virginia Woolf and Dorothy Richardson, were preoccupied with 'inner sensibilities', West was attempting to write about, as she puts it, 'the real world'. She was then in her early forties.

This 'real world' was largely American. West's long association with the United States had begun in 1923, when she travelled around the country on a lecture tour. She subsequently worked for the *Herald Tribune* as a staff writer and spent two months of every year in New York and elsewhere in the States. She did not visit the States between 1928 and 1935 (when she returned soon after the American publication of *The Harsh Voice*) but continued to contribute regularly to American newspapers and journals. At this time she was contemplating a book on America, which she told the journalist S. K. Ratcliffe, 'I've always been hankering to write'. She mentions three pieces which would have been part of this book. Two were published in *Harpers* in 1925, entitled 'These American Men' and 'These American Women', and the third was her introduction to the *Selected Poems of Carl Sandburg* (1926) which so richly evokes the city of Chicago.

The book on America was never written, but we have in *The Harsh Voice* a fictional record of Rebecca West's experience of that country. In a recent article in *New Fiction* she has written 'Fiction and poetry are the only way one can stop time and give an account of an experience and nail it down so that it lasts for ever.' The title of the collection is significant. It comes from a poem by Richard Wynne Errington and its lines,

> 'Speaks the harsh voice
> We hear when money talks, or hate,
> Then comes the softest answer.'

Journalism has always been a drudgery for Rebecca West: 'I needed money . . . so I had to engage in journalism', and although when she wrote these stories she knew she could place them in American magazines, they were written primarily for her own pleasure. They enlarge on the themes of her earlier creative writing. Her view of the world had always been dualistic, concerned with adversaries. She opposed the forces of life to the forces of death, of love to hate, good to bad. In a simple and, as it were, natural manner West's good people, (Margaret in *The Return of the Soldier,* Ellen and her mother in *The Judge,* Harriet in *Harriet*

Hume) are all poor. Poverty and goodness are one. In *The Harsh Voice* Rebecca West examines the world of the rich, the subject also of *The Thinking Reed* in which her exquisite, immensely rich heroine Isabelle remarks 'I am a cad because I am a privileged person, and the two things are bound to be the same.'

But this book is also about hate and wedlock. That hate is not necessarily a result of wealth; it is bred by marriage. In a much earlier story, 'Indissoluble Matrimony' (1914), published in Wyndham Lewis' Vorticist magazine *Blast*, there had been a rehearsal of this theme. A couple are bound together more closely by their hate than by their love; only death can release them. In her 1930 essay, 'Divorce is a Necessity', Rebecca West calls an unsuitable marriage a 'life sentence'. This is the title she uses for her first story in *The Harsh Voice*. When Corrie Dickson, a gentle, unassuming man, marries his fiancée Josephine through the sheer force of her will and against his better judgement, 'in time to his heart-beat' he says to himself 'This is a life sentence, this is a life sentence.'

Corrie is weak, like many of West's male characters: in Josie we see a new kind of American woman. Corrie was drawn to her as a vulnerable little girl. She becomes harder and strident. She finds her capabilities not in the family but in commerce. She cannot be content to be a wife and mother after she had learnt to 'brood over Wall Street lists'. She is then gripped by ambition, though she is calm and relentless in her property developments. She attains social command of Montarac City through deft entrepreneurship. This is the type of new woman that Rebecca West observed in America in the twenties when she was working for the *Herald Tribune*:

> The American woman began to discover herself as an amateur of business. Sitting back on the throne of prosperity her husband had built up for her, she could bide her time and pick her chances, and see her money increase and multiply in a way that seemed the happiest miracle to a sex which had been tied down since the beginning of time to fixed homekeeping allowances.

In her way, Josie is splendid. We admire her tall beauty, her command over life, but we feel no warmth for her and we cannot trust her. With Corrie, we grieve for the shyer, kinder woman she once had been. One of the points of the story is that she has taken on male characteristics. Jill Craigie's observation in an unpublished interview is pertinent. She found that Rebecca West 'in conversation . . . gives the impression that she would prefer men to make good wives rather than women transmute themselves into good male company directors and politicians'.

Rebecca West wrote to Edward Sackville West that these stories were written 'in the depths of gloomy contemplation of the destinies of the inarticulate damned'. Failure of communication is a constant theme. Corrie and Josie's marriage fails because, as Corrie says, 'We can't talk. Nobody but writers knows, how to put things into words, and everybody goes around stuffed up with things they want to say and can't.' The title of the second story reiterates this bleak message, as does the author's plain statement that 'There is no such thing as conversation. It is an illusion. There are intersecting monologues, that is all.' Literary art is put to the description of the misunderstanding and misinterpretation, between two people, two sensibilities and two cultures.

In its concern for art, 'handing round a pearl', as well as in its Parisian and American settings, the story 'There is No Conversation' is reminiscent of Henry James. The French streets and interiors are personally known to West, however, and are not derived from other fiction: they are described with the impressionistic richness of the Paris of her 1928 essay 'The Strange Necessity'. As elegant as any of his settings in the *beau monde* is Etienne de Sevenac, 'fifty and an inveterate beauty', an aristocrat for whom life is a series of amusing games. He was confident of the rules and *manœuvres* of such games before the appearance of a middle-aged, mannish American businesswoman, Nancy Sarle. He feels sorry for her, but his sympathy is trite and egocentric.

Awkward and plain, how can she extract any pleasure from life? Indeed life to her must be 'inconceivably monotonous, spent in servitude, in duties faithfully performed'. In order to give her pleasure and alleviate his own boredom, de Sevenac carries out a little flirtation, then stages jealous quarrels after which he would 'instruct her in the art of reconciliation'. A lover of de Sevenac's type reappears in West's 1936 novel, *The Thinking Reed,* as Isabelle's suitor André de Verviers. Theatrical and scheming, he lives vicariously off false emotions. Rebecca West is perhaps suggesting that only violence and hate can be the true feelings in such as relationship, or in a marriage based on such a relationship. In 'Divorce is a Necessity' she describes this kind of man:

> No one who has not been through it can know the full horror of being tied to a man who craves war instead of peace, whose love is indistinguishable from hate. The day is poisoned from its dawn by petty rages about nothing, by a deliberate destruction of everything pleasant.

In 'There is No Conversation', which is not specifically about marriage, such feelings underly wider concerns. Etienne and Nancy's misconceptions of each other are a result of their cultural differences. She cannot see that he is merely a volupturary, and therefore bored: he cannot see, nor even imagine, that she is strong-minded, manipulative and self-possessed. 'There is No Conversation' ends on a note both mysterious and arid.

The result of the third story, 'The Salt of the Earth' is death. Like Conrad (who, with Henry James, nourished her earlier ambitions in fiction) West uses the thriller form to make a serious moral statement. Again like Conrad, she employs the device of continually building, then destroying, suspense. It was a technique she would later use quite brilliantly in her report of the trial of William Joyce in *The Meaning of Treason* (1949) and in her last novel *The Birds Fall Down.* The present tale finally resolves itself in death because the situation allowed no other resolution to the truthful novelist. When I discussed this story with her recently, Rebecca West pointed out that although American couples would divorce at that time if their marriages were unsuccessful, their English counterparts would not. Divorce was not socially acceptable. In 'Divorce is a Necessity' she wrote, 'I myself can only think of three English friends of mine who have dissolved their marriages. It is different in America'. The totally English setting of the story is part of its theme. So is the unflinching examination of a character so little in contact with those who surround her that she cannot see that she is hateful. If Alice Pemberton had any understanding of herself or had been able to listen to others she might have been saved. But she is blind to her own imperfections, her cruelty to her husband, mother, siblings and servants.

In the final story of this quartet, the destructive power of money is modulated by the softer power of love – Errington's 'softest answer'? Sam Hartley is a self-made man. With his wife Lulah at his side he has fought his way up from Butte, Montana, to Park Avenue, New York. By the time they have attained this commercial zenith they have also reached middle age. Through some unkind trick of corporeal fate, Sam is at his radiant best while Lulah's kind face has become lined and wrinkled, worn out by years of struggle. Sam takes a mistress, a chorus girl named Lily with a past that 'probably included everything but tears'. She treats love as a business proposition. This is what Sam wants, or thinks he wants, for 'sentimentalists get punished'. A shared female perspective on such a situation is of interest. Sam Hartley resembles Robert Grant in Christina Stead's *A Little Tea, A Little Chat (1948)*. Both her subject and West's are successful, dishonest businessmen living in America at a time when riches were there for the taking. Christina Stead and Rebecca West were both married to bankers. This, West feels, gave them a bond, a clear-eyed vision of the world of international affairs and finance. But Sam Hartley is a better man than Robert Grant because he is open to the influence of love. As Lulah fades from Sam's life, Lily gives him a kind of tenderness and support. When Sam fails in the Wall Street

Crash it is Lily who prevents his self-destruction, who gives him new life through her female nurturing powers. 'The Abiding Vision' is Rebecca West's own favourite among these stories because she feels 'this is how it was'. In this case it is a good record that, in its reserved way, it is also the most optimistic of the collection.

Each story in *The Harsh Voice* is highly polished and ingenious with a plot that twists and turns, leading the reader to an ending that is always unexpected, and often shocking. Perhaps finally, however, the stories are most remarkable, and indeed satisfying, for the sheer technical skill of the writing, for the strength of Rebecca West's authorial voice, as H. G. Wells put it, 'the MASTERY of these stories'.

Alexandra Pringle, London 1981

LIFE SENTENCE

ONE evening a year or two before the war, when most people still took it for granted that the overwhelming tragedies of life related to the private affairs of individuals, a very pale young man crossed the lawn of a large house in Montarac City and stopped dead when he came near enough to see that on the porch was standing a young woman who was far from pale. Her glowing colour was one of her chief beauties: that and her stature, which would have been sturdy if she had not been as near goddess size as would have enabled her to hold her own on a pedestal in any art gallery, made her definitely superb. On the score of complexion and height the young man was a worthy match for her. This had been said by everyone from the first. But just at the moment he was so disorganized that he felt miserably at a disadvantage before her mere physical state. There were some vases on the folding table before her, and a heap of roses which she was stripping of their lower leaves and cutting to convenient lengths; and from a certain wildness about her hair, of which she carried an immense amount on the nape of her neck, it could be guessed that she herself had gathered them from the very extensive flower-garden behind the house. She liked being in the open air; she liked altering the look of things with her hands. She was therefore as contented at that moment as any human being could be. Perception of this made the young man paler than ever.

He did not call to her; and he had been standing for some moments at the foot of the steps before she looked over her flowers and saw him. It did not occur to her that there was anything ominous in his silent and rigid presence. Had she been under the necessity of breaking important news, whether good or bad, to any person standing on a porch, she would not have stopped at the foot of the stairs. Therefore she assumed that he was standing there because he loved her and everything that was hers, including her beauty, and had found the sight of her from that angle specially pleasing. This assumption she candidly betrayed in her proud and happy smile.

That fetched out of him a queer little noise; and he walked up to the porch. There he came to a standstill, lounging in front of her table with his hands in his pockets. It was the unbearable continuance of her gay serenity that made him mumble, with a greater embarrassment than he had ever felt in a conversation with a girl since the day he left dancing-class, 'Hello, Josephine, how are you feeling?'

'Pretty good, pretty good,' she murmured, not looking up, continuing to smile, because of coquetry, because of assurance.

He put both his hands to his temples and groaned.

There can have been no human being since the world began less acquainted with trouble than Josephine Houblon at the age of twenty. First her mouth opened quite round with fright, as if she were a very little girl. Then she asked strongly enough, 'What's the matter, honey?' But indeed she was only reproducing the accent in which her coloured mammy used to speak those words when she was a very little girl, so there was nothing so grown-up about that.

He said, 'Josephine, you'll think me just the dirtiest skunk in the whole world, but I can't help it. I've got to tell you. Josie, I can't marry you.'

There was a curious sound. The scissors she held had cut through a rose instead of a stem.

'Corrie, what do you mean?' she breathed.

'Oh, Josie,' he said. 'It isn't that I don't think you're the grandest girl that ever lived. You're just as lovely as you're beautiful, and I know it. But I don't care enough. I don't care. Not in that way. And it's better to face it now than leave it till after we're married.'

He had to admire the way she did not change colour. Though her head had dropped back on her throat and her face had become a tragic mask, with the brows brought together in a straight line, her cheeks and her lips were as they always had been. Yet they were not painted. It was as if her flesh had confidence that the order of things was not inimical to it, and refused to let the mind stampede it into panic.

Aching with pity, he went on, 'You've got every right to think me the lowest dog in town, leaving it till two days before the wedding. But I didn't know before. It's just come over me. I woke up knowing I couldn't go through with it, yesterday. And it's no use trying to fool myself. I can't do it. I just can't.'

She laid down her scissors on the table, carefully, so as to make no noise, and stood regarding them.

'Maybe we could find some way of stalling the whole thing that wouldn't have all the old cats talking,' he suggested weakly. 'After all I had pneumonia last fall, and everybody knows my mother was a lunger. Maybe I could go up to Saranac for a spell, and say I'd been sent. Then they'd all understand that your people couldn't have you marry me.'

A pause left him trying to account for her silence. It was not accountable in one who was so quick on the trigger in all her responses unless he admitted that he had stunned her with pain. To make himself seem a little better in his own eyes he stammered, 'Mind you, I'm putting it this way because I think you're a wonderful girl, and it seems a pretty poor game for you to have to marry a poor fool who feels the way I do, just not man enough for anything. But if you're willing to go through with it, why, I'd think myself the luckiest man . . .'

As his voice trailed away, she raised her head with a jerk and looked into his eyes. Her brows still met in a straight line, but he was surprised to note that the mask her strong feeling held over her everyday mild and smiling face now reminded him not of tragedy but of command. She made him think of some great general scowling in a history book.

Her eyes left his and looked over his shoulder. She muttered, 'Wait a minute.'

She brushed past him, not looking at him, and went down the steps into the garden. The way she held her head and her shoulders had not changed any more than her colour. As he noted that she walked swiftly out of sight round the corner of the house to the right.

'She's gone to fetch Mrs Houblon,' he thought miserably, 'she'll be out among her flowers at the back. Or maybe it's Mr Houblon who's out there now. I'll feel the rottenest kind of piker whichever it is, they've always been so decent to me. But the worst will be when I have to tell my own old man.' He shuddered, stared down at his boots, and thrust out his lower lip sullenly, but swung round, looked up at some birds that were flying high in that quarter where the mellowness of the afternoon was being stained with sunset, and cried in his heart to them and the clouds that raced behind them, 'All the same it's good to be free! Oh Lord, I am glad to be free!'

At that moment he perceived that Josephine had come back. She had just turned the corner of the house, on the left, and was walking along the path in front of the porch. She was alone. Of course she had not fetched her mother or father. She never did anything unnecessary, and neither of the old people could have contributed anything to resolving the situation. Simply she had walked round the house to give herself time to take the blow. Apparently she had taken it well, for she was still unbowed; and yet, while he looked at her and remarked this, he remembered that the path round the Houblon's house ran very close to it at one point, where a bow window protruded, and he had an immediate conviction that she had had to stop there and cling to the window-ledge. He felt sick with pity, but told himself stubbornly, 'It had to be done,' and looked up again at the birds and the racing clouds and thought, 'It's good to be free! Lord, I am glad to be free!'

She mounted the steps briskly and took her place behind

the table again, and stood there with her hands clasped in front of her.

'I guess we'd better do the way you suggested,' she said; and added, 'and I think it's handsome of you.'

A sinking feeling came over him. 'How?' he asked, as he had not done since his father had boxed his ears for saying it when he was ten years old.

She began clipping the stems of her roses.

'Why, you said you were willing to go through with it,' she coldly reminded him, 'and that's what we're going to do.'

When he could speak he made a pleased, assenting noise. 'That's just swell,' he told her heavily. 'I'm real glad you've come to this decision, and I'm sure . . .'

She cut in before he could finish. 'You'd better be going now. Joan Hunter and Edna Allison are coming along with some of their crowd. I don't suppose you want to come in on a party right now. And I wouldn't be seeing you to-morrow in any case. So good-bye. Till our wedding day.'

There was a minute while his feet shuffled. 'Well, good-bye, Josie,' he mumbled.

'The girls will be here any minute,' she said.

'All right! all right!' he exclaimed, showing a little spirit, and went down the steps. He remembered to walk slowly across the lawn, and to turn and wave his hand when he got to the street; but the first moment he knew himself to be out of sight of the porch he mopped his brow and groaned aloud, 'I never knew Josephine was that kind of girl! I never knew there was a kind of a girl that would do that to a man! Keeping him to it!' He shook his head as he went on his way. 'It's a life sentence,' he said. 'It's a life sentence.'

Two days later he derived a further melancholy pleasure from the repetition of that phrase, when he took his place beside Josie in the Houblons' drawing-room, under the bell of white flowers which was the symbol of wedded love in that generation. Then, like a flash, it went out of his mind: it and all that lay behind it. As the minister's voice twanged on he became more and more conscious of Josie and what the other people in the room were thinking about Josie. They were all thinking how beautiful she was, of course, but he didn't believe that any of them were noticing that the way she was standing was the way a shy little girl stands, looking down at her feet, which were pressed together as close as could be, the toes very nearly touching. Nobody but himself understood that though Josie was so tall and dignified she was really just like a little girl inside, full of funny little feelings, wonderfully easily pleased, wonderfully easily hurt. He was swallowing a lump in his throat and making extensive vows to guard her from all harm, when it suddenly came to him what he had done two evenings before. Those of his friends who facetiously told him afterwards that he had looked just terrible during the ceremony were not speaking an untruth.

Thus it happened that when they were left alone together that night Corrie Dickson threw himself on his knees before his bride, who had shown signs of wrapping sadness round her like an old woman's shawl, and cried out:

'Josie, I didn't mean what I said the other night. I guess all that happened to me was that I got scared, the way lots of men do before they get married. Only this morning Dad told me he'd have given anything in the world to have got out of town the night before his wedding, and he and Mother hadn't had a cross word till the day she died. Josie, I didn't mean one word of what I said! You must have known I didn't. You can't have thought I'd forgotten that night in the woods when the moon . . .'

'I gambled on it, I gambled on it,' wept Josie, nuzzling her face against his shoulder.

'And you were a brave girl to do it,' he told her, when his lips had left her wet eyes. 'God, it must have taken pluck not to let me go my own way and lose what I wanted! And don't think I don't know how I hurt you! Why, you got me out of the way so that you could cry, didn't you, by saying those girls were coming round, and they weren't at all! I saw Joan and Edna myself right after I left your house, driving up to the Club with the Frazier boys . . .'

But she had wrenched herself out of his arms, and had run to the other side of the room, there to hide her face against the wall. Puzzled, he watched her, and thought – as she was to make him more than once in later years – that a big woman can be more pathetic than a little woman, for the very reason that she is so ill-adapted to assume the attitudes of pathos. At this moment anybody who did not know Josie might think she was mad about something, instead of being very nearly wounded to death. Her hurt might easily go unlamented but for him. With wide arms, with his unique understanding, he went towards her.

'Will you never quit talking about it?' she sobbed.

Corrie promised that to the end of his days not one more word concerning it should pass his lips.

But that vow proved not to be so easily kept as he imagined. There were days, weeks, months of fine weather in the Dickson home, when it seemed as if in spite of being a respectable automobile manufacturer he had two wives, and both of them perfect. There was the shrinking virginal Josie whom nobody but himself knew; who would approach him unheard across a twilit room and give him grave lips, and as his answering kiss established her a woman would shiver and withdraw, back into the shadows, back into childhood, from which she would return only out of kindness and much against her timid will. There was also the superb Josephine whom everyone knew, who rode before the waxing prosperity of her husband and the ordered luxury of her home like the figurehead of a clipper. Sometimes he would raise his head to listen fearfully for the coming of misfortune, what he had was so much beyond the common lot. But there were other times when he had to bow his head because he could not bear to look on the misfortune the coming of which, it seemed, he had himself provoked. It turned his Josephine into a tortured woman whose tallness was no glory to her but merely an encumbrance that kept her from creeping near enough earth to hide her shame; it made Josie's perpetual maidenhood of spirit no longer an allurement but a special ability to pain, since it prevented her from practising ruses to save her pride.

Always these provocations were involuntary. There was nothing farther from his mind than the intention to offend when he complained one June evening of the way the waitress had arranged some roses he had brought home. 'Look at the way she's bunched them all together,' he grumbled away, well on the right side of good humour. 'I've seen a clump of bananas look more graceful. Why don't you fix them yourself, darling? I've noticed you never take any notice of the flowers nowadays, yet you used to make your mother's house look like a flower shop. Oh Lord, what is the matter now?'

She had put up her hands to her head and was asking him with her eyes how it was that he could do such things.

It was unfortunate that both of them could perfectly recollect what a strange sound scissors make when they cut through the moist substance of a rose.

She turned and went from the room, though he had just poured out cocktails for them both, and they had been meaning to spend the half-hour before some guests came for dinner in talking over an amusing deal he had just finished that day.

'Does she still feel it all that badly?' he marvelled. 'My poor little girl . . .' He set down his glass and went after her. But something cold in him asked, as he turned the doorhandle of her room, 'Is she going to go on feeling as badly as this all our lives long? Will I always have to stop doing what I want to do and comfort her?' And as he knelt by the bed where she had cast herself, and whispered to her that he could not bear it if she would not turn her head that way, that something grew colder still and said, in time to his heartbeat, 'This is a life sentence, this is a life sentence.'

That was, however, not very long after they were married. Corrie told himself that in time the memory must lose its galvanic power over her; and that if she had children she would get a new sense of proportion. Later on he congratulated himself on being right. Within seven years of their marriage Josie had three children, two boys and a girl. One night, eight years after their marriage, she sat at table while a guest described how the Pearsall boy had jilted the Cutler girl a week before the wedding; and calm had not been unseated from her eyes, which travelled ceiling-wards as the baby began to whimper in the room above. Smiling, he waved his highball at an invisible presence, as if he were drinking its health. Later still, he wondered if the new dispensation deserved to be toasted. For when he came to look into it, nothing in it seemed so good as to outweigh the fact that one of his two perfect wives whom he had loved the best had, so to speak, died in childbirth.

Never any more did the tender and virginal Josie creep about the house, sharing with him, reluctantly yet trustfully, the secret of her extreme surprise at life. There was nobody there now but the splendid Josephine who had no secrets and who was never surprised at anything. As she frequently had the air of turning from him and going to the window and flinging it open so that she could hear the music of some band that was passing by, it was very much as if there was nobody in the house at all who was thinking very particularly of him. That music always sounded stirring, he had to admit. Josephine ennobled the world's affairs by the attention she gave them. She belonged to the ambassadress type who has such a gift for pressing social life into a mould of splendid formality that she need never fret if she finds herself elsewhere than in an embassy. Without apparent effort on her part, magnificence unfolded itself in their house. If that had been what he cared for, he might have been happy.

Even though it was not he might have been happy a little later on, when he found that he was altogether wrong and the wife he had loved the best was not dead but merely in hiding behind the superb skirts of Josephine. In her youth she had been tender and virginal because she could not believe that anybody but herself had ever been faced with this extraordinary destiny of being a woman, of having to take the heart out of her breast and give it away to one whom her modesty would not permit her to believe anxious for the gift, of having to accept the heart he had taken out of his breast for her, though it was a man's and she had a quivering disposition to keep herself separate from the male. She might have been the first woman who had ever been loved or in love, so naïve was she about the business. Now she was developing a new set of characteristics because she was being equally naïve about the business of being a mother. She could not believe that this extraordinary destiny of bringing into the world people who had not been there before, and who were infinitely dear to one, could ever have befallen anyone else; and she was perpetually vexed by the fear that Fate would withdraw this unique privilege from her, leaving her anguished and alone. Therefore Josie turned for help to her other self, competent Josephine, who always got what she wanted, and begged her to do everything she could to establish the family. That was the only reason why Josephine was so much around the house these days.

Corrie thought this all out, smiling at his own fantasy, one Sunday evening when he was sitting on the porch, after he had seen Josephine hurry out to pay a call. The reason why she was paying that call had not been mentioned between them, but he understood it perfectly. He had spent the morning playing golf at the country club, and at lunch he had mentioned that Mrs Wellyn had been his partner in a foursome.

'We played old Bradley and Miss Stallbridge,' he went on; and at the last name had seen Josie's face droop till it was just a wistful triangle. Miss Stallbridge was a daughter of an ex-Governor of the State who had gone to New York and Europe and come back with an armful of degrees and the intention of starting a school for little girls, who, it was rumoured, were to be drawn from the twenty best families of the State. In spite of their rising fortunes the Dicksons were not yet on that shelf. He was sorry he had spoken of the woman. He could imagine his silly little wife lying awake at nights wondering if heaven would not punish her impotence to get Diana into the best possible school by taking the whole family away from her. If the waitress had not been there he would have got up out of his chair and kissed her.

'It seems Mrs Wellyn's a cousin of hers,' he continued.

Her head came up. 'I never knew that. How?'

'Old Bradley says so. It seems Mrs Wellyn isn't the daughter of the Mrs Hutchinson we know, but of a first wife who died. And she was a Stallbridge.'

'I never knew that,' said his wife thoughtfully.

'Neither did I,' he said, 'but she's a nice woman anyway. She was saying she hadn't seen you in weeks, and couldn't think why, and hoped you'd come in any afternoon. I think she said something about to-day.'

Josephine lifted her imperial profile. 'I'll go right away,' she said, 'and ask them to dinner Tuesday.'

So now her roadster was carrying her on the way to lay the foundation of a friendship that would assume useful proportions at just the right time; the remoteness of which made Corrie laugh aloud. It was one of the most charming circumstances in the whole episode that Diana was not yet eighteen months old.

But he stopped laughing when it came up in his mind that it was to Josephine that Josie had turned in her timorousness and not to him. There were, indeed, then and later, innumerable indications that she felt for his character almost every conceivable emotion which is related to love except confidence in it. They became quite unmistakable as the affair of Cherry-garden Bluff came to maturity.

It happened that old Mr Houblon died and left his daughter a fortune which was not stupendous, but was nevertheless a large, solid block of dollars bound to make quite a difference to any economic field whither it was transported; and it happened just about the same time that the American woman began to discover herself as an amateur of business. Sitting back on the throne of prosperity her husband had built up for her, she could bide her time and pick her chances, and see her money increase and multiply in a way that seemed the happiest miracle to a sex which had been tied down since the beginning of time to fixed housekeeping allowances. It was the kind of leisured advance towards more and more magnificence that was Josephine's natural movement. She began to brood over the Wall Street lists and look hawk-like and unassuaged. But she never consulted him, and he had no idea of the direction her mind was travelling until one summer evening, when he had been waiting on the porch for an hour or two after he got back from business, and she came in at last with the children.

She sat down beside him, breathing rather fast.

As the children ran past them he cuffed the boys' ears and pulled Diana's hair, and they squeaked back at him with delight, but he did not take his eyes off their mother. 'You're looking fine,' he said.

She said, 'We've been picnicking up by Cherry-garden Bluff.'

He mused, 'Well, well, it's odd to think of my own children picnicking up there! That place meant a lot to me when I was Jim's age . . .'

It was a long low hill that lifted a shining cliff to the sunlight a couple of miles north of Montarac. On the crest of the cliff were the tallest maple woods in Montarac County, and the face of the hill was laid out like a park round a white house built in the Colonial style, with a wooden colonnade and a sunk flower-garden before it.

'It's for sale!' Josephine announced. 'The Forresters are leaving. The man at the lodge told us. They just made up their minds last night. He's sick and they're going to the coast for good.'

'Sick or well, I wouldn't want to leave that place,' he

reflected. 'Did I ever tell you about the good times I used to have up there?'

But he forbore to try and tell her about them. It had happened that fifty years before a young Southern gentleman had somehow infringed the code of his society, or had seemed to do so, and in any case not attempted to justify himself, but had sold his estate and gathered his servants around him, and gone into exile north of the Mason-Dixon line. He travelled disdainfully through the Yankee lands till he found a place so like the estate he had left that it eased his mind more to stay than move on, and there he had built a house and planted a garden and laid out a park like those he had lost. Then he had closed the gates, and with his coloured people had set himself to play a game of pretending that they were still living in the South. For thirty years that game had been going on when Corrie, just turned twelve, had climbed a fence because a boy with a white gash of teeth in a black face, riding a piebald pony bareback in the paddock beyond, waved at him arms thin as hawthorn branches, and in a voice like the cooing and hooting of night birds had dared him to do the same. Perhaps because the game had been played so long, it had come to rank alongside of reality. The South seemed to hang on the hillside like a patch of mellow afternoon, and things went easily there as they do in the South. When he fell from the pony and a trickle of blood ran down his chin it did not matter very much. It ceased to matter at all when he was taken along to a mountainously fat Mammy with a red handkerchief tied round her grey fuzz, who was sitting in the trellis of a cottage shelling peas into a china bowl that had bright flowers on it, and she had washed the wound and clapped a cobweb to it, uttering sage words as to the efficacy of this hygienic precaution. Then she gave them hunks of bread and molasses, and they ate them on the porch while she moved about within the cottage, singing and humming tunes that seemed to take up every emotion in the world and show it for what it was and drop it before it became

23

tiresome, and clicking pots and pans that presently began to send out heavy savours into the twilight. Presences, tall and short, came as white smiles out of the shadows, and sat round singing, shooting craps, doing household chores dexterously and casually. None of them took much notice of him, there was no suggestion that he was a stranger. At that date there were not above twenty coloured people in Montarac, and they were segregated either in rich folks' kitchens or in the squalor on the wrong side of the railway tracks. It was his first experience of the dark magic that excludes nothing from its circle but robs all of the ultimate sting by taking it easy. He did not feel he ever wanted to go home, particularly after he had had supper, but his new friends accepted sleep as simply as everything else, and were yawning and stretching round him, so he had to set forth on the moonlight road to Montarac, thinking out what explanations would go down best at home.

Such as he found were not too successful, but he went back to Cherry-garden Bluff the very first afternoon he could, and on many another. The groom and some of the boys taught him a kind of polo that left him for the rest of his life a match for most horses. He learned a great many songs, and a manner of speech that puzzled his elders and set them off on unsound speculations concerning heredity, based on the assumption that his Virginian grandmother was now speaking through him. He acquired a passion for Southern cooking, and a wealth of sometimes inaccurate but always interesting information about plants and birds and beasts, and a liking for people who showed what they felt and on the whole felt genial. At last he met the old master of the house, slashing at the long grass round a statue in the park as if it were an enemy, and grumbling a long-delayed rebuttal of some charge. He looked at the boy with the bewildered eyes of those whose saner parts have died first, and spoke to him in soft ceremonial accents that seemed to clothe too fully a shrunken will, like the fine white suit that flapped about his emaciated limbs. He took the boy up to the house, and would have taught him how to play chess with jade and coral chessmen on a damp-warped board, had he not suddenly fallen back asleep in his high-backed chair. The boy did not know what to do, and had sat stiffly until he had heard, far away but somewhere in the house, Thaddeus singing 'Go down Moses'. He had tiptoed out along the shining floor past the fine old things, and opened a door or two, and had found the old butler polishing the silver with plate powder and his bare hands instead of a cloth; and in this delicious occupation he had joined him for an hour, listening to a long story about how a horse once went to heaven. It was the picture-book South, and recollecting it he had the same joy that comes to those who fall in love, of finding that a reality can keep its freshness though all its expressions are infinitely trite. All these things he would have liked to tell her, but they were difficult to put into words, and he had come home tired from the office, and anyway Josephine had something she was all set on saying.

'That's the most valuable real estate in the district,' she declared.

'Why do you think that?' he asked. 'Nobody wants to live right out there.'

'They don't now,' she said darkly. 'But they will – in five years' time. When you come to think of it, where are the rich people in this town going to live, day after to-morrow? There isn't a house to be got round here for love or money, and they can't build out farther west on the other side of the river, because it's swampy. You just can't drain it. Three people have tried. I've looked into that. Well, where else are they to live? They can't move out south on the plains. It's too hot in summer. They can't go east to the hills, with all your factories and the rest of them lying there just where the view ought to be, and they can't go north-east because the Italians and the Poles got there first. They'll have to go farther out, and the ideal site where they'll all want to be is Cherry-garden Bluff. See here . . .'

Suddenly he wanted very much to tell her what the place

had meant to him in his boyhood, because of the way he had lost it. His possession of it had lasted only eight or nine months; then his mother had fallen sick with the grippe and had made a poor recovery, and he had been sent to keep her company through a winter's exile in the desert. The first free afternoon after he got home he sought his Paradise. But it was gone. There was a gang of Wops laying down a broad automobile road through the park up to the old house, and a man with spectacles overseeing them who ordered him off the place. It seemed from what the people at the garage at the crossroads told him that the old man had died round about Christmas. The coloured folks had been in a terrible way, they said: were like a lot of lost kids, didn't know where to go. Blindly Corrie had turned aside from the road to a coppice and stood for a long time with his arms round a tree and his head burrowed against the bark. It is queer the bad times boys can have without anybody knowing about it. Maybe their boys had gone through something just as bad as that, and Josie and he did not know a thing.

For this reason, and because he wanted her to know about him standing with his head against that tree, he tried to tell her what Cherry-garden Bluff had meant to him. It is unfortunate that, because he was casting about for the right words, he failed to show a proper interest in the county map she picked up from her work-table, all scored about and annotated to prove her point; and that, because he had just found them and was trying to bring them out in the right order, he did not at first catch her announcement, though it was made with flashing eyes and uplifted chin, that she intended to sell out her father's securities and buy Cherry-garden Bluff to develop it as a luxury garden-city.

He caught on to it a minute late, when he saw Josie looking at him with very much the same face that he had worn as he turned aside from the road and sought the coppice. But he did not speak quickly enough to prevent Josephine rising to her feet, crushing the map to her breast with irascibly crooked fingers, and crying over her shoulder, before she shut the door into the house with a weary carefulness not to slam it:

'Oh, that is like you! You hold back from everything!'

That was the attitude which she obstinately ascribed to him from that day on in the matter of Cherry-garden Bluff. He tried to explain himself, but all he did was to impress her obstinacy with the new error that he regarded her enterprise as a desecration of a childish playground. This was not true. Corrie was no sentimentalist; and in any case the childish playground had already been desecrated beyond all grieving, since it had been for twenty years in the possession of Mrs Forrester, who had every year attempted to make it resemble more closely the home of her father, a beer baron from Milwaukee. But the error was as sharply engraved in Josie's obstinacy as if it were an intaglio cut in a dark, hard stone; she wore it in her mind as she might have worn a mourning ring on her finger, and turned it over perpetually. For a time it seemed as if he would be able to take it from her by his continued praise. She was so superb in her enterprise that he could praise her fervently and honestly. At first she spent more money than she had done before on entertaining. There was no hurry, no strain. Simply she put down so many dollar bills and took in return the social leadership of Montarac. All her world followed her, therefore, when a year or two later, she moved out to the perfect house she had built on nothing like the best lot at Cherry-garden Bluff. Obviously there were far better sites; this gave every woman who saw it the confident hope that she would have a far better house. Infinite was the guile displayed by Josephine, and also the art. The place never lost its look of being a park. In the morning one could walk along its avenues and look up at the cliff, and not feel that the clean-cut, clean-coloured stone had been demeaned by what man had set below it. At night, the view over the dark plains where Montarac lay like a brilliant foundered star was something that in the Old World would have been famous. The honour in which he held her for the achievement was so great that when he spoke it she had to believe him, and looked at him with her Josie face, smiling and timid, as if to say, 'Yet you know better than this. You know that I am not really competent, that I am young and afraid.' All would have gone well if Cherry-garden Bluff had been the only hill in the neighbourhood. But geology is not so single-minded.

One afternoon Josephine came to see him at the factory, tall, unsmiling, avid-eyed.

'I have been talking over things with Jack Farmer,' she said. Jack Farmer was the real estate agent with whom she usually worked. 'He says that if Flanagan builds a factory here in two years time I can do what I've done at Cherry-garden Bluff up on that hill they call Battle Heights, only for operatives. But I must buy now.'

It was a big venture. Not possibly could either of them or both of them raise the money out of their loose cash.

'Well, go ahead. The banks will lend it to you.'

Sullenly, as one who knows she is going to be denied, she owned. 'I've borrowed every cent I can already.'

'Great guns! What for?'

'Land east and west of Cherry-garden. Flanagan's coming. This town is growing. It will be all right.'

He knew it would be all right. What she said was sense. He nodded approval. 'Good girl. Well, it's a pity we can't have everything in this world. You'll have to let Battle Heights go.'

She flung out a demanding hand. 'But can't you borrow it?'

'What, I borrow it, honey?' He was startled at her forgetfulness of their common enterprises. 'Why, you know I need every cent I can raise for this extension of our works I've planned for next fall . . .'

Her outflung hand turned over in the air. The gesture it described was infinitesimal, but it made Corrie draw in his breath and for the first time consider the possibility that perhaps the final emotion he might feel for his wife was hate. Though they had spoken of these matters many times and at

28

great length it had never before been admitted that he was never going to be a great man in business, that his automobiles were good but not quite good enough, that he and his corporation were headed for a safe but not glorious future in the shape of a merger with some more victorious commercial entity. That tiny movement had, however, stated it once and for all.

Corrie walked to the window and stood with his back to her. Was it perhaps the right thing to take his capital and his credit out of the corporation, and let the merger happen now instead of in three or four years' time? She was reciting figures to him now. With half his attention he concentrated on the financial riddle they propounded. With the rest he noted that her manner was divided against herself. She was putting her case as strongly as she could, yet sometimes there was an overtone in her voice that seemed deliberately to mute what she said, as if she wanted not to win it.

He did some figures in his head. There was nothing much in it either way. Considering the upset he would cause by the precipitation of the merger, and the financial allowances he would have to make to ease his colleagues' feelings, he would rake in little more by coming into Josephine's more attractive proposition than he would by sitting tight. Or, rather, it would be more exact to say that he would make a little more. Just a little more. Not much, but definitely more. Wouldn't it be better if he did get out and help Josephine on her triumphant way?

The window at which he stood looked on a courtyard, used as a passage between two of the sheds. As he stared down under knit brows the doors of one shed swung open and half a dozen men in blue overalls walked smartly over to the other. He liked the look of them. They were on the job, they weren't loitering, yet they were happy: he had seen the teeth of the two offside ones that were Wops flash in laughter as they went by. His men were like that on the whole. The one part of business where he was a master was the handling of labour. Too shy to make contacts easily with

29

individuals, he could manage them in hundreds with the greatest ease. Always he could divine what they were thinking and feeling, and could accept his knowledge in a philosophical spirit. The relationship he had established between his operatives and himself was ideal, which meant that their relationship to their work was all right. It was because of this that when the merger came he would not die with the business but would pass on as a valuable person into the new organization. If at that time he had carried out the extension he had planned he would go in with even greater prestige, for that would bring up his pay-roll to an impressive length. Simply Josephine was asking for his future. And, damn it all! This was his job and he liked it.

He turned round and said, 'No, Josie. I'm sorry I can't.'

She picked up her bag and the papers she always seemed to carry around these days. 'I didn't think you could make up your mind to it.'

'It isn't only that,' he answered coldly.

She raked his office with an eye that estimated the probable importance of everything that would happen in it from the standpoint of justice rather than of mercy, and rose to go.

Nevertheless it seemed to him, as he stood on the kerb saluting her good-bye, that it was Josie who sat with downcast head in the back of the limousine. And he noted as significant that she made no attempt to borrow the money elsewhere. Since her own husband would not give it to her, she did not want it from anybody else. That was like Josie. But when a man named Edelstein made a whole heap of money out of Battle Heights it seemed to be Josephine who read in the papers about it.

After this he had to admit that things were going much worse between them; which was the first time he had ever admitted that things had been going badly. These financial matters were never discussed, but almost everything else was, and that with acrimony. He noticed that nowadays when people at dinners or dances congratulated him on his wife's beauty he felt embarrassed, as if he held some secret information that made what they said intolerably ironical. Quite what this feeling meant he did not understand, but he knew that it made him turn away as speedily as possible and seek a highball. When he did come to understand it, that did him no good, because of the manner in which he made the discovery. One evening he was coercing his dress tie into a bow in front of his glass when Josephine came in, as much more than merely ready as an empress is after she has made all preparations for a public appearance, and sat down on the chaise-longue at the end of the bed. At first she talked about the people they were going to meet that night at dinner, who the guests of honour were and why they were visiting the town; and then she fell silent. Nowadays he was nervous about whatever she was doing at the moment. If she spoke he was on edge for the next word, if she did not he suspected she was biting back some reproach crasser than had yet been made. His eyes shifted from his tie to the shadowy distance behind his head in the glass, and found her handsome face distorted with embitterment. She was looking at his reflexion, not at his eyes, but at a beam of light that a lamp on the dressing-table laid across his fair hair and his broad, high forehead. Since his knowledge of her was as nearly perfect as one human being's knowledge of another could be, he was immediately aware that she was saying to herself, 'Yes, he is good-looking. It is a pity that all that promise his looks make that he is a wonderful human being doesn't mean a darned thing!' That he had been thinking precisely the same thing did nothing to allay his deep sense of grievance.

Nevertheless, because he knew he had committed no offence against her in the way of unfairness comparable to the attitude she took up over Diana's illness, his resentment was greatly increased. It was not true that he had been neglectful. He had seen at once that the child was ill, as soon as he came in and put down his golf clubs and said, 'Well, what shall we do to console ourselves now mother and the boys have left us for the week-end?' For Diana was fair as he was, and had the sort of fine gold hair that announces the physical state of its owner almost before she knows it herself; and now her curls were flat to her head and dark at the roots. He had not let her stay up for dinner, though she had been looking forward to having it alone with him, and he hated to go against her in anything. He had taken her temperature, and though he had not sent for the doctor in spite of its high reading, that was because she had had that degree of fever before now and awakened well the next morning. At least he had given her a dose of aspirin the doctor had prescribed on those previous occasions, and had gone into her bedroom several times during the night, and had taken her temperature again in the morning, and when that showed no fall had telephoned for the doctor right away. He had defensively recapitulated these points so often that the recital of them produced all those feelings of guilt that even an innocent man experiences in the dock. But there was nothing whatsoever in the charges Josephine brought against him. Standing out in the garden in the spring sunshine which the words 'pneumonic infection' had in a second made monstrously ironic, he had asked, 'Shall I send for my wife?' and the doctor had answered, 'What does that mean? That she gets here twenty-four hours earlier and drives home in a state of panic? It isn't worth it. The child's fine.' He had murmured assent, and shuddered, seeing a vision of Josephine, hawk-faced at the wheel, forcing her automobile round the hairpin bends of the road down from Torquand, intent on having her will to get home in disregard of the nature of automobiles and hairpin bends, and the safety of the boys behind her.

Maybe he would not have imprinted on her mind such a vivid image of himself as dealing with this crisis frivolously, if it had not happened that when she came home, jumping wildly out of the roadster because she had seen the doctor's automobile outside her house, he was on the lawn talking to Judy Mandeville. She was the niece of the people next door, a girl of twenty-one who had come to them to rest up after her first divorce, a slender creature who had the bright colour and the air of being coated with syrupy juices characteristic of canned fruit; and it certainly seemed unlikely that she should have come forward with such handsome offers of help that he had been obliged to thank her at length.

When Josephine started these accusations he would have liked to walk out of the house and never see her again. But there was Diana; and during the first week of the illness there were hours in the middle of the night when fatigue seemed to whirl his wife about as if they were stripping her of a dress of metal brocade and heavy jewellery and uncovering the naked woman. Then he seemed to be getting back into a sane world, a world full of horror, but nevertheless possible to live in because there was an identity between what existed and what was alleged to exist.

Corrie tried to pretend that that was going to be their permanent habitation when, on the first night that Diana was definitely out of the wood, they went in to see her before they went to bed. She was asleep, but Josephine could always move as silently as a squaw and during the last few days he had learned to do so. The only sound that might have awakened the child was the 'Sh!' she flung over her shoulder as he approached a table which he had every intention of avoiding.

They stood together at the end of the bed. 'Isn't she blonde!' breathed Josephine in an infatuated whisper. While she was still tranced in admiration for her child she put up her hand and touched his hair above the temples. When she realized what she was doing she trembled, and though she left her finger-tips where they were she crooked her fingers as if they were claws. She might have been trying to tell him, 'Yes, the texture of your hair is dear to me, but nothing else, believe me, nothing else.'

As they tip-toed out of the room he said to himself, 'This is just silliness, it is a habit she has got into, I must snap her out of it.' Once they were out in the corridor he slipped his arm through hers and held her to him, and begged her,

'Now it's all over, Josie, won't you own that there wasn't a thing I could have done for the kid that I didn't do?'

Over her eyes that were still wet with tears from looking at the child her brows contracted furiously.

'Well, say what it was!' he challenged.

She jerked her head from side to side like a rogue horse that is being ridden on the kerb.

His temper rose, 'Yes,' he pressed her sternly, 'just tell us what it was.'

For a minute she was unable to speak, but not because the accusation had struck home; simply because she was amazed at the impudence of the accuser. 'Why,' she cried, 'if it had been left to you there wouldn't have been any . . .' A sob choked her, she shook loose his arm and ran to her room.

It was some time before he realized what she meant: 'Any Diana at all.' Then, though dutifully he forced his mind into the groove where he lamented that pain he had caused should last so long, he had an exasperated feeling that his mind had been brought down from something very big to something very small.

Some weeks later, as Corrie sat alone at the dinner table, he reflected that this business of the sick child joining its parents' hands over the sick-bed was all bunk. That afternoon he had gone down to the station to see Diana and her mother off to the shore, and the thought of the cold cheek Josephine had turned to him made him mix himself a very stiff highball. For months now all he had seen of his wife was her profile. Barely had he seen more than the tip of her nose and the point of her chin when she had told him that she was sending the boys to stay with their cousin while she was away, and had hinted by an acid arrangement of the overtones that only thus could she be certain they were in trustworthy hands. After she said that he would have given something to be one of his Wop or Bohunk hands who, when they were displeased with their wives, beat them. A shudder of hatred ran through him at the recollection, and left him cold and dispirited. The furniture gleamed through the gathering dusk at him with whitish high lights, and he could not turn on the lamp because he had looked at himself in the mirror before he came down to dinner, and had seen that his face was more haggard and enraged than he cared the servants should see. The famous view of the plains framed within the widest windows was covered now by creeping mists. Everything was cheerless, and made no promise of anything different. He pushed away his plate, since he found difficulty in swallowing, and drank some more Scotch.

Instances of Josephine's unfairness crowded into his mind. He recapitulated the most flagrant examples with full details, as he had done often enough lately when he woke up in the early hours of the morning. Shaking all over, he said, 'Why do I stand it? I'm a fool, that's why. I'm just a fool. But a man can always quit being a fool. And, by God, that's what I'm going to do.' He took another highball, and set himself to consider what exactly was to be done. With a glow of exaltation he told himself that he must do nothing that would hurt Josie. He must get clear, of course, but he hoped he was man enough to say that he would not help himself to what he wanted at the expense of a woman: particularly when she was such a lovely person as his wife. His warm and luminous thoughts were for some reason not easy to compress into any definite mould of intention at the moment, but he knew that he meant to behave with the utmost generosity, and felt confident that the parting would flower into a beautiful display of tenderness. After all, their lives had not been destitute of beauty, even in those passages which to the outsider – whose opinion he suddenly violently resented – might seem most ugly. There was that time, to take just one case, when she had turned on him in the corridor after they had stood by Diana's bedside. People who did not know Josie might call her down for that, but if one understood the way her mind worked it was just pretty and appealing. What she had said just before she ran away couldn't have meant that if it had been left to him she wouldn't have had children, for she had been the acknowledged belle of the town and could have married anybody she liked. It must have meant that if it had been left to him she wouldn't have had any children that were like him: and the implication was that that was the sort she much preferred to have. He began to laugh uproariously. It was so like a woman, he thought, to hate a man because one loved him so much that one couldn't bear to think of having children by anybody else. As corroboration for his theory he remembered the languorous satisfaction in her voice as she said of her daughter, 'How blonde she is!' and the slow slide of her finger-tips over his hair. He longed for the moment to come back so that he could put up his hands and catch hold of her fingers and kiss them before she hardened that movement into something hateful and repelling. A mellow regret suffused him at the reflexion that something was less possible, but as he gave himself some more Scotch he resolved to tell Josie all about it next time they met.

But then Corrie made a great discovery. This was not surprising, for his mind had become very clear. It felt as if he had in his head a great glittering ice palace like the ones they have in Canada, with thoughts dashing about as quickly and smoothly as if they were on skates. He said loudly and wisely, 'No!' and sat shaking his head doggedly and bravely, as men do when they are sturdy enough to face a disagreeable reality. It would be impossible for him to tell Josie about it next time they met, for the reason that he would not be able to find the proper words. That was what had been the matter with them all along. Things kept on happening to them that they could not describe. He had not been able to tell her what he really felt that awful evening when he went along to her home and found her fixing roses on the porch. If he could have said exactly what he meant she would never have taken it the way she did, and if she could have said right out what it did to her, then she would have got it off her chest, and it wouldn't have eaten her away inside like a cancer; and if he could have told her he knew quite well what was going on in her mind, the way you told people in business when a situation gets balled up, that might have soothed her. 'That's what's wrong with us!' he exclaimed, getting up and walking about the room. 'We can't talk. Nobody but writers know how to put things into words, and everybody goes around stuffed up with things they want to say and can't.' It seemed to him that he had put his fingers on the secret of all human sorrow. He wanted to tell not only Josie but the whole world about it. After he had poured himself another highball, he went out through the glass doors on to the porch, because steep steps led down from it, and the garden below fell away in a steep slope, so that standing there was like being on a raised platform in a hall.

He stood there sipping and nodding into the darkness. 'That is why people quarrel about nothing at parties,' he told himself. 'Things happen inside them that they can't talk about, and they simmer and simmer and simmer, and then they get hold of some liquor and they just go full steam ahead. But they can only yap at each other the way they feel; they can't put what's troubling them into words. It's the words, the words.' His personal troubles had now assumed lesser proportions, and he was able to look at them loftily as an infinitesimal part of a great universal misery. 'What is to happen to a world where nobody can talk? I don't know anybody who can talk. Who can put difficult things, the kind that really matter, into words? What is to happen to us all? We will go along getting balled up, and it will get worse and worse, the more that happens.' He did not entertain any serious hope that this deficiency in the human equipment could be changed, but he felt that the trouble it caused might be mitigated if everybody loved human beings the way he did at that moment, and was very kind to them. For his eyes were wet as he looked down on the black plain and watched the dazzling lights of the automobiles thread the invisible roads from Montarac; and the light-hearted sounds made by young people and victrolas and radios that came to him through the trees from his neighbours' houses seemed to him heart-rending in their irony. 'I build them automobiles, Josie plans them houses,' he told himself with a lump in his throat, 'but what's the use? They aren't happy, because they can't talk.'

He was so completely saturated in his mood that it did not leave him when he heard footfalls on the steps up to the porch, and when, after switching on the light, he found Judy Mandeville standing there. She was now even more brilliantly coloured than a canned fruit. Her evening make-up and the prospect of adventure made her as luscious as the advertisement of a canned fruit. But it was not because of that he went and stared into her face, gripping her wrist with the hand that was not holding his glass. Nor was it because she was holding out a volume to him; for literature played its part in Judy's life, since she often borrowed a book when everybody was at home in order to return it when everybody but one was out. It was simply because he had the intention of saying to her:

'Here you, you're as simple as can be. You're as simple as a monkey in the Zoo. You needn't try and fool me, I know all about that, and I don't care. What I'm trying to say is that I want to know if even you find it easy to put what you want to say into words. Don't you ever get all balled up because things happen to you that you can't straighten out by talking about them?'

But he found he himself could not put what he wanted to say into words, and he could not straighten out the situation by talking about it when Judy, leaving his left hand just where it was on her wrist, took the glass from his other hand and silently set her lips to it.

The next day he did what he could by getting the works manager, who was a bachelor, to come up and stay with him till his wife came back. But somehow the news got round; and indeed he found he could not get rid of Judy in a minute. All the time he knew that Josephine would hear of it, and he presumed that she did, though she never spoke of it. Only on her return she went about looking sick, so sick that the lipstick on her mouth looked pathetically gallant, and at times she drew in the air through her teeth as if she were too tired to breathe.

So it happened that he was standing in his office, looking out of the window and thinking, 'I must talk to her about this or the bottom will drop out of the world,' when she came in and said: 'Corrie, I'm going to Reno next week. I want to divorce you. I want to marry Jack Lambert.'

Again he was without words, and did not find them until he burst into her bedroom at eleven o'clock that night.

'Did you mean it, that fool thing you said to me down at the office?' he asked.

As she cowered against the end of the bed, a velvet negligée winding round her and trailing in front of her feet in a fish-tail point, she looked like a Renaissance lady fearing a Renaissance crime.

'It's no use you looking as if you were going to be murdered,' he said. 'You know damn well that if there's a murder done in this house it's more likely to be you than me that does it. I'm asking you if it's true what you said then, that you want to divorce me and marry Jack Lambert?'

She answered that she did.

'God! That college boy who's never learned enough to put away his coonskin coat,' he jeered. 'It would have saved me a lot of trouble if I'd known what you wanted. You don't want a husband. You want a cheer-leader. Jack Lambert will be grand at that. He'll just stand up in front of the crowd and fling himself about and get them to holler their heads off. Gee! that will be fine. You'll love that, won't you? Everybody cheering the great Josephine. But there should be more to it than that. There should be a whole heap more.'

He sat down heavily on an Italian chair that happened to be behind him, and remained for some time with his hands over his face. 'Gee!' he said. 'That bell of white flowers we got married under!' When he looked up again Josephine was standing erect, her brows meeting as she looked down on him in a steady stare of disfavour, while her hand fluttered in front of her mouth. It seemed probably she was masking a smile of satisfaction of which she was ashamed, but which nevertheless came and went.

He tapped the gold-painted wood of the chair arm and stroked the brocade. 'Well,' he said. 'This is a grand room, and I'm glad to leave it.' He got on to his feet and shook his head at her. 'And you're a grand woman, and I'm glad to leave you.'

She continued to press her fingers against her lips.

'God! you are the meanest, ugliest woman that ever lived!' he suddenly burst out. 'And what makes me sick is that you might have been great if you'd only been a fraction better than what you are! You've missed it by a hairs-breadth. But, by God! you've missed it. There can't be a woman on the streets who's such an unmitigated nuisance to everyone that she's tied up with as you are. And the pity is you started fine. It's because you started fine that you've turned into the hard-mouthed pest that you are. You were big enough not to let me make a fool of myself that evening when I wanted to cry off our marriage; and ever since you've been smaller than your own little finger. You were big enough to say that you wouldn't let me throw away my happiness just because I had cold feet, even though I'd put you in a position when convention almost forced you to do it. But you weren't big enough ever to forgive me for the insult to your pride, even though I've done everything I could to atone. You've tried to prove me a poor dog so that you can feel that an insult from me doesn't matter. That's why you've fixed this real estate business the way it looks as if it was something you'd pulled off with me like a dead weight on you, though you know I was behind you all the time, except when you asked so much that nobody but a eunuch would have given in to you. That's why you've faked all this damn nonsense about the children, though you know as well as you know your own face in the glass that I care about them

40

the way you do. That's why you've carried on this way about this thing with Judy, though you know damn well that I couldn't help it more than I could help a skunk coming and dying in the yard. But of course it wasn't like another man's slip, because other men haven't done to their wives what I did to you two days before our marriage. You had to give me hell, hadn't you? That's why you had to tear up everything good that we'd done together, and let heck happen to the children, so that you could have the fun of putting that poor flat-fish Jack Lambert in my place, and saying to the world, "I know them both, and, believe me, this is the better man." Well, have it your own way. It suits me. Sure, it suits me.' He walked towards the door and turned there to cry: 'You can't believe how well it suits me. I thought I was in for a life sentence, and now I'm free. God! It's good to be free!'

While he had been unburdening himself he had not paid much attention to the impressions his eye was recording. But once he had banged the door it seemed to him that from the moment he had mentioned that which was never mentioned between them, Josie's gown had suddenly ceased to seem a part of her easily handled magnificence and had hung about her in unmanageable, hostile folds, as if she were a little girl who had put on her mother's dress, and had been caught, and would have run away if it had not been for this great horrid train. He tried to go back and see if it were so, but found that Josephine had locked the door.

So the merger happened, after all, some years before he had planned. As soon as Josie had got her divorce and had started for home again, he himself packed his traps and went West. For the corporation that had taken over his business were trying to ginger up the Coast market by starting a factory two nights and two days on the other side of Chicago, where an ambitious state was backing its newly developed coal and iron fields, and they had offered him the job of organizing it. He was very glad Josie and he had split when they did, for now he could go right to taking the job. And it was grand. It meant turning a mixed crowd of crusted farm and ranch workers on the one hand and raw immigrants on the other hand into a modern industrial army. It meant housing them and feeding them and clothing them and seeing they had the right sort of place to go nights to keep them sweet and efficient. In fact it meant making a city and its citizens.

When he got out there the job did not disappoint him; and he found that he was one of the Easterners who, if they have been afflicted by a slight melancholy from their birth up, can blame it on the fact that it was the West they wanted all the time. His factory stood half-way up a winding valley looking down over irrigated plains to a great lake that stretched silver to the skyline and overpassed it. For his operatives he built houses low down on the plains, but he himself lived a mile or two up the valley, where he could step out of doors and find himself at once on trails that led from the hills to the mountains, to the feet of the great peaks that have their own names and own characters, and wear their snow-crests as if they were orders. All his life he had felt about high ground that if one went on and on climbing it one would come to a region where the air was pure with an eternal and positive purity that could never be polluted by human breath, and yet was not inimical to man like the snake-breeding desert. When he sat on a ledge of black rock, listening to the wind in the high pine forest and looking down on the great lake which still, even when seen from the heights, overpassed the skyline, it was apparent to him that he had found this region. But every circumstance alike of his new existence enchanted him. 'It's a great life!' he used to say, setting his hat, which he now wore with a rather wider brim than was necessary, farther back on his head. 'It's a great life!' By this he meant, among other things, that nobody who saw him in his present could have guessed anything about his past.

A little more than a year after Corrie settled in the West he married again. She was the prettiest girl in the town and she had a nice steady temper. She did not even get cross when he kept on calling her Josie around the house. But in that, of course, she showed her good sense, for it was just a slip of the tongue. He hardly ever thought of his first wife, or Cherry-garden Bluff, or Montarac. There was no reason why he should, for he was so conscious that his wife had instilled in his children her legend of his weakness and worthlessness that he fought shy of them in his thoughts as one does of people whom one knows to have a mistaken and unalterable contempt for one. The only times that he ever spoke of Josie came when he and his second wife were alone together, and an unexpected beauty broke on them. Perhaps they might be strolling around the house with the dogs the last thing before bedtime, and the moon would rise above the far peaks and cover the hills with a thin snow of moonlight and strike a clean, cold radiance from the face of the cliffs. Then he would fall silent and walk at some distance from her, with his head down, as if he were listening compassionately to the whimper of the coyotes. Presently he would jerk up his head, as if he were weary of listening to their complaints, come back and say how good it was to be with her and be able to enjoy good moments when they came, and how all such things had been spoiled for him in the past because his first wife had trailed her grievance-bedraggled beauty between him and them.

Never did he speak of her in any other connexion until one October morning when the papers carried headlines telling of a crash in Wall Street such as had not been known before.

'I am worried,' he said at breakfast to his second wife.

'Why?' she asked. 'I thought you hadn't got anything on margin?'

'Sure I haven't,' he answered. 'I've got enough put by in bonds to take care of us for the rest of our lives, and there's my salary, and I guess we can wait for the stock I have in our corporation to right itself. But I was thinking of Josie.'

43

'Why, what stocks has she got?'

He was surprised to find that he had no idea. Simply he was certain that by this time she must have launched out into complicated financial adventure on much too large a scale to be confined to Montarac, of the sort that was most likely to be punished by this collapse. He knew it as an engineer who has studied a river can know years after how its course will be affected by the current weather. He also knew that ruin inflicted by this blind and senseless disaster, against which her will would raise no defence, would cause her the most unspeakable agony.

'I guess she's always playing the market,' he said evasively. 'There couldn't be a crash that wouldn't get her somewhere where she lives.'

He read on down the list of stocks and said 'Ah', as if he had recognized a pet holding of hers. But really it was not so. It was only that he had seen the name of a motor corporation that he had heard Jack Lambert speak of years before.

'I am worried sick over this,' he said. 'It affects the children, you know. Would you mind if I made a date with her in Chicago some day soon? I guess she could meet me there easy enough, she goes over there all the time to stay with an old aunt. And this is a thing that ought to be gone into. Do you mind if I send her a night letter fixing this up?'

'Why would I mind?' said his wife. 'I know the way you feel about her.'

But he sent a straight telegram, after all, instead of a night letter. The thought of seeing her again made him feel so nervous that he could not bear the delay. And when it was crossed by a telegram from Josie in which she asked if she could see him in Chicago three days later he became more nervous still.

He called up his wife and said, 'Darling, I guess I'll have to go to Chicago. Josie's telegraphed me right now to say she wants to see me. She wouldn't have done that if she hadn't lost the hat off her head. I'll have to fix things up for the children.'

'Do you want me to go down town and get your reservations, or will the office do it?' she asked.

'I'll do it here,' he answered. 'And you're sure you don't mind me going?'

'I'm only sorry you have to go,' said the voice at the other end of the telephone, 'because I know how you'll hate it.'

She was as good to him as the West had been. When she drove him down to the station the next afternoon he said with conviction, 'I can't tell you how I loathe leaving you. But I'll tear back the minute I can. It seems she and this chap Lambert are on their way through Chicago to stay with his folks up in St Paul, and they haven't but an hour or two between trains, so I've told her to come along to the Greenland where I'll have a room. We'll get through our talk and run. I guess I'll be back Tuesday.'

'Won't that be grand,' said his wife.

'You don't know how grand,' he told her, 'because you haven't been through what I have.'

'Well, I can see that going away is making you look sicker than I've ever seen you,' she said. 'I guess a man never hated a woman worse than you hate her.'

As he looked down on her from the Pullman windows he found himself thinking in a patronizing way that her face was rather too round and simple. He was shocked at himself for being critical of a face that was smiling to say a loyal and kind good-bye. That he should be capable of doing it showed that he had fallen again into the atmosphere radiated by Josephine, who would never suspend an intellectual judgement because the object judged had a claim on her emotions. That was unlovable. Everything about Josephine was unlovable. His wife had been right when she guessed that no man hated a woman worse than he hated Josephine. He hated her so much that he could not eat any dinner, either that night in the dining-car or the next night when he had to wait for a few hours between trains in a small town where the Rockies give way to the plains. Instead of

45

eating there he had a bath and as he combed his wet hair in front of the glass he noted how the prospect of meeting Josephine had scored old-man lines on his forehead; and later he had walked in the dusk through the town which with its rickety timber houses and its hiking posts had not altogether lost the character imprinted on it by the lead mines, and was therefore to him the embodiment of the kind West he loved. Tall people strode through the shadows, calling to each other in deep even-tempered voices. He felt sure that there were lots of men and women in this town who would understand what this trip to see Josephine meant to him, would see that it was like going down into the pit. But it was no good, one cannot put anything that matters into words. He thought he would like to stop here for ever and lose his name, and take a job as a soda-fountain clerk and stand there all day face to face with these people whose kindliness he trusted, though his knowledge of the limitations of speech would save him from ever trying it unwisely, shaking for them the innocent sweet things they liked to drink good and sugary. But that was foolishness. His adult destiny was different and abhorrent. Though this was the West, it was the end of the West. To-morrow he would wake up and find the Middle West flat around him, and every moment would bring him to the terrible, acid, energetic East.

He got into Chicago in the middle of the morning. All the previous day he had such a blinding headache that even the tender monotony of the Kansas plains was intolerable to his retina, and he had sat all day in the Pullman with his eyes on his knees, eating nothing. All night the wheel of Josephine's misdoings had revolved in his head and he had cried silently to the darkness, 'Why have I to give any more of my life to this woman? Why do I have to see her again? But I suppose a man must look after his children . . .' Yet when he stepped off the train he felt well and full of quick decisions, easy power. He went to his hotel and made them change the suite they had given him for one that looked over the lake. It struck him as pretty silly that now he had to have a sitting-room to see Josie in, or they would have been thrown out. There was a telegram from Josie waiting for him, saying that her train was an hour late and warning him to be sure and wait in for her, since she must leave the town by an early evening train. He felt slightly exasperated by that, and got busy telephoning for his own reservation on a West-going Limited that started about six. He told them to come for his bags about half an hour before the train started. Then, having settled everything, he had a bath, and got a barber sent up to give him a shave. He told the barber he ought to go West. He felt young and victorious and well fitted to direct other people's lives. Everything in life seemed unusually pleasant, and putting on his clean underlinen gave his skin a shock of delight. He could not think why he had worried so much about meeting Josie. He would settle her affairs, at least as well as she deserved, for if she had dipped herself too deeply she would just have to learn her lesson. But at any rate he could increase the children's allowance. It was the children he cared about.

He went out presently and took a turn along Michigan Boulevard, but the wind got in between his skin and his shirt, so he hurried back to the hotel. There was a florist's shop just beside the entrance, which lit up the greyness with a show of yellow and red chrysanthemums, and he stopped as he might have to warm his hands at a fire. Soon he noticed one of the girls inside the shop watching him through the flowers, and he felt a fool, so he passed on. But that, he reflected, left him still looking like a gaping fool, so he went back and walked into the shop.

'We don't have flowers like this where I come from in the West,' he told the girl, as he chose some chrysanthemums. It was not true, for his wife always had the house full of flowers: but it excused him for staring like a boob into the window. He bought quite an armful of chrysanthemums, and came out feeling foolish. He had no use for them. It meant a lot of trouble giving them to a bell-hop to take up to the chambermaid with a message about fixing them.

47

There was no reason why he should care whether a girl in a florist's thought him a boob or not.

In the restaurant he ate for the first time since he had left home, a large, elaborate meal. There was something like a storm raging out on the lake. He watched it through the vast windows without perturbation, for he liked violence in nature almost as much as he disliked it in human beings. 'Why did I need to get all wrought up about this?' he wondered. 'I will simply go into whatever statements she has brought along, and figure how much she needs, and then I'll write to her lawyer and her broker. I'll feel the same as if I were dealing with anybody who'd once been in business with me and isn't any longer.' He would have stayed down there longer if he had not remembered that his wife had packed a flask in his bag. He went up and got it out, and had a couple of highballs. There was nothing to worry about. The room looked fine with all the red and yellow flowers. By the clock set in the wall he saw that it was much earlier than he had supposed. He had ample time to have a sleep, so he lay down on the couch and closed his eyes. The clatter of the windows in their frames soothed rather than disturbed him. The only time he had ever been to Europe, a few years after he had married Josie, he had enjoyed as much as anything a few days on the homeward crossing when a storm picked up the great ship and rocked it from side to side without cease.

Corrie slept; but awoke the minute the telephone bell started ringing. When they said that Mrs Lambert was downstairs he stared into the transmitter, seeing that instrument which is hardly ever seen by its users. He felt an acute desire to say, 'Tell her to go away.' There was a type of man who would do that if he felt like it. While he reflected on what else he knew about that type of man, and whether he would enjoy belonging to it, the clerk testily repeated the information. He could imagine Josephine waiting impatiently, tapping long fingers on the desk, marking up the delay to his discredit, even though she had come to him for his help. He barked his directions to the clerk.

While she was on her way up he went and looked at the storm, biting his lip at it as if he had to reduce the angry confusion to order by argument. He must not lose his temper with her. Even if she took this thing in an ugly way, he must not try to get back at her, because he must keep separate from her ugliness. It had overwhelmed him for years. Now that he knew what life could be without it he must not go under again for a minute.

Then Josephine was standing in the doorway. There was always a suggestion of something spiral about her, as if under her clothes and her flesh there coiled up a spring, and the long dress she was wearing made this seem so more than ever. Neither her body nor her head were bowed, and though it was four years since he had seen her, and she must now be thirty-eight, she struck him as having kept hold of her looks. She had not easy possession of them: she had easy possession of nothing. But in spite of her massaged look and the too regular crenellations of her hair that showed under her hat on each side of her face, she had still a great deal of her high-coloured beauty. 'Women do not lose all they say they do when they lose their youth,' Corrie grumbled to himself.

Yet she had lost something since her youth. As he scrutinized her to see how she was bearing up under the situation, he noticed that she raked the room before her with a quick, defensive glance, as in old days a man with enemies might rake darkness with his sword; and realized that this was without particular significance, for that was how she always looked when she went into a room, or when a stranger came in on her. He remembered how years before she had proudly and happily smiled at him when she found him watching her from the foot of the stairs as she tended the roses. That expression had been missing from her repertory ever since.

'After all, I did that to her,' Corrie thought. 'It wouldn't have had the same effect on a nicer woman, but she's as she is, and I did it to her. I must try to make up for it.' So he

49

went forward and crushed her hand as he had learned to do in the West.

'How are you, Josie?' he asked heartily.

'Fine,' she said. She had difficulty in drawing her dry lips back from her teeth, so that her smile looked insincere. But he knew her well enough to have learned that it was the insincere smiles that Josephine could manage as easily as an empress acknowledging the obeisance of her subject, and the sincere smiles that seemed to hurt her face. 'I guess it's been a help to her through this bad time to feel that I'll be right behind her,' he thought. 'I guess she feels grateful.' Kindly he said, 'Come right in and sit down, and I'll mix you a highball.'

Her breath was driving through her teeth very quickly, as if her heart were bad and coming up in the elevator had been too much for her. But the colour on her lips and cheeks was still the colour of health made visible, and when she sat down in the arm-chair there was nothing wavering about the hands with which she opened the heavy coat and straightened her fine woollen black dress so that a diamond pattern formed by silk stitching lay in its right place on her waist. She looked so exquisitely neat and dustless that it flashed across his mind that she could not have come there direct from the train, that she must have stopped in somewhere to bathe and change. But looking up at the clock, he saw that she had not had the time for this.

'How are the children?' he said, busying himself with the Scotch.

'They're fine,' she answered. Her voice was a little unsteady with excitement. 'They sent you their love.'

'Uhuh,' he said, but went no further.

'Diana's going to Bryn Mawr next fall,' she added brightly.

'That so?' he said. 'Worth while if she's got your brains.' He thought to himself, as she sipped her highball and flashed up a quick eye to see what he was thinking, 'She seems pretty chipper considering the way things are. I guess that's Lambert. He hasn't the guts to take a beating and he'll have fooled her into believing that he's got some plan that will put them on their feet again. I remember how he was in business. But if her holdings are what I think they are they'll be sunk for a year. She ought to have more sense than to listen to Lambert. But, Gee! she looks well. She always did love a fight.'

Corrie took his highball and walked about the room. The storm shook the windows and he grimaced at it; then turned back to her, smiled and lifted his glass to drink to her. Her answering smile was slow and almost voluptuous. He put down his glass smartly to show he was ready to talk business.

'Well, Josie,' he said. 'How much are you dipped on this thing?'

She answered, 'Not a cent. I guess I can let you have all you want.'

He picked up his glass and twirled it, looking down into it though it was empty. 'Do you mean that, Josie?'

She jerked her head high. 'Not a cent. I guess I can help you out with all you're likely to have had on margin.'

'So that's why you came,' he said, and laughed for a long time. 'Well, I haven't lost a cent either. I came here . . .' He laughed again uproariously, 'to lend you money.'

'To lend *me* money?' she exclaimed, jerking her head still higher.

He thought to himself, 'Yes, lend you money, and damn it all, why not? You might have been caught like the rest of the world. If you weren't it must have been by accident, though I suppose by now you've built up a legend that it was just because you're the wonderful Josephine that's above everybody else. I guess Lambert's helped you get that way. I said that boob was just a cheer leader.' He realized that he was glaring at her, and had to turn aside and pour himself out another highball. 'Well, it's a shame this isn't April the First,' he said lightly.

Josephine seemed stunned. 'Did you come all this way to

51

lend me money?' she asked. 'That was good of you. Corrie, that was real good of you.'

'Oh, it was nothing, no more than what you've done,' he said. 'I guess we can always look to each other for that sort of thing.'

Before he had stopped speaking she had brought her brows together in a slight scowl. 'Why didn't you wire the position?' she asked.

'Why didn't you?' he answered. It was beginning to hurt him, the strain of keeping in order his good-humoured smile. For he was saying to himself, 'I know damn well why you didn't wire. You took it for granted that you would be up and I would be down. I know that feeling you have.'

There must have been some tartness in his tone for she murmured, her great eyes looking hungrily about the room, 'I only meant that you might have saved yourself that terrible long journey.'

'Isn't so bad,' he assured her brightly. 'I'll be back Tuesday. I'm pulling out this evening early. My new place needs me to look after it pretty badly.'

'Why,' she said vaguely. 'Are you building a house?'

He could have choked. It was as if, grown tall as the skies, she had knelt beside his white town and spat into the central square. 'No, a garage,' he said.

'We had to come anyway,' she went on.

'Who's "we"?' he asked.

'Jack Lambert,' she answered.

'I suppose you left him sitting down in the lobby,' he said. 'Too bad, with all the bell-hops falling over him. Shall we have him up?'

'He's over at the Brownrock,' she answered.

'Well, that's a whole heap nicer for him,' he said cheerfully. 'I'm glad about that. Well, we've made a couple of fools of ourselves. Haven't we?'

Her head was downcast. 'Yes,' she said.

'But a couple of nice fools, running to help each other out. Nice fools, aren't we, Josie?'

She nodded. Her face was childish in its sulkiness.

'So we'll just shake hands with each other, and say that we like the kind of fools we are, and turn round and go home, and never have another moment's ill-feeling against each other. I haven't any ill-feeling against you. Have you any ill-feeling against me, Josie?'

'No,' she said.

'We would have had if we hadn't parted when we did. We're both the same kind of nice fool, but we weren't the kind of fools that need each other. I said that from the beginning, and I guess I was . . .'

Oh, God in Heaven, why had he said that? But maybe she hadn't heard. For she had raised her head and cut into his words: 'How did it happen you didn't get hurt in the crash?'

'I put a whole heap in bonds,' he said.

'When did you do that?' she asked.

He saw what she was after. 'Oh . . . I guess a year ago.'

Her eyes rested on him a second, then slid to the corner of the room. 'Say right out you know me so damn well you know I'm lying and I sold out two years ago!' his thoughts raged. 'But what's the harm of me taking the chill off for myself? I've got a right to lie like anyone else.'

'Too bad,' said Josephine.

'What's too bad?' he asked pugnaciously.

'Too bad you shouldn't have raked in some of the profits that have been lying about these last few years,' she explained.

'Well, I should have lost the lot if I'd hung on, wouldn't I?' he burst out.

'Sure, sure,' she agreed, in a humouring tone.

'Well, I would, wouldn't I?' he cried.

'Oh, sure, that's what I'm saying,' she assured him. But when she fell silent the corners of her mouth turned up as if she held back a complacent smile.

'How did you keep out of it?' he demanded. 'Something damn smart, I suppose. Yes, you wouldn't be you if you

53

weren't damn smart, would you? Well, let's hear about it! Out where I am now in the West I don't meet smart people any more. Tell us about it, Josie. It'll take the hayseeds out of my hair.'

She kept her head down and murmured. 'I just had a hunch.'

'Well, wasn't that smart!' he said. 'To have a hunch that no one else had, and that everybody else would have given their eyes to have! Gee! if that isn't smart, what is?'

'And anyway,' she told him, still murmuring and keeping her chin on her breast, 'I had to sell out about then.'

'What's that?'

'I had to sell out about then,' she repeated.

He knew perfectly well from the silken sulkiness of her tone that he was wresting from her a secret which she was quite willing he should know, and that she was willing because there was some implication in that secret which he would find profoundly humiliating. Yet he could not stop.

He went and stood over her. 'What do you mean, you had to sell out? Are you putting all your eggs in one basket?'

She lifted her head and looked into his eyes. 'They're my own eggs.' Her chin went back to her breast again.

'Say, Josie, you didn't have to tell me that! I never put my hands on your money! But I would just hate to see you making a fool of yourself!' Something cold and remote in him said, before the words were out of his mouth, 'You know she never makes a fool of herself. That's one of the reasons why you hate her,' and a new muscle in her cheek twitched as if she were thinking the same. Yet he had to go on. 'I'd feel easier in my mind if you'd tell me about it!'

With a detestable, affected reluctance she said, 'Jack and me have joined up with some folks in Cincinnati to handle that Quintin River Power Scheme.'

He had to put down his glass. 'But, Josie,' he stuttered, 'that's a terribly big scheme.'

'We didn't see why Wall Street should get away with

everything in these United States,' she said with a gloating dourness.

'But, Josie,' he expostulated. 'You and Jack Lambert'll never ...'

She rolled an ironic eye on him. 'What's that?'

'It's too big, Josie, it's too big!' he cried. He paused for a second, his mouth open. Before him there appeared, in the bright colours of washable paint, an image of her enterprise; and he recognized its essential characteristic as success. He was familiar enough with current financial adventure to guess who the folks in Cincinnati would be. They were a sound crowd. He was fair enough, too, to recognize that Jack Lambert was the kind of guy who, though he never initiates anything, never loses his head. Put him in charge of big things and he will deal with them as coolly as if they were little; and Josie had put him in charge of the big things all right. They would pile up one of the great outside-New-York fortunes. He knew it. And why should he feel sore at it? Why shouldn't he feel grand about it? He wasn't mean. Yet he found himself protesting, 'Why, Josie, it's a wild-cat scheme I wouldn't have thought you would have fallen for! For crying out loud, why Josie ...'

'There's more to do with money in a new country than put it into bonds,' she told him icily.

'Holy smoke, Josie, one couldn't tell the difference between you and a rattler if one went by the tongue!' he groaned. 'Would you like to know why I put my money in bonds – some of it? Most of it's where it ought to be, in the business where I work. But I put some of it in bonds two years ago – a year ago, because I wanted to see my wife was all right whatever happened, and she's a real woman, the kind that can't look after herself; and I work so damned hard these days that I hadn't time to watch the stockmarket. I suppose you don't believe that?'

'Oh sure,' she said, 'you always worked hard.'

'Meaning that the poor dumb beast always had its nose to the grindstone. It wasn't that that was the matter with it.

Just that it had no sense. Well, I'll tell you that maybe I wasn't much when I was with you. There are things that eat out a man's guts. But now I'm doing a man's work.'

'Sure you are,' said Josephine. 'I know that, though I don't know much about your corporation. I just see it in the stock lists, that's all.'

Corrie drew in his breath with awe. 'My God, you are mean. You are so mean that there's a kind of grandness in it. You said that because we aren't where we ought to be yet. Gee, we can't be, laying the foundations the way we are out West. But you wait till 1932. You'll know about us then.'

She breathed, hardly audibly, 'Sure.'

'God in Heaven, I want to kill you quite a lot,' he told her, and walked the length of the room. For a minute or two he stood and looked out of the window at the storm. He turned and said over his shoulder to her. 'That bell of white flowers we were married under . . . ! Funny, isn't it?' Then he went back to the contemplation of the waters, until he swung about and walked back again, wondering if when he got to her he would do something that would send him to the chair. However, words came into his head that he had to say:

'Anybody's got to hand it to you,' he said, 'you're so smart when you're mean. You wait till 1932, you'll know about us then! That's the kind of a line a failure pulls. Only it happens to be true of my corporation, and we aren't failures. But the way you listened and the way you said "Sure" just tagged the lot of us as poor whites. Oh, you've done it. I've got to hand it to you. You've taken away my faith in jobs. I'll have to get back to my work and the real woman I live with before I believe in myself again. Oh, you're swell.'

She grumbled, 'I don't know what you're talking about.'

'Oh, yes you do. You're too smart not to know what I'm talking about. Gee, I hate to think of what you'll do with Quintin River. Money's the big thing, isn't it, Josie? Being

56

great, big, magnificent Josie with nearly all the money in the world. You'll make a grand thing of Quintin River. You'll have Southern niggers coming up and living where they can get in, knee-deep in filth. You'll have Mexicans, too, won't you, Josie? And you'll have Wops, too, lots of Wops. You won't do anything for them, and you'll look snooty when they fester in the rottenness where you've put them. You'll put welfare workers on them then and go all Nordic. You'll have labour troubles that'll cost the corporation a fortune and could have been avoided if you hadn't done the heavy all over them. You're mean and you're dumb. And always you'll get away with it. You'll hold your head up and people'll think you're grand.'

She said, still keeping her head down. 'I'm just awful, amn't I?'

'You're so awful,' he told her, 'that it makes me sick to think of my children being brought up by you. God, I wonder what you'll make of them.'

Suddenly she stood up. 'You needn't worry. They look like you and act like you all the time.'

'That must be terrible for you,' he said. 'What do you do about it?'

'What I can,' she answered. 'And thank God they've got a real man living with them now as an example.'

'What, have you left Jack Lambert and picked something better?'

'I'm talking of Jack Lambert. He's a better man than you.'

'My God! My God!' The laughter poured out of him. He was afraid he would not be able to stop it.

'Stop that noise. You're like a hysterical woman.'

'I am not. Times have changed. Hysterical women act large and calm nowadays. You have to watch them before you find out they're just crazy with meanness.'

'I'm going now. Thank God Jack Lambert's waiting for me.'

'Thank God my wife's waiting for me. It tickles me to

57

death the way you call him Jack Lambert. You don't call him your husband, do you?'

'I give him his name because he's a real person and doesn't just tag around with me.'

'You can go back to him when you like. But I wish you'd tell me why you hate me so. I never did anything to you.'

'I guess you're right. I hate you. I hate the bones in your spine that don't stand up straight, the blood in your veins that isn't red. I hate the silly hair on your head that isn't like a man's hair. And you've done a lot to me.'

'I never did a thing. Yes I did, though. I hated you the way you hated me. Do you know that out West we have to make roads up on the hills and every once in a while we come on great outcrops of rock. They're hard and they're mean and they aren't any good. They're just in the way, and you can't get on till they're gone. They always put me in mind of you. Whenever I see one go up with the dynamite I say to myself, "That's a good divorce!" ...'

'If I'm like a rock, you're like a swamp. You're like those swamps down by the river that you can't drain. You're weak and sloppy.'

'What's this lie that goes on and on about me being weak? I'm not weak. What have I done that's weak?'

'What's this lie that goes on and on about me being hard? I'm not hard.'

'You're so hard I want to kill you, Josie. Now I've seen you I can't think there'll ever be anything decent in the world so long as you're alive. God, you are mean. I want to kill you.'

'I wouldn't mind being killed if they got you for it.'

'Yes, that's you. Hell! you're mean. You're so mean you wouldn't mind giving your life to get me into trouble. All the same I'd like to kill you.'

'How'd you kill anybody? You couldn't do it. You haven't got the guts.'

'Haven't I? I'll show you.'

They were shouting so loud that for some time they did

not hear the knocking on the door. When it penetrated to them they stopped and watched the door defiantly.

'Hell, they won't stop me,' said Corrie. 'Let 'em knock.'

But a service key clicked in the lock, and a bell-boy stood and looked at them.

'Say, what did you want?' asked Corrie.

'Come for the baggage.'

'Will you get to hell out of here?' said Corrie. 'I told the desk to send half after five.'

'Well, sure, it is half after five.'

Corrie flung out his hand at the clock on the wall. 'Does that say half after four or does it not?'

With the insolent pride of the young who find themselves able through secret information to put their elders to shame, the bell-boy squawked, 'Sure, it says half after four, but it's an hour slow. The central do-funny of them clocks ate something this morning, and there isn't one in the house that isn't fooling.'

Corrie looked at his wrist-watch. 'I guess you needn't get to hell. Take my bag. It's in the other room.'

They stood still, listening to the buffets of the storm on the windows, till the bell-boy came back through the room again. Corrie said, 'When do I have to leave this hotel to catch the six o'clock Limited?'

'It takes all of twenty minutes.'

'I'd best leave in ten minutes, then.'

'That's right.'

As the door closed Josie dropped on her knees. Tears were running down her cheeks, and she seemed about to fall forward on her face. Corrie knelt in front of her, so that he could take her in his arms.

Her lips against his fair hair, she whimpered, 'I thought we had another hour!'

He groaned, 'Ten minutes; we've only got ten minutes. Josie, how are we going to bear this?'

They rocked together, body to body, and looked into the years ahead.

THERE IS NO CONVERSATION

THERE IS NO CONVERSATION

I

THERE is no such thing as conversation. It is an illusion. There are intersecting monologues, that is all. We speak; we spread round us with sounds, with words, an emanation from ourselves. Sometimes they overlap the circles that others are spreading round themselves. Then they are affected by these other circles, to be sure, but not because of any real communication that has taken place, merely as a scarf of blue chiffon lying on a woman's dressing-table will change colour if she casts down on it a scarf of red chiffon. I am talking now of times when life is being lived, not when it is being talked about, not when the intellect is holding the field. Then, of course, ideas can be formulated, can be passed from one mind to another. It is not easy, but it can be done with care, like handing round a pearl on which you wish an opinion to a circle of experts. You cup the palm to hold it, you keep tne hand very steady. No such caution is possible when one is really living. Then there is no conversation.

Nothing ever demonstrated to me more effectively that such is the case than the story which was unravelled to me not long ago by a series of incidents which began on a September afternoon, in the Champs Elysées, when I met the Marquis de Sevenac.

I tried not to see him, because meeting him always involves me in one of those insincerities to which people who are interested in character constantly find themselves committed. When we are together I cannot help watching him with a fascinated fixity, because he perpetually struggles with a comic dilemma. Étienne de Sevenac is older than he likes to be, for he is fifty and an inveterate beauty. When one looks at him one gets a terrifying intimation that age exists as an isolated and devouring entity, that it is not just

63

the name we give to the running down of the old machine, the lining of the skin, the dimming of the eyes, the blanching of the hair, the decrepitude of the skeleton; for his skin is white and smooth, his deep-set eyes are bright as a boy's, and therefore those white streaks in his hair have that look of prematurity and contrast which is so attractive, his body is straight as if he were a young cavalry officer. Yet youth has gone out of him. How does one know it? I cannot say. One just sees age ingrained in him. It cannot be described because it is unlike anything else. One can imagine him looking in a mirror and checking up all the different warnings of old age and saying, 'Yes, I'm all right, ask that, there's no sign of that coming on; and yes, I'm all right there too; yes, and that's all right too', and in satisfaction turning away to some other occupation; and then suddenly arresting himself, because there was a tingling in his mind, as if something he had seen in the mirror had struck a chord of apprehension in his being that was going on vibrating and vibrating and vibrating till he could attend to nothing else, till he was shaken and shattered . . . till he got up and performed some of those ministrations to himself which were responsible for his marvellous appearance: rubbed creams into his forehead with the fingertips of a masseur; fitted the little cup full of boracic lotion to his eye and tilted the head sharply backwards; wrote a letter to his electro-therapeutist to say he would come and have the ultra-violet rays on the scalp to-morrow at seven; raised his arms straight above his head with the grimace of disgust which the voluptuary feels when his body has to do anything but describe curves encircling curves, and let the muscles of his stomach clench and shut the torso down close to the legs like the blade of a closing jack-knife, gesture loathsome to him in its tempo so different from that of seduction; then hit the floor again and again, first with the palm of the hand then with its back, in a way that could not have been borne if it had not been the only way he could tell that he had extended himself to the extent that it was understood was absolutely necessary if he was to keep really . . . Then he slipped his feet into shoes that were a little narrower and longer than was necessary, and hurried out to find some people who were beautiful and gay and young, who obviously would not bore themselves for one moment with the society of anybody who was old . . .

Then the dilemma declared itself. For however great a success, Étienne honestly paid for, and should have received if there was any justice on earth, however quickly and loudly he talked, however often he was witty or burst with immediate comprehension into laughter at the wit of the youngest people present, however he remembered to sit up straight as if he too had just been playing tennis, and to keep his waistcoat from sagging in front of him like a sail that the wind had forsaken, sooner or later the talk began to stream past him, just as he had noticed in his youth that it did past the people who were outmoded. It was as if that isolated factor of age, which had been the salient characteristic of his image in the mirror, although his skin and his hair and his bearing had refused to lend themselves to the expression of it, was now looking out from interstices between his jokes which he could have sworn he had carefully closed by a continuous animation.

At such moments – I had been present so often that I could interpret the signs quite easily – an expedient for laying hold of the attention that was rushing past him would occur to him. He would for a brief space be entirely silent, his eyes would fall on to his long, narrow shoes, in which he would wriggle his toes as if he had forgotten that he must never show they hurt him or it was no good wearing them. His waistcoat would fall forward like the deflated sail, his face would turn a curious dead white, like a paper flower. He was impaled on a choice that to him, poor fellow, was a really horrible necessity. You see, he had been born of a great family, his mother had maintained for several generations one of the most famous salons in Paris, in his youth his exquisite though vulgarly indubitable good looks had caused all kinds of society in every capital to make much of him; in fact, there was no interesting European personality for the last fifty years of which he had not some first-hand memory. Young people are interested in that kind of thing to-day, it is the fashion. One can always get them to listen if one tells them what the valet one's father took on the recommendation of Robert de Montesquiou said when he was reproached with indiscretion committed with the laundry maid whom one's mother had taken on the recommendation of the Princesse de Caraman-Chimay. But memories are like furniture. If they are only five, or ten, or fifteen years old, they make no appeal. To enjoy the present one must believe that one has just emerged from the banal; but one can concede the qualities of romance to a past so remote that one had no part in it. Young people will listen if one speaks of twenty, of thirty – oh, the little brutes – of forty years ago. But to have such memories is to admit that one is old ... The toes wriggled in the shoes. Either he would jump to his feet and go, with an air of being forced to leave this place where he was having such a tremendously good time because a woman (and perhaps there are too many women in the world) was waiting for him. Or one would hear his voice gathering body in the still air of an entranced room, 'That reminds me of the first time Marcel Proust ever came to see my mother, when he was a boy of sixteen...' Then victory had been gained, but at what a price...

It interests me to watch such conflicts. I cannot take my eyes off one if it is enacted in front of me; and that fixity Étienne de Sevenac, who was not unobservant, had recorded but had misinterpreted. He thought I liked him. As it happened he could not be under the delusion that I loved him. But he believed that I regarded him as a pleasant person, that I was full of kindly wishes for his well-being. In this he was wrong. I felt no pity for his distress about his age, because in fact he was not old. He was at most a year or so over fifty and in a physical state that would have contented anybody who had not had some gluttonous dream of being a young Antinous for decade after decade. He was just being a bore, like those film actresses who from the age of twenty-five utter no words except, 'I've got to have my face lifted. Don't you think I ought to have my face lifted?' Also I feel that people are bound to have accumulated interests and responsibilities which leave them no time for these narcissistic excesses unless they have lived with an appalling coldness and selfishness. I do not like him at all. But although I have no pity for his distress I do not want to increase it by being disagreeable; for I know that then he would say to himself, 'She was not like this last year. Ah, I suppose I have aged a lot since then.' Therefore, when I meet him, I am insincerely agreeable. Therefore, when I can, I avoid meeting him.

But that day I submitted quietly. For when I first saw Étienne he was walking quite close to the trees, in the shadow and with his face turned to where it was darker, although the other side of the pavement, where by the rule of the road he ought to have been walking, was golden with what would probably be the last strong sunlight of the year. A tyreburst made him turn towards the road a face that I thought haggard and wild. It was then that he saw me. He cut incivilly across the path of some prettier women than myself to get to me; and it seemed that the line of his footsteps somehow traced a diagram of misery.

He said, taking my hand but forgetting to smile, 'I didn't know you were in Paris.'

I answered, 'I arrived only last night from my house in Provence.'

Perfunctorily he said, 'You look wonderful. And how wise you are to give up those eternal sports clothes and wear a tailor made. You can wear that sort of thing.' A pause fell because he was so preoccupied that he had lost all touch with his own conversation. He knew he had embarked on the sort of remark which he believed obligatory at that stage of the conversation, but he could not tell what he had said, or whether he had said enough and could go on to the matter regarding which he really longed to speak. He remembered to ask me, 'How is your husband?' and then he stood beside me in silence while I felt like a pillar-box in which an absent-minded person has posted letters which he would like to recover so that he could see if he has properly addressed and stamped them.

Then he said, 'Come and have a cocktail at my flat.'

I objected, 'I was just about to take a taxi to the Rue de Ranelagh to see Violet...'

He said, 'But you don't understand. I want you to come and see my pictures.'

Dumbfounded I said, 'But surely I've seen your pictures often enough!'

He gripped my arm and shook it, and exclaimed, rather as if I had become hysterical in a shipwreck and were refusing to leave the deck and get into a boat although there was no longer a moment to spare, 'Yes, you've seen them often enough! But they're sold! They're going to be taken off my walls to-morrow! I want you to see them once again!'

I gasped, 'They're sold!' That was inexplicable. Étienne adored his pictures, he surely could have no need to sell them, for he was a very rich man. I had known him many years and in many places, and I had never known him not to spend vast amounts of money. 'Why did you do that?'

'I had to,' he said, 'I'm ruined.' And as I still regarded him in amazement, he added, 'I haven't anything left, I have had to give up my flat, I'm going to London on Monday to help Uncle Léon in the Bank. I have always detested that place.' He made as he spoke the large enveloping gestures I had often seen him use when he was compelling people to give him their attention by providing them with some anecdote so remote and so compendious, so successful in forcing Zola and Yvette Guilbert and Rostand and Hérédia and Degas on to the same sofa in his mother's drawing-room, that everybody was sure to find something for themselves in it. I was conscious that he was receiving a certain amount of pleasure from holding the interest of another human being by his present instead of by his past, but it was not nearly enough to offset the desolation, the sense of wrong, that was flattening his voice to a kind of drone unnatural to a Frenchman, specially unnatural to him.

I murmured, 'What a shame! I am so sorry! Your lovely flat.'

'Yes,' he said, 'you always loved it, didn't you? Come and see it for the last time!'

I had never felt the slightest emotion concerning his flat, and indeed at the moment had but a faint recollection of it, as the last occasion I had visited it was distant by perhaps seven or eight years. Still Étienne was so obviously near to tears at that moment, and so eternally under the temperamental necessity of doing whatever he had to do, whether it was weeping or anything else, before an audience, that I was quite willing to fall in with his ideas and go back to his flat with him. But unfortunately I had not only forgotten what his flat was like, I had even forgotten where it was. So I had to stand pretending a vacillation that I did not feel, that was plainly inappropriate to the consideration of a visit that was to be purely one of condolence, until he laid his hand on my arm and gently compelled me in the right direction. In point of fact his flat was quite near, it was in one of those side-streets on the right as you go up towards the Bois. He had moved to it years and years ago, on the occasion of his divorce, from a much nicer house he had had in the Faubourg St Germain, to be near the Villa Saïd, when he was thinking of writing a book on a journey he had made in Syria with Pierre Louÿs, and Anatole France had promised to help him: a reason insubstantial in all but the richness of its elusiveness.

He walked alongside me, with his head down and his hands clasped behind his back, silent most of the time but occasionally breaking out in excitement to say the same thing over and over again. 'I can't believe it's happened yet. I can't credit it. Fancy having to go to live in London at the beginning of the winter. You see, there isn't one thing where my luck has held . . .' It was like a man taking a doctor home to his wife, 'She's dreadfully bad, doctor, she's dreadfully bad.'

It was on the fourth floor. Étienne did not mind any more going up slowly, he forgot to be afraid that I might think he could not run up fast. I remembered the sitting-room once I had seen it. It was lined with a pitted silver Japanese wallpaper that made one feel as if one were sitting cheek by cheek with the moon. It had been furnished some time before the war, when there was no nonsense about period decoration or austerity. There was a Dutch marquetry escritoire, and an Italian refectory table, and some Louis-Quinze chairs, and an Empire cabinet, all very good, and brass table lamps with fluted silk shades, not at all good, and thousands of things lying about on everything, snuff-boxes, scarabs, some very fine trifles in old Dutch silver, cameos, jade and soapstone carvings, small bronzes, most of them priceless but all insignificant. I don't know why he had never had the place refurnished; perhaps because to do so would have been to admit that the taste of his maturity already belonged to the past. And indeed at this moment there was a beautiful architectonic quality about the pointlessness of the room, seen from the armchair he had pushed forward for me. On my left this pointlessness was focused at the doorway, which was hung with portières made of a very beautiful piece of Persian embroidery which had been intended to be hung not vertically but horizontally, so that in its present state it made the onlooker squint with its lines of flowers lying on their sides, its birds and beasts that did not reveal their nature until one had found which way they were lying. One of the portières had been torn down from the rungs at one point, where it formed a scalloped pouch which added to the craziness of their appearance. On the other side the same tipsy treatment of matter was secured by one of those mirrors that I had never seen anywhere else except in the country, in the houses of very simple people, of old maids who can no longer get about, of dressmakers who have to keep their nose over the needle all day. You attach them to the side of one's window by a nickel arm, at an angle to the wall, projecting into the air, and they at least enfranchise you from the view of the house opposite by showing you what is going on down the street. This presented me with a bright little view of high, white, pompous houses ending like cliffs above the tawny confusion of the Champs Elysées' chestnuts under which passed a fugue of little figures, man, woman, child, child, woman, man, child, man, woman, child, the concentration of the mercury surface exaggerating all colours, so that the falling chestnut leaves looked like sovereigns thrown from an at last remembering Providence to the mob, the women's flesh-coloured stockings seemed pink as blush roses, the children's balloons had apparently lights glowing in them, the men's black coats were black as coffins. It was characteristic of the room that what seemed most intense in the room should in fact not be there at all. Between this portière and that window Étienne walked like the governing principle of confusion, waving a shaker with that curious lateral motion which the elderly Frenchman of fashion believes to be the Transatlantic way of preparing a cocktail, but which actually resembles nothing so much as the English coster's way of playing his concertina. You could not say that there was not a kind of harmony about the scene.

He was looking about the room at points where I could see nothing, and I perceived that there had been much in my idea that he was like a man bringing the doctor home to a scene of suffering. Something had happened in this room which had caused him such enduring misery that to him it was as if it was still happening. It was here, I supposed, that he had first heard that he had lost all his money.

I murmured, taking the glass he gave me, 'Oh, all those lovely pictures? My poor dear, I am so sorry, so very, very sorry.'

71

He sat down and drank, his chest concave. 'They go to-morrow morning. People are coming to pack them up at ten o'clock. Charles de Frélac has bought them. He didn't give me enough for them. My father always said old Madame de Frélac was a Jewess.'

We stared at them gloomily. They were really very nice pictures. There was a Toulouse-Lautrec of a pale handsome boy, sickly with excess of race, holding a wolf-hound on leash beside a stormy violet sea; there was a Manet of a girl in a limp white dress sitting in a boat on blue waters crumbling under the assault of heat; there was a Monet, too late, too deliquescent, but fine enough with its parrot-plumaged sunset; there were two Renoirs, one sticky with the juices of a Provençal landscape, the other spherical with the shapes of peasant women resting under a hedge; there was one of Sisley's *sage* little canals. I like them, but I really felt too puzzled to enjoy or regret them.

How in the world could Étienne, who was sanity itself about money, have become destitute?

I turned to him with the intention of asking, but it struck me that he would have told me at once unless the cause was so loathsome to him that he could not bring himself to speak of it; and indeed as he sat and looked round at his pictures his mouth was drawn down as if his cocktail had been a nauseous medicine. Then his eye, travelling from a portrait of his little sister on the left of the doorway to a drawing of Gauthier-Villars and his secretary (in the costume of Little Lord Fauntleroy) at a bar at Wimereux, crossed the portières and seemed to be arrested. He shot forward his chair, spilling his cocktail over his knees, pointed a stiff finger at the pouch of portière that hung loose from its ring, and wheeled round at me.

'Americans!' he exclaimed. Just that. But the word explained just why he had crossed the pavement to me with such urgency, just why he had importuned me to come back to his flat. Étienne de Sevenac never does anything without a conscious purpose. He cannot spare the vitality from this perpetual nagging preoccupation with his age. If he had lost his money in speculating in oil wells in Mesopotamia, a subject concerning which I know nothing, he would have informed me of it and passed on. But he knew that he can discuss Americans with me to his profit. This is not because my husband, George Templeton, is an American, for Étienne is not so simple as to suppose that one learns to understand a nation by marrying one of its children. It is because I am English by birth, and he knows that the Right Wing of the English temperament stretches towards Europe and touches France with its tip, and that the Left Wing stretches all the way to America, and that therefore I can tell him about the United States in terms which his French mind can comprehend. It was for that he had called me in this afternoon.

He cried, 'Americans! American women! You have always told me that they were civilized!'

'So they are.'

'I will tell you! I will show you they are not. Have you half an hour? Can you wait? I will tell you!' He set down his cocktail glass on the table, went to the portières and thrust his body out between them, calling, 'Guillaume! Guillaume! I am not at home to anybody!' He came back towards me, then on a second thought thrust out his body crying, 'But, Guillaume! Guillaume! You can come in yourself if you want to!' Then he settled down again in his chair, pointing his forefinger at me like a schoolmaster.

Perfunctorily he remembered to say, crooking the forefinger and wagging it as if he were beckoning to a dog, 'It is such a consolation to tell you all this. You always understand so perfectly.' Then he got going with his story.

'It began last Easter. I was very unhappy about that time, because Léonie had gone out to the Argentine to spend a year with her old father and mother, and you know my temperament. I must have a woman friend, a close woman friend. It is not at all because the physical side of love means so very much to me, it is because I need sympathy, because I like to be tender. All that. It is queer how it is always one's virtues and not one's vices that precipitate one into disaster.

'It was when I was in that state of loneliness, of frustrated tenderness, that I met a woman named Mrs Sarle. Nancy Sarle. You know there's an American woman living on the first floor flat down below. We meet in the hall sometimes and speak sometimes. She knows my Cousin Lucie quite well, so I don't care to be disagreeable, I often go to stay with Lucie at her villa in Cannes. This American woman has a son and a daughter who are quite young, they look charming, though as it turns out they are not. Well, I met her in the hall one April morning, and she asked me to lunch the next day, and I accepted, because the son and daughter were home from college, and I wanted to meet them.

'Mrs Sarle was at this lunch. I would not have taken any notice of her if it had not been that the young people were not at all agreeable, and had a lot of friends of their own age who occupied them entirely. They had apparently not been educated to be polite to their mother's guests. So I was thrown back on this Mrs Sarle, though she was not beautiful, not beautiful at all, and had a very bad figure, too broad, short but with shoulders like a man's, and was not at all elegant. And she was quite old. Forty-two. Forty-three. Perhaps forty-five! That is all right if a woman is elegant. But if she is not it is disgusting. I should have been warned by her lack of elegance! For a woman who does not care for that shows herself callous, cruel, vehement . . . But I was at the mercy of my loneliness, which had turned me back into myself, which had made me forget all those qualities one assumes for one's protection when one has dealings with others, so that I was just as I fundamentally am, foolishly kind, indulgent, anxious to spread happiness wherever I go. And she had eyes that excited my pity: blue, very blue eyes, that she seemed to use for no purpose but seeing. When I spoke to her she looked straight at me, as if she wanted to see me. They were her only feature, and she had not the ghost of an idea how to manage them. It was pathetic to think of how little could ever have happened to her, particularly as there was something in those really extraordinary blue eyes which told of an immense appetite for life. She would have adored to be somebody, that little thing! To have been elegant, to have had lovers, to have known passion and adventure in romantic surroundings, her heart was craving for it. She was one of those women who in spite of their fine minds read *romans de concierge* because there is that in them which is more insistent than the mind. When she told me that this was the first time she had been in Europe, because her late husband had hated travelling and had added that this was due not to selfishness or stupidity but to his age, since he was over seventy when he died, I could have burst into tears. Pity is my dominant characteristic. Pity which expresses itself sometimes without due thought for the consequences to myself. I often think that Dostoevsky's *The Idiot* might have been written about me. Prince Myshkin, *c'est moi*.

'I resolved then and there that I would help the poor little thing, that before she left Paris she should have some of the things that till now she had lacked. After lunch I drove her back to her hotel. She was staying as they all do at the Ritz. Just before I left her I felt a positive gush of pity for her, like the rising of a warm fountain, because when I happened to say to her that I had seen so many beautiful women of her country when I had gone into the Ritz bar the day before for a cocktail, she said modestly that she did not dare to go, all the people there seemed so perfectly dressed and so sure of themselves. Think of it, to feel unworthy of entering that place where distinction has never been seen, which is so exactly comparable to those show-places in the corridors of the hotel outside which exhibit with the extreme emphasis obtainable from crystal and electric light goods which make a dazzling appeal to the eye and speak of ingenuity and industry and even invention on the part of those who make them, and which no person of refinement could regard without derision! She was of course right. She came up to the standards of no world. Filled with tenderness, I asked her to lunch with me the next day.

'She seemed surprised. Certainly she belonged to the order of women who are accustomed to meet men only once. Her expression made me see as by a flash of lightning a life inconceivably monotonous, spent in servitude, in duties faithfully performed and requited, by not one romantic generosity on the part of fate. No doubt she had been wooed by this elderly husband because of her value as a sick-nurse, no doubt her marriage had been but an extension of a familiar bondage under another name and slightly more remunerative terms. No wonder she could not believe that I was interested in her. Positively I had to insist on her accepting my invitation.

'We lunched at Armenonville. It is an obvious place, but I have often found it pleases very simple women inordinately. The shepherdess idea persists in nearly every woman, if a man takes her out in the open air to eat she immediately feels as if she carried a be-ribboned crook and all her sheep will come home behind her. It was so with my little Nancy Sarle. Sitting there at the little table she blossomed. As I looked there seemed fewer of those dreadful little lines under the eyes which are the cruellest misfortunes of your sex. (You have none yet, none at all, my dear.) She began noticing the dresses of the women at other tables, asking me if I approved of them. I can't tell you how pathetic it was. Then she began questioning me about my life. Who I was. Very naïvely. I told her. Always with this woman I was simple and honest, like a child. She pretended to be a little shocked at hearing that I did no work, she kept saying, "But what do you do all day? How do you pass the time?" bringing her brows together as if she disapproved. But really she was enchanted by everything I told her of our

Parisian life, so different from anything in her poor little experience. I could tell that by the way that she opened her blue eyes very wide every time I mentioned anybody with a title: particularly if I said that they were related to me. She tried to control it, she was not so naïve as all that. Always the shutter slipped back, a little child looked out, then the shutter was barred again. What a fool I am. Do you observe I am still speaking of her with tenderness?

'I asked if she would come with me to the theatre. It must be so difficult for a woman without a man to see Paris. I gave her to understand she would be giving me an immense pleasure by going. Then too the shutter slipped back, a shy little child looked out, then, naturally enough, since the life of a plain woman must be more full of humiliation than people like us can ever realize, the shutter was barred again. But she came. I took her to see the Guitrys. She didn't understand a word, of course, but how she loved Yvonne Printemps, with the infinitely touching reverence of a plain woman for a beautiful one. I felt nearer to her than ever, more paternal, more anxious to give her a little happiness. Though she demurred, we lunched together again the next day. During the following week we were perpetually together. I did everything I could for her, out of my knowledge of the life she hungered for I was able to give and give and give, and I gave without stint. I taught her how to eat, I took her to Voisin, to Larue, to Lapérouse, to Foyot. I taught her how to drink, not always that abominable champagne. I took her to Chanel and said quite simply, "For my sake, dress this lady". And Coco did some things for her in which, really, she didn't look at all bad. I honestly was not at all ashamed to be seen out with her.

'I even introduced her to my friends. I gave luncheon parties for her. I felt so pleased that my position in Paris enabled me to do that. People will accept anything I do. And it gave her such joy. I wish you could have seen her sit down at a table and look round and say to herself with that adorable shutter, little child, shutter again look, "Why, everybody here but me has a title!" She was so naïve that she actually said that to me once. I went mad, I pestered friends of mine to invite her to their *soirées*. Some of them obliged me. Even the Duchesse de Draguignan let me bring her to a ball. I tell you, I gave to her with an insane generosity.

'It was the day after that ball, I remember, that I made my two mistakes: that I put myself doubly in her power. Usually she would not see me till twelve. I don't know what she did till then. I suppose she wrote letters to relatives and friends, women without elegance like herself in places with incredible names like Cincinnati and Tallahassee; boasting probably about me. Do you know, I am not vindictive. It quite touches me to think of those letters. Well, this morning she would not see me until one. I went up to her sitting-room to have an *apéritif* before lunch. I always felt touched by this sitting-room. It was so big that I was always infinitely touched by it. She must have paid a fortune for it: you know how we make Americans pay. It was obvious that she must have a great deal of money; and that a woman with money should have made so little of herself! Specially I felt this that morning, for, no doubt because I was making her keep later hours than was her custom, she was looking pathetically old: or rather she was making no disguise of how old she looked, that was what seemed so dreadful. I was running my eye round the room, noting without censoriousness, simply with pity, how utterly incompetent as a woman she was, how she had added to that hotel room not one article, not one photograph, not one *objet d'art,* which made the claim a woman who knows her business ought perpetually to be making, "I have personality, I am unique, I have charm". Suddenly I caught sight of an object that surprised me. On the top of the writing-desk was a toy engine, very nicely finished, with gleaming paint and steel as bright as silver, quite a good size, about twelve inches long. It occurred to me that perhaps my poor little Nancy was a mother, that she had children, whom of course she adored, but of whom she had never spoken to me, because she feared that it would make her appear in a less romantic light, not knowing how little of that sort of thing there was between us.

'I said gently, "You have been buying toys?"

'She looked at me with those blue, blue eyes. "Toys?"

'I waved my hand towards the engine.

'I should have taken warning. She looked at it and then back at me, and her eyes were like steel, like two steel drills. "That's not a toy!" she said in a grim, rough voice like a man's. "That's a model. That cost a thousand dollars, that did. Pretty dear for a toy. And what it stands for is going to cost me dearer still." Quite abruptly, she turned her back on me, went over to the writing-table, and stood looking down on the little engine for a minute. With a gesture horrible in a woman she knocked the ash off her cigarette on to the carpet, not caring where it went. I do not think women understand how repelled a man feels when he sees a woman wholly absorbed in what she is thinking, unless it is about her child, or her husband, or her lover. It . . . gives one gooseflesh. I made a violent movement in my chair, I struck my glass against the table, so that she recollected I was there, and turned to me with an exclamation. She said, "I am still very much interested in this. It's a new type of locomotive we are putting on the line. And I am not sure about it. Not sure at all. I have a hunch . . ."

'She went from me again. I said, "I do not understand. What have you to do with railways?"

'For a minute she did not answer, but just looked at me with those eyes that were like two drills. She repeated, "What have I to do with railways?"

'I laughed. "Yes! This interests me extraordinarily! I am dying to know what you have to do with railways!"

'She took a step towards me, several steps. I should have taken warning from the way she looked at that moment. Her eyes were of this astonishing hardness, her face was furrowed with lines like a strong old man's, she moved like a man. When a woman gives up her grace . . . In a rasping voice she asked, "Don't you know what I have to do with railways?"

'I stammered, "No!" I could hardly bear to look at her, but I dared not take my eyes off her, in case it suddenly flashed over her that she was repulsive. I was afraid that if I once let go my pose of infatuation my true feelings would disclose themselves and her heart would break.

'She said, "Don't you know that Mr Sarle was President of the South-West and West-South Route from New York to Los Angeles by the Mexican Border?" She spoke with immense pride. I could see she adored her wealth. "And that I still potter about with the concern?"

'I cried out laughing, "No! I knew nothing of that! But I rejoice, because now I know there is another link between us as well as my love for you. For I too am concerned with an American Railway!"

'Still very thin-lipped and mannish, and old, and leaning over me like a schoolmaster over a pupil he suspects of cheating, she said, "How may that be?"

'And I told her. Think of my demented folly! I told her. I put into her hands the weapon by which she has destroyed my life. Still laughing, I said, "I hold half a million dollars' worth of stock of another American railway. The St Louis and the Los Angeles United. When my father died I realized every penny of my inheritance and on the advice of my uncle Léon de Férodoville, I bought this stock which just then had happened to come on the market."

'She said, "In 1911. Old man Watkins had died. It was his holding. My, you have made some money since then." Then she turned away, and bent over some flowers . . . Do you know it is a strange thing that in the same five minutes I saw the worst and the best of that woman? Still bending over the flowers she looked across at me, and her eyes did that shutter trick – the shutter opening, the little child showing herself . . . but this time the shutter did not close. The little child continued to confront me, with her innocence, her faith in life, her gratitude for kindness, her belief that if she was a good little girl God would send her all sorts of lovely things. She said, you cannot think how prettily, "These are your flowers, I haven't thanked you for them yet."

'My heart turned over in me with compassion. I forgot what she had been a minute before. I saw only the little child to whom I desired to be kind, and for a second time I delivered myself into her hands. I stood up and said, "Let us go to lunch at once, because I am going to ask you to do me a favour this afternoon. I am going to ask you to come to my flat and look at my pictures."

'Do you know, that affair was at moments quite charming. She was not so utterly without temperament as one might have supposed. And I had the joy of giving her so much. I conveyed to her how many marvellous women had been her predecessors, how by meeting me she had in a sense allied herself with the most beautiful and charming figures of the time. I taught her all she could possibly learn about civilized relations between men and women, even I got her to understand a little about subtlety, to grasp the nature of *finesse*. I staged one or two little quarrels for her, I instructed her in the art of the reconciliation. It was delightful to see her blossoming like a flower, not a very beautiful flower, it is true, but such as it was in a full state of blossom. I took so many little lines away from her face.

'But she stayed in Paris too long! You know how brief their visits usually are, these Americans! Unless they take a house here. Then they stick here interminably, they don't seem to want to leave Paris, as we Parisians do, for the south in the winter, and the north in the summer. But she went on living at the Ritz. Every day I expected her to say something about going home, but it never came. I had relied on a month, on six weeks. Two months even I could have stood. But April went, May went, June was going . . . and not a word. I ask you, can a man go on being kind for ever? I could not keep it up, in a sense it was not to be expected that I should. I had brought romance in her life, what more

81

could I do? I could not keep it there! After the victory has been gained, there is nothing to do unless one can live some sort of common life, that is unless one can go to certain places together. One can do that with a married woman of one's own class; one can do it with an actress, with a *cocotte*, though the places one goes to are different. But this woman did not belong to any world, she did not fit in anywhere. When I was no longer inflamed by my own kindness I found it too much of an effort to try to contrive a place for her in my world. And when I was beginning to be thoroughly irked by the situation I fell in love. With the most delicious woman in the world. Who is quite young. Almost a girl. Who left the Duc de Cortorenia, who is very young, who is in his twenties, for me. I cannot tell you how the chain I had forged out of my own generosity dragged on me then. One day when I saw for the first time definitely that I could make this adorable creature mine if only I pursued her, and I had the chance to spend the evening with her, I had an engagement to dine with this Mrs Sarle. I excused myself with the curtest *petit bleu*.

'I went to see her the next day. I don't do things brutally. I was prepared to confront her reproaches coldly, to shrug my shoulders when she cried, to point out that romance had got to come to an end when there was no real basis for it; and at the end, when we had got all that over, to have said one or two things that would have convinced her that in me she had a real friend. Mind you it was entirely her own fault that any of this had to happen. If she had gone back to America in reasonable time all this need never have happened. Then I would have gone down to the station with roses perhaps all the way to Cherbourg if she had seemed very upset. That would have been much pleasanter for everybody.

'When she received me I thought there was going to be a lot of trouble. There was a curious stillness about her, like that which falls on some women when they are going to be violently hysterical. Her blue eyes looked curiously blank.

They moved slowly from object to object, they rested on my face with deadly intensity. But all she said was, "To-morrow I am going to Carlsbad to do a cure."

'Do you know, although there was absolutely nothing I could do about it, I nearly burst out crying! To go to Carlsbad for a cure in the middle of June! Why, the hotels would hardly be open. No, I could see too well that she was pathetically trying to apply some of the method of *finesse* in which I had instructed her. When a man seems to tire of you, don't pursue him, withdraw so that he, piqued, may pursue you . . . To something as crude as that she had reduced my suggestion that in love there can be the most delicate interplay, that a woman may dance a psychological minuet with her lover, to a fine filigree music like Couperin's. It was pathetic! I spent the whole day with her, and took roses down to the train next day.

'I got a note in a few days, of course, which I answered shortly but amiably. I had an idea that by the time she returned to Paris I should be at Deauville with a very agreeable little party, and that the whole thing could pass off without the need for any explanation. I felt entirely happy about it all, I had brought a great deal of joy into her life, and evidently I was to be rewarded, for the affair that was nearest my heart was prospering. Consider my distress when after another few days I got a letter from Nancy Sarle, asking me quite crudely and stupidly if I loved her. I wish I had kept that letter, but it embarrassed me so that I tore it up at once. Also I felt so sorry for the poor little thing who had made this desperate attempt at self-control and *finesse* and had not been able to stand by it. But I would have liked to show it to you. You could not have believed that a woman could be so . . . not immodest, because that sounds as if the letter had too much consciousness of sex, whereas actually it had too little. It was the kind of letter a woman might write to you asking if she had understood you aright in conversation at lunch the other day and it was correct that you were prepared to let her your villa at Cap Martin

83

for so many thousand francs a month. But it was nothing to the second letter I got a few days later. That . . . Oh, I'll tell you what it was like. The kind of letter your lawyer writes you when he has sent you some papers to sign and you have been too busy or too happy to attend to them. You know the kind of hectoring irritated tone which implies, "This is your own advantage that you're neglecting, you know!" She had taken what I told her as seriously as that. Naturally I didn't answer either of these letters. I couldn't. I felt she was making a fool of herself and a fool of me, and I wanted to bring the whole thing to an end as quickly as possible.

'I don't believe that whatever I might have done could have succeeded in averting the horrible thing that happened here in this room, one evening about six, about a fortnight after she had left for Carlsbad. The affair that was nearest my heart had prospered as well as I could have hoped. In fact, I hoped that that very evening it was going to come to its divine climax. The delicious woman of whom I had told you had the evening before said to me, in that exquisite and absurd locution which never loses its charm, "Yes, I will come to-morrow and see your pictures . . . if you promise you will not touch me." So I had everything ready. I had the rooms full of flowers. I had tea with little cakes and cocktails if she cared for them, I had laid out my new dressing-gown that Chanel made for me from a design by my friend Jean Cocteau. I was walking up and down as one does waiting, watching, listening for the taxi to stop in front of the house, more crazily in love than one ever is again . . .

'Then suddenly the disgusting event happened. I heard Guillaume, who had been given instructions not to admit any but the one visitor, speaking to somebody at the front door, disputing with somebody. I heard a voice, the last voice in the world that I wanted to hear at that moment, raised almost to a shout, I heard – it's too loathsome – a scuffle. I stood up, paralysed by my sense that here in my flat the decencies were being violated, facing the doorway.

Then the portières were torn apart, and Nancy Sarle stood looking at me.

'It hurts me to tell you what she looked like, because I have always loved women. I have always dealt tenderly with their defects and their misfortunes. But in these circumstances, since she has wronged me as I would not have believed that any human being could wrong another, I will tell you. She had on a hat that I had not chosen for her; one of those hats she had brought with her from the United States; and the stupid piece of felt had slipped to the back of her head, so that a greyish tangle of hair appeared across her forehead. Her face had the muddy look that a woman's skin has when she has put powder on her face without first cleaning it properly. I do not think she had even tried to freshen herself up with rouge. She had remembered her lipstick, but carelessly, without first stretching her lips so that there were crevices where the natural colour of the mouth showed brown beside the artificial red. This flat always remains perfectly cool in summer, so I had forgotten that it was in fact a very hot day; I became aware of it when I saw the little beads of sweat in the furrow of her upper lip. She was wearing one of the unspeakable garments she had bought before she met me, and it was crumpled and dusty and glazed as if it too was perspiring. I was incensed at a woman I knew presenting herself before me in that condition. I would have been ready to kill her even if she had not been wearing the expression she did, which was impertinent in its desperation. I was about to cry out in rage at her presence when she made a gesture so awkward and so odd that I found myself just gaping at her, to see how it would end.

'Keeping her elbows close to her side, she put out both her hands sideways and gripped the portières. Tilting her head right back, which exposed her already wrinkled neck, but fixing her enormous eyes on my face, she began to move her red-and-brown lips as if she were speaking. But no sounds came.

85

'"What are you saying? What do you want?" I screamed at her.

'A clicking noise came out of her mouth. Then she said – I do not know if you will believe this, but these are literally the exact words that she used. I will unfortunately be unable to forget them until I die – "Do you care for me or don't you?"

'I shrieked in amazement, "What is that you are saying?"

'She repeated in a horrible, flat, rasping voice: "Do you care for me or don't you? Don't you understand me? I'm asking, do you love me?"

'Of all the imbecile questions! When I had not answered her letters! I was transported with fury. I had heard a taxi stop in the street below, and it occurred to me that at any moment Yvette might precipitate herself into the midst of this really horrible scene. And that would be fatal, because it was essential that nobody should see her. She is so young that she still has an unblemished reputation. Also if she saw this appalling woman and realized as she would be bound to do from the detestable nature of the scene that we had been lovers she would perhaps refuse to belong to me, as women do sometimes out of a queer sort of pride when they find that the men who are making love to them have had mistresses who are not beautiful or charming. My happiness hung by a hair. Can you imagine the feelings of a man in love?

'I advanced on the American, making such movements as people use when they are driving off animals. I shouted, "No, of course I do not love you! Go away!"

'Her head dropped forward, but she kept her enormous eyes fixed on me. She made no movement to go, though I was waving my hands in her face. Suddenly her hands, which had nearly relaxed their grip on the portière, which had seemed likely to fall, tightened in the stuff again, dragged it down, so that one side was torn down from its hooks. Look, I've never had it mended. Then – will you believe it – she tilted back her chin and said with brutish persistence: "You don't love me. But don't you care for me? Haven't you any feeling for me at all?"

'I was almost out of my mind, I was almost sure I could hear the lift coming up. I shouted, "No! None! You are nothing to me, you are less than nothing! Go away!"

'Her eyes left my face. She appeared to be looking at something over my left shoulder. An expression which I could not understand passed over her; and before I could say anything else she pulled the portières together in front of her. When I parted them she had already left the house.

'I was utterly shattered by this scene. In fact I had not entirely recovered when Yvette arrived to pay her visit half an hour later, and it is to that I ascribe the extreme brevity of our idyll, which came to an end very shortly afterwards. So I would have had reason to regret my foolish generosity to Mrs Sarle even if she had not done the vile and monstrous thing which, as I learned ten days ago, she had left my flat to do. For my uncle Léon de Férodoville tells me that it was the very next day on which there began (by her instruction, he has ascertained) the complicated operations on the stock market which reduced stock in the St Louis and Los Angeles United to waste-paper; which made me a beggar.

'Can you think of the blackness in that woman's soul? To turn and rend me in that way, me who had given her so much, just because an affair had come to its natural end! I never would have done a thing to hurt her, I never would have said a word to wound her, if she hadn't thrust herself into my flat like that, imperilling my happiness. I ask you, is it fair, is it just? I cannot understand it, almost it makes me doubt the kindness of God . . . My dear little friend, are you cold?'

With his unfailing instinct for doing the inessential kindness, Étienne had noticed that I was shivering.

'Yes, you are shaking all over! Shall I tell Guillaume to

light the fire? You wouldn't shake like that unless you were cold . . .'

He bent over me, laying his fingers on my hand to see if it was warm. Looking up into his face, I saw how things had changed with him. For always before, when he looked distressed at anyone else's discomfort, it had seemed insincere, because the expression had been thinly painted over a more fundamental expression which spoke of the complete satisfaction with all the arrangements of the universe; there was of course his age, but that could be circumvented, that had been circumvented. But now, when he looked concerned because I was cold, he seemed insincere because that concern was plainly as nothing compared with the profound and embittered dissatisfaction with the whole of life which determined his fundamental expression.

I said, 'No, it's not that I'm cold . . . It's because I'm so sorry . . .'

That was however not quite true. Why was I filled with thoughts of miserable, sterile chill as I sat in Étienne de Sevenac's room? Was it because the wallpaper was silver and pitted like the surface of the fruitless moon? Or perhaps it was because the little mirror on its nickel arm was now concentrating in its frame the evening, as it had concentrated, when I first came, the afternoon; and showed me now women and men and children garbed in a common greyness, lagging with fatigue, under trees that dropped leaves which at this time did not seem to reach the ground, but to melt in the course of their descent into the twilight. But it could be nothing in the place nor the moment which accounted for my depression, since I had felt it before in places quite different from his, in moments belonging to another age. It had appeared on all these occasions to be provoked by consideration of Étienne's soul, which was really not sufficiently unlike a desert.

II

I ADORE people who have strong feelings, so when I got back to America I found myself haunted by the strongest possible desire to meet Nancy Sarle. I did not approve of her revenge, but I liked the intensity of the emotion that had inspired it. Apparently I liked it very much indeed, for quite often at parties I found myself looking round the room and wondering whether, if I knew the names of all the women, I would not learn one of them was Mrs Sarle. But it never proved so. I neither met her, nor heard of her, although she lived in New York. At least, I thought so, because I had once given way to an impulse to look her up in the telephone-book, and I found a Mrs Walter Sarle at an address in Park Avenue, who, I felt sure, was Étienne's friend. I could not quite understand why I never met her, because the kind of woman Étienne had described – wealthy, dowdy, unsophisticated but not by any means abashed or unable to look after her own comfort – was exactly the kind of woman that I meet at my mother-in-law's home. Sometimes I supposed that she had retired from social life, owing to the shock of this tragedy in Paris.

Then just before Christmas I had the shock of my life. I learned that Nancy Sarle had been married three times.

I learned it at a dinner party to which we were asked by some people who have interests and relations out west. My neighbour at table was an oldish man, patently an obligatory guest, a not to be dodged old friend of a rich uncle, who hardly held my attention till he began to talk about railways, which were apparently his line in life. He gossiped about the giants of the old days, Hill and Harriman and Patten; and then, while I was wondering how I should frame the question, he came to a more recent generation, and said the very name that was in my mind.

I sat up straight. 'Did you know his wife? Did you know Nancy Sarle?'

'Sure I did. And Nancy Gott. And Nancy McFarlane. And Nancy King.'

'Who are they?' I asked stupidly.

He chuckled with the provincial's enjoyment of a local joke that the town dude cannot see. 'The same as Nancy Sarle. And changed very little in the process, I guess.'

It didn't seem possible: but he stuck to his facts. He'd known Nancy ever since she was a little girl in Seattle, the daughter of a widow-woman who had been his mother's minister's wife's help at one time. When she got older she had gone as clerk to the biggest hotel in Seattle: that must be thirty years ago now. Then she had married a young fellow called Sam McFarlane, and she had pushed him on wonderfully. In the end he got a fine position in Denver, and they lived there quite a while. 'But she couldn't make anything of him, he wasn't the kind of fellow that ever goes big. Just a nice boy. She got him up to a point maybe, I guess that before she left he was pulling down fifty thousand bucks a year. But that was no good to Nancy. So she quit and got a divorce and married a fellow called King – Dwight King – and they settled in Chicago. But he wasn't right for her. He had no sense. Should have been a steamboat gambler. He would make his pile all right, and then lose it all in some fool speculation. And Nancy was always a sensible girl. So she gave him his chance and when he showed he couldn't take it she quit, and made her little trip to Reno all over again, and married old Sarle. He died on her three years after, but I guess she's got what she wanted. Making money's what Nancy likes. She hasn't let any of his interests drop, runs the whole show herself.'

I was amazed. I was not quite convinced that the economic preoccupation of my adopted country had determined Nancy's matrimonial career as much as the old gentleman from Seattle suggested, for he had reached an age at which people are apt to find the sexual proceedings of their juniors incomprehensible and to invent motivations for them. But even had that been true, it appeared unlikely that she

should have been as much in need of education concerning the voluptuous possibilities of life as Étienne had
believed.

Had he been altogether wrong about Nancy? Had his
resentment at her revenge on him been so great that it had
distorted his view of her?

I asked, 'What is she like, this Mrs Sarle? Is she pretty?'

To which the ancient from Seattle replied, 'I can't
figure out how any man would ever look at Nancy for
pleasure. She's little and stocky like them English terriers
that my fool sons and their fool wives pay all the money in
the world for.' He added, 'She had pretty eyes, mind you,
mighty pretty blue eyes.' But his tone suggested that he was
throwing Nancy's appearance a lifebuoy.

I pondered. 'Is she . . . a good sort?'

'I never came across a better. She's a grand woman.
She's been a good wife to all her husbands, too; and is still
in a way. The wife Sam McFarlane's got now told me herself that they never would be where they are now if Nancy
hadn't now and then tipped them off on to something good.
And I don't know how Dwight King, who fancies himself as
a big operator and couldn't run a hot-dog stall on his own
power, could keep offices open in Chicago and New York if
some more important guy wasn't behind him. Oh, she's a
helluva good fellow.'

'Oh, she is, is she . . . Have you seen her lately?' I did
not have to guard my conversation from suspicions of undue
curiosity or of inconsecutiveness, for it was only too plain
that the old gentleman took remarks with as little inquiry
into their nature as a dog takes biscuits. Simply they were
as stimuli to his garrulity, to which he extravagantly
reacted.

'Sure I have. Old George Parsons and Senator Sorley
and I went out to her place a week ago last night and she
gave us a grand time. She has the best rye in the United
States, has Nancy.'

'Where does she live?'

'Oh, here in New York all week. She goes down to Wall Street every day, just like a man. They say she's got a swell apartment up on Park Avenue and Seventy-first Street. I don't know. We didn't go there. We went to her country place.'

'Where's that?'

'Way down on the end of Long Island. Cedar Corner they call it . . .'

That was where Hildegarde Pierce had built her new house. I noted it with resolution.

'Does she really carry on all her husband's business? I mean . . . had she anything to do with that railway business last summer . . . when the St Louis and Los Angeles United went phut?'

He laughed. 'I'll say she had. That was Nancy.'

Frantically I cultivated Hildegarde that winter. The affair, you see, had become infinitely more dramatic and exciting in my eyes. Étienne's story had been confirmed. Indeed, it had been shown to be even more extraordinary, and more flattering to him, than he had imagined when he told it. He had apparently been wrong when he had imagined that Nancy Sarle had not been sought after by the amorous male; but then again it could be argued that perhaps he was not so wrong about that. The ancient from Seattle had talked of her appearance as if it was inconceivable that she should ever have entered for the beauty stakes, and he had added no rider to the effect that in spite of her looks she had charm. It had evidently never crossed his mind to consider her as a sexually attractive woman; and from this and that in the bad old man's demeanour I would have backed him to be no fool in these matters. After all, it was extremely unlikely that Étienne, who had spent his life running after women, should have made a mistake of this sort about a woman he knew intimately. The old man's economic interpretation of her matrimonial career must have been correct, and Étienne had reason in supposing that he had awakened her to love. This had been a greater triumph than he supposed. For from the conversation of the old man I had realized that he was hard as nails, and that he looked up to Nancy as rather harder. Furthermore, Étienne had been right in believing that she had deliberately ruined him. When the old man had said, 'Yes, that was Nancy,' I could hear in his tone that he was recalling a complicated transaction and giving credit to her not only for brilliance but for ruthlessness. And the revenge had been a greater compliment to Étienne than he had realized, for it had represented the supersession of a habitual tendency to generosity and fairness. I could tell that from the old man's tone when he had spoken of her kindness to her former husbands, which had that peculiar shade of reverence one may notice in the voice of mean people when they are talking of a liberal person whom they know to be no fool. It is as if, being ignorant of the governing principle of generosity, they had to invent some situation that would account for it otherwise; and found that they could do this most satisfactorily by imagining that the person in question was so enormously rich that for him or her to give money away was a positively selfish act, a motion of disembarrassment like taking off one's coat on a hot day. As a result of listening to him I did not know whether he was right in thinking Nancy prodigiously wealthy, but I knew I was right in thinking that Nancy's usual disposition was very different from that which she had manifested when she had revenged herself on Étienne.

I had to meet this woman. I had to meet this marvel who had felt an emotion so strong that it had been able to break the mould of her character when it had hardened for nearly half a century; so strong that it had demanded for its expression not a day's hysterics, not some nights of weeping, but weeks of complicated and murderous operations on the stock market. As I have told you, that is the kind of thing I like. It amused me. And until I met Nancy Sarle I felt as a collector might who knows that somewhere, say in one of six small towns in the province of Lombardy, there is a lost

Donatello. Therefore I practised on Hildegarde Pierce, whom I scarcely knew, a guileful amiability that, about April, got me my reward: an invitation to spend the week-end at Cedar Corner.

'Mind you,' said Hildegarde, 'it takes hours to get there, and there's nothing to do when you've got there. The only reason we go down is that it's so quiet that my husband can paint for days without an interruption. No neighbours, absolutely none.'

'But isn't there a Mrs Sarle who lives down there?' I asked.

'Yes, there is. She's got the very big house in the place, the only big house other than our own. Do you know her? Oh, you'd adore her. We might go over and see her on Sunday afternoon. Roland revels in her. He says she looks to him as if she had advanced to her present position in life by saying with proper firmness on a certain number of occasions, "You getta hell outta here!..."'

That was as a matter of fact what I was afraid she was going to say when, on the following Sunday afternoon, I at last came face to face with her. We drove over to her house after tea, ostensibly to ask her to come to a lunch-party next Sunday, to which Hildegarde knew she would not be able to come, since one of the servants, who was carrying on amicabilities with one of her chauffeurs, had said that there was to be an early departure for California. The expedition was framed entirely to gratify my curiosity, which I had explained by telling a story which amused even me as I told it (though I don't know why I should say even me, for I was in exactly the same position as the rest of the party in never having heard it before) of how Nancy Sarle had been courted in Paris by a gigolo whom she had dismissed with Western candour in a phrase that had (I said) been the most repeated *mot* of the season. I wish I could remember it, it really was quite funny.

We entered her estate through wrought-iron gates set in brick walls that must have been brought from Europe and re-erected, so sun-steeped were they, so mellowed by the seasons, and came on a very fair imitation of a Tudor manor. It did not interest me very much, because they were saying that she had not built it, that she had taken it over as it stood from Jack Purvis' widow. A Japanese butler told us that Mrs Sarle was out by the shore, that she was alone, that he was sure she would like to see us, that if we liked we might go through the house and the garden. We passed through a lounge that told us little enough about even Jack Purvis, so purely was it the creation of an interior decorator; and into a veranda on which were comfortable chairs and convenient tables and portable electric heaters and all the devices by which a good hostess makes it possible for her guests to sit out of doors as early in the year as can be. Suddenly I realized that I was learning something about Nancy. It showed a certain independence of spirit, a refusal to be drawn into the orbit of certain established harmonies, to have a house that was so definitely equipped and organized for entertaining a large party of guests, and just at that time of year when it seems most natural to take people out into the country to ask nary a person. If you come to think of it very few of us who have such houses have the strength of mind to do that. But as we went through gardens strongly marked with that something which is the opposite of *je ne sais quoi*, which might be described as *je sais précisément quoi*, appertaining perpetually to the result of the unsupervised garden architect's skill, I reflected that perhaps the little thing sometimes felt like moping alone in the shelter of her vast possessions, since that experience in Paris.

It did not lower my spirits that when we found her she was utterly without distinction. I do not suppose that the collector who finds the lost Donatello minds if it is not a very good specimen when he finds it. It is what has happened to it that gives it its interest. We came on her in a quadrangle of high tamarisk hedges which was open on the fourth side to the sands and the sea, plainly a place where in warmer weather people sat and looked at the breakers while keeping out of the wind; a sturdy little figure in a grey pullover and riding-breeches of a particularly ugly slate-colour, who was throwing a ball for four or five young Sealyhams to fight over. We watched her for a few seconds before she saw us, so I had a good look at her. Her coarse, short hair, which was losing nothing now it was turning grey, for where it had not yet turned it was an indeterminate fawn, stood out from her head in little tufts, very much as the Sealyhams' coats were doing; and her features were so far from clear-cut that if one had seen her only at ten yards' distance one could never have been able to recognize her at a second meeting. Though her get-up was mannish it had nothing picturesque or gallant about it. These were just warm and durable things she had put on for country use, that was flatly all. Her movements forbade one to suppose that she had within her some distinction which would express itself in other fields than appearance, for they were common and clumsy. But I noticed that they were all very good-tempered. When she retrieved the ball from her puppies' mouths, an action which usually betrays what depths of teasing malice exist in a dog-owner's soul, it was with a slow, unruffled amiability. My pride in my discovery fairly blazed. That such an ordinary woman should have been capable of feeling such extra-ordinary emotion, and that it had been as complete a reversal of the customary trend of her character as I had suspected, this was meat and drink to my appetite for human oddity.

Hildegarde stepped ahead of us and went towards her; and it was then that she flashed on us this look which made me, as I have said, apprehensive that she was going to say, 'You getta hell outta here'. Decidedly, once she had made up her mind to take revenge on Étienne de Sevenac, she would be able to carry it through.

Hildegarde said prettily, 'I hope we're not intruding', and held out her hand, and Mrs Sarle gripped it and answered with a Western drawl, 'Sure, ya couldn't do that!' and widened her smile to take in the whole of our party.

Her eyes really were remarkably blue; though they suggested, as eyes very rarely do, coarseness of texture. One could imagine that if one dropped a thick blue china cup on a gravel path the fragments might look as those eyes did in the setting of her sandy fairness. Hildegarde rather laboured her point about intrusion, mentioning that we had noted the absence of guests as we came through the house and had wondered if this was a sign that privacy was wanted there this week-end, and that brought Mrs Sarle back to her. She said that there not being any folks around didn't mean a thing except that she and her secretary had brought down some work that just had to be gotten through before they started for their trip on Monday, and that she was as pleased as could be to see us, and thought it real kind of us to come. There were overtones in her voice and an indefinable quirk in her expression which convinced me that she thought Hildegarde was rather blatantly talking nonsense. I don't mean that she was so naïve as to comment to herself on the obvious fact that Hildegarde would really have suffered no anguish whatsoever if she had found that her presence caused her hostess inconvenience. The humbuggery of that she took for granted, it was on a par with her own expressions of gratitude for our visit. What struck her as nonsense, I fancied, was Hildegarde's assumption that anyone might want to be alone for any other purpose but work. 'If I'm out here, with the dawgs,' I could imagine her soul slowly saying, 'why should I mind you and your friends butting in? Don't be silly.' She didn't violently object to it. Her placid brows were even. But she did think that even if society did place on one an obligation to talk humbug, at times there was no need to overdo it.

There followed politenesses about her house, and envy was expressed on account of its propinquity to the beach, and concern lest automobilists should spoil its seclusion at week-ends, to which Mrs Sarle replied that she had taken her pups for a run all of two miles along the sands, and they hadn't met a creature. Then Roland Pierce waved his hand at the clouds and the sea, whose several sorts of greyness were divided on the skyline by a violent hem of storm, and said that was the kind of thing he would give his eye-teeth to be able to paint. Under cover of our sympathetic exclamations Mrs Sarle, who had been standing with her back to the sea, slewed round her head and gave a look at it to find out what on earth we were all talking about. I fancy that during that scamper on the beach she had run with her nose nearly as close to the ground as the dogs. In the conversation that followed about the characteristic beauties of Cedar Corner I noticed that her remarks, while conveying a courteous assent, showed not the slightest real consciousness of their existence. She kept on using such phrases as, 'When I found I could get this place way down at the end of everywhere,' and, 'Yes, I kinda like being way out beyond everywhere,' which showed that in fact no such consciousness had brought her here. Simply her need for going farther than other people, which had expressed itself in financial terms when it committed her to her life work of becoming very rich, had expressed itself for a change in crude geographical terms. The ease with which one could read this, from the broadening and deepening of her drawl when she talked of this covetable outdistancing, from the clear yet dreamy ambition in her eye when she looked at the horizon that outdistanced us all, made me detect a certain characteristic in her. I have said that her hair behaved in the wind just like the coats of the Sealyhams that were chasing a ball round her feet. That was not the only point of resemblance between them. She was like a dog in the way that she had a more than human power of expressing her inmost feelings without words. You know how a pup can twitch its left ear. Keep it pricked, and drop it, and by that motion and certain wigglings of its muzzle will say, 'I want another piece of bread and butter, but I daren't beg because I know I've been enough of a nuisance, and I'm afraid you might sling me out. You're not going to give it to me? Ah, well, you wouldn't. Louisa, now, would. She has the nicer nature of the two.' Even so did Nancy Sarle, by the not so great rise and fall of her not so modulated voice, from the expressions of her not so very mobile little face, give away completely what was going on in her mind. And she was like a dog in another way. What she had more than the usual human power to express was simpler than what is the usual human matter for expression.

If there was anything contemptuous in this judgement, which I should be ready to dispute, it was immediately swept away by the sweetness of the smile she gave when she said that she guessed we had better go back to the house and have highballs and that she had some mighty fine rye. She was a generous woman, who liked giving of her best to people who were neighbourly and came visiting. She had an even more touching, more childlike kind of generosity than that, for, when we started to make our way back through the gardens, she saw to it that she walked beside me and at the first opportunity, which came when we paused to look at an old lead cistern in one of the sunk gardens, she smiled straight at me to show she meant well by me. I knew that this was because, as I had observed from the way she had run her eyes over my clothes when we had first been introduced, she liked the soft, bright primrose-leaf green of my silk jumper. She thought it was nice of me to choose such a jolly colour and nice of me to bring the result of my choice along to her, she preferred me for that reason to my more soberly dressed companions, she liked to give as proof of it this special smile, which as they did not see it could do them no harm. She set us round one of the hearths in deep chairs, some of which she brought forward herself before the men could help her, with an amazingly quick, stubby strength, and kicked up the wood fire to a further extravagance of flame with the heel of her riding-boot. In a soft-mouthed roar to the butler she ordered cocktails for those who liked them, and drank some rye herself in the old-fashioned way, taking the rye neat from one tumbler and drinking another tumbler of water on top of it, as I had never seen a woman do before. Then, in the general atmosphere of amiability that creamed and mantled the group, the bogus invitation to lunch was rather shamefacedly given, and refused with regret by Mrs Sarle, who announced her trip to California, but hoped she might be asked again on her return, which was to be soon, as she was going to stop at the Coast for only five days.

When asked if she was not appalled at such a long journey for such a short visit, she replied that she felt anything was worth while when one was going back to one's home town. She began to recite a poem entitled 'That's where the West begins' which alleged that where Mountain Time begins, there is also noticeable an increasing purity of morals and generous effulgence of manners. Running my eye wildly round the room during this embarrassing resort to the arts for illustration of her emotions, I had to admire it, for the long rays of the late afternoon sun lit up the port-and-sherry tints of the Dutch marquetry tall-boys and grandfather's clock that were the special features of this end of the room, turned into jewels such touches of colour as there were in the Mierweldt portrait of a burgomaster that hung over the mantelpiece, met the firelight on Mrs Sarle's crossed riding-boots; but I thought I saw, in the deep shadow between a tall-boy and the grandfather's clock, the tortured pallor of Étienne de Sevenac. I was perhaps empowered to see it so plainly because of my lively sense that she had got her Mierweldt, for which I do not think she greatly cared, and that he had lost all his beloved pictures.

I courted her favour quite outrageously. When they told her I played the piano, I consented, I almost volunteered to play then and there, and I gave her all the tunes she asked for with an affectation of enjoyment like to her own, although they were as unholy specimens of peroxided Jew-jazz as you could hear in twelve months at a night-club. And shamelessly, because of certain cordialities at parting, I called her at the very first moment I thought she could possibly have got home after her Californian trip.

She wasn't at the Park Avenue apartment; she was at Wall Street. I should have guessed that. And when I got her there, thanks, she didn't lunch. She didn't think lunch was wholesome, she just had a cup of cawfee in the awfice. But when, in my infatuated curiosity, I told her I had to be down in that part of the world anyhow at noon, to see my broker, she bade me come in and see her. At twenty-five to one I was there, sitting facing her broad smile across a desk on which – thrill of my life ! – there was the model of an engine about eighteen inches long. It didn't look very new, it probably was the very one. At my exclamation over it, she murmured, 'Folks not in our business always seem to find them kinda cute,' smiling and sly as people are when they dissimulate tremendous pride; and her maroon coat-sleeve slipped over the shining surface of her desk so that she could touch the beloved thing. That maroon coat was cut exactly like a man's; and she wore a soft linen collar and a tie no doubt bought from Abercrombie & Fitch, which was correctly dented with a diamond pin made in the shape of a Sealyham. But again I noted there was no implication regarding the gallant or the picturesque in her assumption of masculinity. By no means was it a case of George Sand's cigar and trousers. It was simply that she had seen here an opportunity for gratifying her passion for the commonplace and her passion for going a little farther than anybody else. By nature and nurture she was a commonplace woman, and she must have enjoyed using all the clichés of speech and behaviour current in the varying worlds to which her successive marriages introduced her. She must have liked serving salads the way which was favoured that year in that district, and having the tea-napkins of the size and pattern recommended in the woman's magazine that she and most of her friends bought, and talking to them about the convenience of canned goods and the purifying girlishness of Mary Pickford. But by becoming a man so far as was possible she doubled the number of such clichés that she might use; she could now talk and react not only to salad and tea-napkins but to the stock market and corporation law, to Wall Street as well as to the Woman's Club. At her elbow was an indication that it was not the independence, the force of man that she envied, but the standardization of his mind and manners, which is usually more complete than that of a woman, because an office has usually a larger crowd in it than a home. She cannot really have thought that a large cup of coffee with cream, and two heavy sandwiches, one with ham and the other with cheese, were more digestible than the kind of light luncheon, mainly of vegetables and fruit, that sensible people eat in their homes or order in restaurants. But she had heard innumerable business men say virtuously that they didn't eat lunch but had a cup of cawfee and a sandwich in the awfice; and she wanted to belong to their army, their great safe army.

I recognized this without unkindness: simply to give her prodigious act its due of prodigiousness. I could not possibly have felt unkind towards her, for she was so nice! She was nice as she sat there at her desk, smiling at a world in which so far nothing seemed to be going wrong, but without smugness: rather as if she were standing at a country porch, and looking up to clear sky over hills, and thinking that the day was going to be fine, and the children would surely have their picnic. She was nice, too, when at my departure she took me to the door and looking down at my coat, stroked it with her forefinger and said, 'Why, isn't that the prettiest colour? And it's so soft you'd hardly think it was woollen goods. You do have the loveliest clothes . . .'

I said, 'I'm glad you like it,' and added, hesitating till I was sure I dared add it, 'I got this in Paris.'

She burst into a little gentle, unhurried gust of laughter. 'Paris,' she repeated, 'Yes, they've got good clothes there'. She stood for a moment with her hand resting on the handle of the open door, swinging it to and fro, smiling partly because she liked my presence there, and partly because she was contemplating some memory that quite definitely did nothing but amuse her. She gave another little gust of

laughter, even more leisurely and more carefree than the
first. 'Chanel,' she said, and again her laughter rose.
Positively she sounded innocent, like a child, like a bird.

I will own I recoiled. Yet she was nice. I swear she was
nice, when a sudden thought made her pull to the door and
say: 'Here, are you like all you ladies of leisure and eat
breakfast in bed? Because if you aren't, and you start the
morning the way good Americans should, sitting straight up
in your chair eating cereal, I might come and eat it with you
one day. I can't go up to your part of the town for lunch or
for tea, and I don't reckon to dine out, not during the week,
and week-ends I go to my lil place on Long Island. But I
do ride horseback in Central Park mornings, and I'd be just
tickled to death if you'd let me come in and eat ham and
eggs along with you . . .'

And she was nice when she kept her promise and came to
breakfast, very stubby and Sealyhamy in riding-breeches.
She did not mind showing how much she liked my apartment, with my Sheraton and my Chinese wallpaper and the
sea-green linen curtains that I myself embroidered with the
design I found at Holkham Hall. She admired it in a way
which seemed to admit candidly that here I had achieved
something superior to the range of her imagination; just as
her admiration of my breakfast-table, with its Georgian
silver, my two daughters and their four plaits, and my lean,
composed husband, seemed to admit as candidly that here I
possessed something that at any rate was superior in texture
to her own destiny. When the door opened and the nurse
came in to take these two daughters to school, and they
slipped down from their chairs, shaking their plaits with a
dexterous and uncoquettish gesture from the front to the
back of their shoulders, and said good-bye to the visitor in
soft voices, looking at her with civil, uninquisitive eyes for
just the right second less than what makes a stare, and then
gave the whole show away by bursting into Yahoo shouts
the minute the door had closed, her amusement was without the slightest trace of the sneer that a person might

excusably feel at the breakdown of an enterprise so different from anything they themselves would undertake. She was nice then, and nice too when she lounged about in an arm-chair after breakfast was over, frankly regretting that she had to leave us and go down to the office. Few of us when we leave a place which is good do not try to suggest that, good as it is, our lives are so full of the good that we shall hardly miss it. Her eyes crinkled up with pleasure, she generously made no such suggestion. Even George liked her; and part of the value that my husband has for me is that he does not like too easily. He examines life with a fastidiousness which, owing to certain circumstances in my earlier life, is valuable to me. But he thoroughly liked Nancy Sarle, and said that the only thing which worried him about her was that she reminded him of someone, and he could not think who it was.

That somebody turned out to be Texas Guinan. He discovered the missing name during a week-end that we spent down at Cedar Corner not long after. The identifica-tion was made more easy by the presence in the Tudor mansion of a vast number of the friends of the late Mr Sarle and companions of Nancy's youth, who had been at some Convention at Buffalo and had whooped across country in special cars to have a look at her. They decanted themselves from brimming automobiles all over the front of the house just when we were making our mouse-like arrival. In the hour before dinner they seemed simultaneously to be running a greater number than their own of steaming baths and (though I am sure their modesty was impeccable) visiting each other in their rooms. At dinner they ringed a great round table with a circle of faces round which there ran a little train of spurting shrieks and giggles that every now and then resolved into a chorus of laughter, under the conductorship of Nancy, in a bright blue satin gown. She was very like Texas, then and later, when she spread out her flock over the vast continent of her reception rooms: seeing that the few sons and daughters that had come with the older people were getting their dance music all right, and that there was not too much drink in that room; rounding up the most rowdy spirits into a little library so that they could clink glasses and smack each other convivially without scandal; corralling the more genteel just as dexterously. All with the right circus-master quality, the glass held perpetually aloft but hardly ever emptied, that jovial and animated assumption of good will to all men whose source one felt to be a hard and tried recognition that this was an occasion when bad will could not be turned into real money; very much as I remembered Texas Guinan on the one occasion when I went to her Club. And there was the same feeling that beneath the hard and tried recognition there was perhaps a layer where good will again was dominant: that she was brutal only because she had such a mountainously high and austere standard of reality, because hardly anything seemed to her important enough to need dealing with by mercy and love, though she would fully admit that that was how one should deal with affairs of valid importance.

There was also something about her false *bonhomie* which raised it nearly to the ranks of real things, for as its instrument she used shrewd appreciations of the truth. I fancy she could have made no remark about my husband which was anything more than a specimen of the Western tradition of indiscriminate praise, of the tendency to gush which is (contrary to what one would expect) less a habit of the over-civilized than of those who live close to the earth and know the perils of nomadism or pioneering, perhaps because in the midst of innumerable human and natural threats to their safety they find rare and precious all that which they perceive to be amiable. Yet after dinner her eye lay on us just for a second, and she immediately set us down by the three or four members of her party who could give George real pleasure: old men who had been prospectors and adventurers in the Old West, when lakes were still bright with being unvisited, and mountains had not lost that integrity of aspect which, as one may see in Switzerland, can be looted from a place by the eyes of admirers. Of course he sat thralled while they yarned away, telling how they had seen life itself presenting that appearance of freshness, of clarity, of simplicity, which is what he likes; not being used and second-rate, which is what he fears with an almost ridiculous intensity. None of these things could she have put into words; but those were the appropriate neighbours she gave my husband.

He was so thralled that when Nancy came back and stood resting against the doorpost he did not see her. She was a marvellous sight. The blue of her satin dress, though not the same blue as her eyes, seemed likewise to be coarse for its own texture, seemed more appropriate for thick china. A ribbon of silver lamé ran obliquely across her heavy bust, which was compressed into a roundness shaped like a bandbox. Her hair had been maltreated, according to a fashion the supersession of which she had not noticed in the hurry of her marriages and her business life, into a sandy festal fuzz. For a minute she did nothing but rest, leaning backwards, breathing deeply; as well she might, for it must have been a good hour since she had sat us down and began to run about herself. Then her eyes came to me, travelled to George, saw him entranced, travelled through the open doorway to the rooms she had left, narrowing as if the noise were an obscurity through which they had to pierce, to see that the people there were in one way or another as well held as he was; and returned to me. There was a moment when she gauged the quality of my replying smile, and made sure that I was not entranced as George was, that I did not so greatly want to stay with my group. Then she crooked her finger at me.

'I shoulda told you not to come when I heard this crowd was all headed for here,' she murmured in my ear, 'but I kinda wanted you to come. Not that they aren't a grand crowd,' she added, cutting into my assurance that we were enjoying every minute, not so much from loyalty, I think, as because she believed them to be a grand crowd, and to her justice was everything. 'And the whole bunch of them would do anything in the wide world for me . . . Except one or two.' Without haste she corrected herself . . . 'two or three . . .' Her eye ran back through the doorway to a tall shock-headed man standing by the fireplace with his back to us, flicked off him, travelled through the archway to two fattish baldish men who were sitting at a table laughing while a little blonde pretended to read their hands, flicked off them, and came calmly back to me. It was like a bit of trick shooting, and I am certain that each time it was the bull's eye that was hit. If ever I hear that Nancy Sarle's fortunes have been levelled by the machinations of her enemies I shall be tolerably sure that the conspirators are one tall shock-headed man, two fattish baldish men. Dropping her voice still lower she said, 'Listen, I have some liquor upstairs in my room you might like. I have been noticing all evening you don't seem to like the Scotch or the rye or the champagne. But this is a funny stuff, just terribly European, and I've a notion it might be the kinda liquor you like. It's called Tokay. I bought it off a fellow who said he'd got it out of the Emperor of Austria's cellars, maybe he was just talking. Come on up and see.' Her gaze flashed to George. 'I won't ask him to come along because I wanna take off my shoes and I guess he likes it where he is. Don't your feet hurt, ever? But they don't look as if they did. I'll get me body-maid to hunt out an old pair and feed these I got on to the cows. They couldn't hurt them worse than they do me. We won't be missed. This crowd won't go to bed till God knows when. I'd better sit down and rest myself while the going's good.'

Her hand lay on my arm lightly. She took a look round the room and saw that indeed the going was good, and the pressure of her hand grew heavier. We passed up the staircase, along corridors, in dusk hardly dispelled by lighting deliberately contrived to be archaic, past pictures, tapestries, pieces of old furniture, at which I passed a perturbed backward glance, because it seemed so wrong that they should not have affixed some number or explanatory slip which would show that the museum was properly catalogued. Seen in this luxury to which they were irrelevant, they appeared as desolate as if one had perceived them in precisely the contrary circumstances, associated with destitution, standing in the rain outside some tenement during a removal. Her bedroom, curiously enough, made nothing like such a desolate impression, because of various intrusions her personality had made on the eclectically prepared scene. For some reason the four-poster looked much more as if it could be slept in than it would have if there had not been beside it a large steel safe; and a roll-top desk seemed to hold at bay spectres of a hovering custodian of tourists strolling behind red woollen ropes on their way from the Prince's Bedchamber to the Queen's Gallery.

There was an elderly woman in maid's dress doddering about who did not turn her head as we entered. Mrs Sarle shouted as one only does at the very deaf, 'Hi, Martha! Git me some other slippers! These hurt!' And, as the maid scuttled into a further room she pushed forward a deep chair for me. She went to a massive cupboard, flung open its doors, rooted about among the shelves, came out with the right slim-shouldered bottle.

'I don't know whether it's the right stuff,' she grumbled, 'I guess these fellas fool us all the time about this kind of liquor.'

She poured it out into a fine Waterford tumbler, that was in the cupboard too.

It was divinely the right stuff, and I told her so.

'I guess I'll have some myself,' she said, poured out a second tumbler, and took it over to another deep chair, facing the triple mirror on her dressing-table. She switched the chair round till it faced me. 'Haven't really drunk anything this evening. This sort of party isn't any use unless you keep kidding 'em along. Oh, gosh, my feet! My feet!' With an exasperated movement she kicked her slippers off so that they somersaulted into the middle of the room, and wriggled her toes luxuriously. 'Ah, that's better! And you're right this is good liquor.' Perniciously she began to smoke as she drank it. 'Da-de-da, da-de-da,' she carolled in contentment.

The elderly maid doddered back, knelt with an air of pious devotion at her mistress's feet, and began to fit a pair of slippers on her feet. But Nancy yelled, 'Aw! For the love of Mike,' sent them to join the pair. 'She's cuckoo, just plain cuckoo,' she said to me, 'look at what she's brought me.' They were black day-shoes. I had noticed before that often very rich and important people, especially those who have concentrated their lives to the worship of efficiency, have for their most close attendant those who obviously must owe their appointment not to any merit whatsoever, but simply to the chance that they happened to present themselves for employment at a particular place, at a particular hour, with particular words on their lips, which were spoken in a particular way. That I have always found charming, a kind of sacrifice they make to the Gods who have been displaced by efficiency, the gods of good luck and reciprocal benevolence, whom races and individuals worship in their childhood; and the presence of the incompetent Martha in my robust friend's household was as touching as if I had found that she had retained her belief in Santa Claus. 'Martha!' she shouted, 'I can't wear black suede with all these doodads on! Go git me something gold or silver!' And as the door closed on the dodderer she took another sip at Tokay, and another puff at her cigarette, and complained comfortably, 'All the trouble I had fitting those slippers in Paris, and when I turn round there isn't one of them I can use . . .'

That reminded me, of what I had tended to forget during the last few phases of our increasing intimacy, because of the real liking I had conceived for her sturdiness. Nevertheless it was still what interested me most about her. While Martha returned and fitted on a pair of gold kid slippers, and mistress simultaneously petted and bullied her, and told her to leave them by so she could put them on after she had rested her feet, I thought out a new opening.

For a minute I hesitated to use it. The matter I was going to raise related after all to something definitely savage, to something concerning which almost any person who was responsible for it would feel guilty. Almost certainly she would tell me nothing about it, quite probably she would feel such pain at being so directly reminded of it that she would for ever afterwards withdraw herself from me.

But I was precipitated past my own hesitancy by a sudden alarm that came upon me. As we sat there resting in the silence, sipping our Tokay, liking one another, the orchestra, which was in the room beneath us, started playing again. I was thinking how odd it is that dance music heard in such a position, from directly above or directly below, often loses all of itself in the walls and floors save the wail of the saxophone and an unidentifiable thudding like the mallets of roadmakers, so that a person who only heard it in this way would be unable to associate it with anything but human suffering and labour, and would be incredulous if they were told what part it actually played in our life. But suddenly I saw that she too was listening to it, and I feared that probably it would remind her that she had no right to cease being a hostess for so long, and would send her to go on kidding them along. It was really to prevent this and not to continue my detective work that I stumbled into the opening I had prepared and said:

'I like this room . . . I like it very much . . . It reminds me of a room in my home in England . . . though it's a long time since I called it my home. You see, I didn't come straight to America from England. I lived in France first, for quite a long time.'

She asked, as I had known she would, what I had been doing in France.

I told her. I mentioned the names of various people who

had been associated with my life there. I mentioned Étienne de Sevenac.

Her fingers, which had been closing on the glass that she had set down on the dressing-table, thumbled and gave up the search; and instead stopped her cigarette from falling out of her mouth.

She said, stopping me as I went on with other names, 'Did you say Étienne de Sevenac?'

I answered, 'I did.'

'A fella rising fifty? With a white face and black hair? Has an apartment up past that Arc doing?'

I nodded, 'Yes, do you know him?'

'I'll say I do,' her fingers found the glass, she took a drink and set it down. 'Well, what do you know about that!' she exclaimed with a full measure of that Western slowness. 'Well, well, well! Fancy you knowing that fella!'

Her eyes followed the smoke of her own cigarette. I was not quite sure, but I thought there was something odd about her confusion: something comfortable, something not really very confused. I was prepared for it when she uttered words for which I was totally unprepared, which nobody in the world who knew the situation would have imagined issue from her lips: when she cosily settled back in her chair, gave a satisfied, reminiscent chuckle, and said, coyly:

'You know that fella nearly had me making a fool of myself. But I got out of it in time.' She drew a deep breath. 'Phew! I had a close shave!' Her laughter was pure contentment.

I gazed at her in incredulous wonder. 'You know that fella nearly had me making a fool of myself. But I got out of it in time. Phew! I had a close shave!' How could that superb, barbaric act of vengeance, which, if one rose or sunk to the pitch of committing it, would surely leave one crazed with pride or shame, make any human creature utter those words?

I stammered: 'What do you mean? What happened?'

Mildly she answered, as one who thinks confession is good

for the soul, and has in any case nothing very damaging to confess, and will enjoy a cosy chat with the confessor: 'I don't mind telling you. It's all over now, but while it was on I nearly lost the dearest thing in the world to me. Lord, I was scared! For somehow I felt . . . I guess I better tell you all about it from the beginning.

'Last summer I learned two things I hadn't known before. One was that when you're getting on in middle life you need to take vacations like they say you do. And the other was that if you've gone and got yourself prominent you can't take a vacation right here in America. Your executives won't quit bothering you. The way those boys think nothing of climbing the Rockies when you're trying to take a vacation on top of them is a great advertisement for the American spirit but it makes it darned hard for the boss. So I sailed for Europe.

'One of our boys in the office worked out a swell trip for me. He travelled over there with his parents when he was a kid, being educated. Of course he's no good, got no punch, he's just a nice boy, and we like having him round. He reckoned I oughta see London, and Paris, and Rome, and Venice, and Vienna. I guess I oughta too but I didn't. I went to Paris and I stayed there. I kinda liked Paris.' A dreaminess came into her eyes, and I think she retreated into the memory of a real romance, of one of those passions for places which can be every bit as sentimental as passions for people, since she hastily gathered round her her mantle of masculine clichés. 'Say, if all our cities situated on our rivers and the Great Lakes would do what Paris has done with its water-front, the United States would be a very, very beautiful place . . .

'Well, I had the grandest time, running around seeing all the old places, and eating all that swell food, and meeting up my executives' wives who were over and seeing how they spent their husbands' money, and falling over folks I knew who had had the same idea of taking their vacation in Europe too, some of them folks I'd known in Chicago and

Denver and Seattle, when I was young. And I met one woman I'd known way back as long ago as I can remember. She was our minister's daughter and my mother used to go round and help out there when they had company. She'd married a guy who had some sort of business in Paris, and he had died, and she still lives over there with her son and daughter. One day I went up to lunch at her apartment, and this chap you spoke of just now was there, Étienne de Sevenac.

'You know I got him all wrong. I don't believe I ever got him straightened out completely, even at the end, but at the beginning I got him all wrong. You know that chap Harry Richman who acts in George White's "Scandals" and runs a club somewhere up by Carnegie Hall? That's the kinda chap I thought this Étienne de Sevenac was. An actor who ran a club. He had that same air of cashing in on himself. Nervous he was, as if he just had to put himself over, as if he couldn't afford to be a flop. This boy and girl of Norrie Thompson's razzed him a bit because he was thirty years too old for them and he kept butting in like he was one of them, and he minded. I was sorry for him like one is for actors.

'Well, when the girl and boy razzed him, he made a bee-line for me. I thought he must be a pretty good actor from the way he acted he'd fallen for me. How I figured it out was that Norrie had been going to this fella's club and hadn't as much sense as she used to have, and had been treating him like a friend, and had spilled to him who I was and how much I had. She hadn't used to be that sort, but you never can tell as people get older. So I kept on kidding him along, and when he said he just couldn't live if he didn't take me back to the Ritz, why, I let him. While I was saving his life this way he said the usual piece about how beautiful American women are, and I let him know right there that I wasn't one of those old women who fancy themselves as what they aren't. I told him I knew how I looked so darned well that I didn't go into the Ritz bar because of all the dolled-up cuties there. Though you could wait a long time before you found me not going anywhere I wanted to go for any reason on this earth. But he came right back by asking me to come to lunch with him the next day. And, gee! I had to go. That fellow's technique was superb. I just had to go.

'And I enjoyed myself. I hand it to that man every time, he certainly did know how to give a person a good time. He took me to some place right out in the Bois, and it was fine. It was a good day, and watching the women was fun and I'll say Étienne knew how to order a lunch, and how to make me feel good by saying little things all the time that didn't amount to much but were kinda encouraging. I waited for him to tell me about where he was acting, and about his club, but he didn't utter. So I asked him straight out, and he came back at me with the bad news that he did nothing, absolutely nothing. Then he began to spill the names of an awful lot of titles, and said that some of them were relations of his. Well, then I thought I knew where I was. All these Europeans think we Americans are just mad about titles. I thought he was just one of these frauds who hang round and get hold of silly old women with a bit of money by pretending to be Counts and Marquises and all that when half the time they are just cook-boys and shoe-shines. We had a very painful incident of that happen right near our concern, the wife of one of our Presidents, a woman around fifty, who wanted to divorce her husband on account of a Duke she met in Paris, who turned out to be a bell-boy. I said to myself, "I got your number", and every time he brought out a title I looked him straight in the eye. Not long enough to be rude, for I guessed this was his business just as railways are mine. But just long enough to tell him that I knew.

'The funny thing is that though he laughed back every time and seemed to know what I meant, that didn't clear him out. He just kept on hanging around. The next thing was that he had to take me to the theatre. And by heck!

He did. I hadn't a dawg's chance of getting away. And, mind you, it was mighty fine going to the theatre with him. He took me to a swell piece, with a good-looker in it who could sing and act like nobody we got over here, and he did it well. The whole evening went as smooth as oil. So I started going around with him regular. I haven't ever met a man who managed things better than he did. And I kept things honest by giving him that look every now and then to show I was wise to it all, so that if he cared to waste his time it was his fault, not mine. And I figured that maybe when I left I'd hand him a tip on the stock market or something that could be turned into real money, for he had helped me to see Paris the way I wouldn't have done if I hadn't known him.

'Well, the funny thing was that these titles started turning up, as large as life. He kept on asking me to lunch and taking me to parties, where everybody was the Prince of this and the Marquise of that and they called him cousin and uncle and whatnot. I thought at first they must be fakes and I gave him my look. I wonder now what he thought it meant. The queer thing is he always looked as if he understood it, used to laugh and pat my hand like he meant to reassure me. But then I saw that these were the genuine article all right. They were too homely to be crooks. And I put one of my secretaries, who's quite a bright boy, on the job, and he found out that they were all right, and that Étienne was all right too, so far as family went.

'I couldn't make sense of that at all. Then it struck me that maybe this chap hadn't any money of his own, and he'd gone his own way all his life, being kept by one woman after another, like they do over there, and had lost caste, and now he was finding it difficult to carry on that way, and wanted to be respectable again, and thought he would find the comeback easier if he had a rich wife, meaning me. I thought that must be the way it was, for he just picked me up and threw me at these people, and he kept on trying to get me to doll myself so they'd think I looked good. He took me to a swell dressmaker, who looked at me at first as if she'd been given the job of dressing Grant's Tomb, but made me some grand clothes. Not that it matters what I wear.

'Then a thing happened that just knocked me silly. I haven't straightened all this out yet, you know. I just can't figure it out. One night he took me to a party that one of his aunts, a great big girl like a camel, was throwing in a kinda museum place on the other side of the river, with tapestries and those shiny kinda chandelier doodads hanging down like those things you see in a cave. It was fun to watch, but it was terribly late. I made up my mind I'd sleep an hour in the morning, get up at nine instead of eight. So I told him to come round at one instead of twelve. He always came round just like a dawg, when you said.

'Well, I had the deuce-and-all of work to do that morning. I had just told the boys to quit when they called up to say he was downstairs, so I doubled into my bedroom and fixed myself for lunch while he came up. When I got back into the sitting-room he was looking at a model of a loco-motive they'd sent me, a thing that just made me feel mad to look at, I was so sure it was the wrong type and not worth our experts' time fooling with it. And he said to me, "You've been buying toys?"

'I thought he was trying baby-talk on me, and what with being mad about this locomotive and staying up so late the night before, I was feeling the oldest, meanest baby in the universe. So I was pretty short with him and told him what it was, and that it made me sick.

'And he said to me, "I don't understand. What have you to do with railways?"

'I thought that this was more baby-talk, and I was ready to knock his nut off. And then I looked at him and saw he didn't know. He just did not know. He didn't know that I was the widow of Walter Sarle, he didn't know that I controlled the South-West and West-South. Well, if he didn't know that, how did he know that I was worth going after? I don't live so terribly rich. I haven't got jewels. I hadn't even got my own car, I was just living in a plain ordinary suite at the Ritz.

'I was so flummoxed I gave him the information on a plate. I said, "Don't you know that Mr Sarle was President of the South-West and West-South Railway, and that I still potter about with the concern?"

'He came right back at me. Laughing like he was saying nothing at all. He told me he was the foreign holder who bought old Man Watkins's stock in the St Louis and Los Angeles United in 1911.

'Well, that just left me silly. He hadn't known how rich I was, so that made my idea of the poor aristocrat running after the millionairess look funny; and what made it look funnier still was that this bit of news meant that he was a darned wealthy man. Not as wealthy as I am, but comfortable; and I knew enough about the kinda man he was to know that he wouldn't want to be wealthier. Lemme tell ya something. The way people talk you'd think that all rich people want to be richer. There's some that don't. If you get a fella that's never had to work, that's got his money from his father and he's a vain kinda chap, you'll find he won't lift his little finger to add to his fortune. If he did that it would be a kinda confession that maybe his fortune wasn't so swell after all. Well, Étienne's as vain as a peacock. And if he'd money I knew he'd feel that way about it. And now he certainly had money. So he couldn't have been after my money at all.

'Then what in heck was he after? I caught sight of some flowers he had sent me the day before, some very good-looking roses they were, and I remember I bent over them as if the darned things could give me the lowdown on what was worrying me. If Étienne wasn't after my money, what was he after? It must have been me. But I wasn't young, I wasn't dolled-up like the women he went with, I never had as much looks as a street-car. So if it really was me he was after it was kinda nice of him. I mean, he was giving me something for nothing. I got all embarrassed and though I couldn't get a real kick out of it because a fellow like Étienne couldn't matter a hoot to me really, I kinda felt one oughtn't to throw anything away if it looks good, and this certainly looked good, and before I knew what I was doing I found myself giving him the high sign that I had fallen for him too.

'Gee! I wish I knew what it was all about. Because it turned out I had got it all wrong. And it nearly landed me into the darndest foolishness. I feel all dizzy, like looking over a height, when I think of it.

'Well, after that we took to going around like a couple of sweethearts. There was nothing wrong, of course. Nothing wrong. And it was swell in a way. He sure did know how to give a woman a good time taking her around. And I liked the feeling he had for me. I used to look at him and think to myself, "You poor, nice fool", and feel that I mustn't let him come to any harm. And there was another thing that was queer about it all. There's just one time in my life when I didn't feel rightly accountable for what I did and said, when I used to find myself acting up. That was when I was first with my second husband, Dwight King. I used to be like I was crazy sometimes then. If I felt sore about something mighty big I'd shut my mouth on it and pick on him about something that couldn't have worried a cat. I used to pick on him for nothing at all so that we could have a scrap and make up. Kinda hysterical, we were. I had to divorce Dwight because I don't like going to bed at night without knowing whether the house is mortgaged or not, and for plumb silliness at that. He wasn't any good. But I liked him. I liked him quite a lot.

'Well, Étienne liked to act up like we were both hysterical. Picking on each other and making up. And in a queer way it was fine. It had the string on it that we didn't have to do it, which is what takes the fun out of golf for me. But it reminded me of the time when I did have to do it because Dwight made me so's I couldn't help it. It is a queer feeling, like going about all day wanting to sneeze and not being able to do it. Oh, one way and another he gave me a grand time in Paris, Étienne did. I had to stop over much longer than I had meant, because the Soviet Government offered us some work to do on the side reorganizing railways in Siberia and I had to see a whole lot of people: to find out how much there was in it. But really it didn't seem so long.

'Then I got news that made me feel like a dawg whenever Étienne was around.

'They cabled me that Mary Martin was sick.

'Now there's a whole long story behind that. You see the South-West and West-South, and the St Louis and Los Angeles – that's the railways I'm interested in and the railway Étienne's interested in – are rivals. We love each other like a coupla wild cats. And the South-West and the West-South has had the St Louis and Los Angeles killed stone dead for a quarter of a century – if it hadn't been for Mary Martin. Gosh, the way I feel about that woman! . . .

'You see, my husband, Walter Sarle, started in business way back in the seventies with a fella from the same town called Tom Martin, and they went on from deal to deal until the early nineties, when they were going to do a merger between the South-West and West-South, and the St Louis and Los Angeles. But on the eve of the deal Walter found out that Tom was a crook, and had been double-crossing him since the day they left their home town together. So there wasn't a merger, and Walter took the South-West and West-South, and Tom took the St Louis and Los Angeles, and they never spoke again, except on public occasions, when they wanted to give the Stock-market a false hunch. And y'know, Walter was right. Tom Martin was a crook, and when he found he couldn't make a go of the St Louis and Los Angeles – and no one on God's earth could – Walter had the low-down on that, and that's why he got Tom to take it when they unhitched – he tried all sorts of crook's games. And we knew all about them, and we could have killed the line dead twenty-five years ago, if it hadn't been for Tom's wife, Mary. Lord! how I hated that woman! She was a toothache to me when she lived, and she couldn't even die at the right time.

'She was one of those professional good women, daughter of a Methodist minister in Cairo, Illinois, wore her hair parted in the middle and brushed smooth. I never saw the woman but I've seen her photograph till I could have cried because the condition of Walter's heart and his great age prevented me from dancing on it. Walter married me because I made him laugh, and I guess a few other ladies have been useful to him in other ways in the course of his life; but he put Mary Martin above us all. I guess men who have been pretty tough often do that. They get worried with all the cuties clustering round them, and the women who'd done real work for them, and they hang up the picture of a woman who isn't a cutie and who hasn't done any real work, and say, "Ah, that's the kind of woman I'm crazy about!" It's an alibi. Well, I was told from the start that we mustn't go after the St Louis and Los Angeles until Mary Martin was dead. Tom had died back in 1915, but he didn't count. It was Mary whose faith in her dead husband mustn't be destroyed. Walter left a note in his will, begging me to respect his wishes in this matter.

'Gee! how I cussed. But I got it all fixed to say, "Go" the minute she died. I had my folks at Washington ready to worry the Government with a true story of what those dirty grafters had been doing for years, and bring the Railway Commission down on 'em like a cyclone; I'd politicians in every State that our lines cut through ready to squeal in the Legislative Assemblies with enough to put every President of the line in jail, I'd bought four newspapers in the West and the Middle West that would just tear the sky down with headlines, I'd got control of enough shares in the St Louis and Los Angeles to dump on the market and start a panic. (And they had nothing on us; not a thing that you could call anything.) And that darned

woman would not die. She just celebrated birthday after
birthday in her home in Indianapolis, sending messages to
Women's Clubs attributing her great age to her not having
done this or that thing that I'd bet my last cent she never
had the chance to do. I hated her so I felt I was keeping her
alive in my hatred like a kinda pickle. That's why all this
hardly came into my mind when I spoke about the lines to
Étienne. It never occurred to me that she wouldn't live to
send a loving, tender, understanding message to my
funeral.

'Then they cabled she had pleurisy.

'Mind you, she was older than Walter. For a minute I
was so glad I could have kissed the bell-boy. Then I went all
gone at the knees. What was to happen to Étienne if I put
this thing over?

'I tried all I could not to face it. I said, "That old Polly-
anna will get better. The girls of Indianapolis, Terre Haute,
and other towns within the zone of her Local Group
Women's Clubs, will get the low-down on the moral effect
of rolled stockings on this September thirteenth same as any
other." I hated her so much I knew her birthday. But the
cables kept on getting worse and worse. She was making a
good hard fight for it, considering how old a woman she
was, but it wasn't going to be good enough. So I sat down
and tried to figure out how I could do as I wanted and not
leave Étienne broke. And however long I sat and however
hard I tried there wasn't a thing in it. The big idea in the
whole thing was that by shooting up the town I should be
able to buy the stock of the St Louis and Los Angeles at
rock bottom prices after the panic and have the merger
same as Walter had planned but leave the Martin crowd
flat. Well, I couldn't do it without cleaning out Étienne. It
just couldn't happen any other way.

'You see, this had to be kept secret. I'd been a clam about
it myself for years. There weren't above three people in our
own organization who knew what I had been planning to
do. The people I have in Washington and in the Legislative

Assemblies, and the newspapers, they didn't know what story they'd got to spill, they just knew they'd got to spill a story when they were told. Otherwise the Martin crowd might ... But that doesn't matter. The point is that if I told Étienne what was on the way and gave him the tip to get rid of his stock he would talk. My Lord! how that baby did talk. His own age was the only thing he ever kept to himself. I used to listen to him by the hour telling who'd been his sweetheart and my blood would have run cold at the thought of how he'd tell about me some day if I hadn't known that it wasn't likely he'd ever meet a soul to whom my name meant a thing. And even if he didn't talk, the mere fact of his getting rid of his holding would have put people wise to the fact that there was something coming to the St Louis and Los Angeles, particularly as we'd been seen about together. And I wanted those shares to fall sudden. I wanted the thing to crash down like a poleaxed steer in the stockyards. It had to be that way, or maybe they'd come back at us. Étienne had to go down with the rest of 'em or I couldn't have my fun.

'And that meant I couldn't have it.

'Believe me or not, I found I couldn't do it. If he felt about me the way he said he did, I couldn't sell him up the river.

'Well, it all got perfectly terrible. The cables kept coming faster and faster, and worse and worse. Mary's pleurisy turned to pneumonia. I should have dined with Étienne the night that cable came and I was in a cold sweat all the afternoon at having to face him. Then mercifully he sent a telegram to say he couldn't come. But I couldn't stand for anything more like that. I pushed off for Carlsbad the next day, to take a cure, I said. That'll tell you how bad I was, pushing off to a country with a name like Czecho-Slovakia when I should have been hareing home to stand up to a deal. Sheer foolishness it was.

'And it wasn't any use. I kept on getting those cables in Carlsbad, and thinking of Étienne. I used to go and take my waters at some godawful hour in the morning, and go one of those beastly walks through those mangy fir-woods that come out in restaurants like something you'd get the vet to come and see, and I would feel so hungry for my breakfast that I would think I would die. Then when I sat down in front of my cawfee and my ham I would just put my head in my hands and my elbows on the table and look at the darned things and groan. If he felt about me the way he said he did I couldn't do it to him. And oh, Lordy, I wanted to do it. I wanted it more than I've ever wanted anything in my life.

'I sicked on that bright boy I got as secretary I told you about to find out more about Étienne, to see if maybe he didn't want a rich wife after all. And I got so frantic that I sat down and wrote a letter to Étienne asking if he did really feel about me the way he'd said he did. But he didn't answer, and the boy said that so far as he could reckon Étienne couldn't want a rich wife or any other kind of wife, because he had had a wife once, who had divorced him, and it seems that in the kind of French society where he belonged they would have turned on him like a dawg if he had got married again, being Catholics. Then I just seemed to lose control. I went kind of cuckoo. I used to see a man coming along one of these paths in the woods, or maybe having dinner across the room in the hotel, and I would think it was Étienne, though it wouldn't be a bit like him when one got near. He still didn't answer, and then I got a cable to say Mary Martin was sinking fast. I could have screamed the house down, because if he felt about me the way he said he did I couldn't do what I wanted, and I just had to do it.

'George – that's the secretary I've been talking about – wired to me to ask if he should say "Go" the minute he got the cable to say she'd gone. And instead of answering I put myself in the train and went back to Paris. I half hoped that Étienne's not answering might mean something funny, but then it mightn't. He had said something about going to the shore. I had to find out before I could do a thing. How I threshed about in that train! And it was hot as Death Valley. And such a train. If you call it a train.

'I wired George from Zürich to come and meet me: and there he was bright as a button when he got in.

'"She's dead," said he, "do we say 'Go'?"

'I just groaned. I said, "We say nothing at all till I've paid a call, and till then I'd be pleased if you'd describe with full detail how your Aunt is enjoying her trip to Palestine with the Moravian Mission Sisters. And don't mention Mary Martin, and what's more regard that as a rehearsal, for maybe we're never going to talk of her again. And tell the chauffeur not to drive to the Ritz, tell him to drive to where M. de Sevenac lives."

'"Why, Mrs Sarle," says George, "aren't you going to have a bath and a bit to eat?"

'"I've lost all interest in being clean, and I haven't eaten for days," I said, "just you go on talking."

'I was yammering when we went up that long Avenoo by the Champs-Elysées. I tell you it would have broken my heart not to have gone for that gang of no-account crooks on the St Louis and Los Angeles. But I couldn't do it if it was as he'd said. So when we had got to Étienne's apartment I just stampeded the elevator as if there was a fire and I hung on to his bell as if I was giving an alarm.

'And then his butler wouldn't let me in. Can you imagine anything that would have made you madder! And I knew Étienne wasn't out because if he had been the butler would have made signs he wanted me to wait like he always did before. I argued with him the best way I knew how, seeing he didn't know any American and I don't know any French, and then it flashed across me that maybe he was keeping me out because Étienne had one of those sweethearts he was always talking about calling on him, and I'd give my eye teeth to find out if he was, because if it were so that would let me out. So I just doubled past him like a wild cat and was into the sitting-room before he knew what had happened.

'There wasn't any girl there. Étienne was there all right, but he was alone. And when I saw him something funny happened to me, like what happens to old people when they have a stroke, I guess. Remember I had had a fortnight of this torture at Carlsbad alone, and I hadn't been taking my food, and I'd been cooking in that wagon-lit like a planked steak all across Europe. And I was up against the prospect of doing something that was as comfortable as cutting off my right hand. And now I'd got to hear him say whether I had to do that or not. I was so scared of hearing that I couldn't get my voice out, my sight went black, I had to hang on to some drapes there were on the doorway. I remember thinking before my sight went that he looked kinda scared.

'I don't remember what I said exactly. I think I said, "Do you care for me or don't you?"'

'He answered something silly that didn't help like, "What are you saying?"'

'It crossed my mind that wherever Mary Martin was she would be laughing herself sick, for here was I tied up from doing the thing I most wanted in the whole wide world through going with just the kind of beau she warned the girls of Indianapolis and Terre Haute against. It came on that the sensible thing to do was to dash out of that apartment and bolt home and do what I wanted and not care a hoot what Étienne felt or didn't feel. But I had to be decent. So I kinda moaned, "Do you really care for me like you said? Do you get me? I'm asking – do you really care for me?"'

'Then my eyes got better and I saw him clearly as he crossed the room towards me, and my heart nearly stopped right then, for I saw it was all right. He looked real ugly and he said something about not wanting me there, and I saw that his being with me had just been some kind of foolishness, and that whatever it was it was over, and there wasn't a thing stood between me and the St Louis and Los Angeles.

'I could have gone down on my knees and prayed and

shouted and sung, I was so happy. Then a kinda doubt came over me. It just couldn't be so perfect. Maybe he was just peeved because he hadn't expected me, maybe he'd come around afterwards and go back on it. So I had it out with him. I asked him a second time, and he said, No, he didn't care a scrap, and he looked so mean I believed him. I guess it had all been foolishness of some sort, and some new foolishness had come and cut the old sort out. I'd rather like to meet him again and find out what it was all about, but I don't suppose he'd be able to tell me himself, and anyway he's probably sore at me. Anyway I got it signed on the dotted line. He didn't care for me like he said he did, so I could go ahead. I just stood for a moment looking into the golden future. Then I remembered that George was downstairs and almost as eager as I was to say "Go". And I felt embarrassed being with Étienne too, knowing that in ten days' time that poor baby wouldn't own more than his shirt.

'So I made a getaway and I ran down to George. He said, "Why, Mrs Sarle, you look a different woman!" And I felt it. I'd been all in when I went into that apartment, and when I came out I was able to go back to the Ritz and get the whole thing moving by midnight. And how it moved! There never has been any big operation of the size run so sweetly. Ten days and we had the St Louis and Los Angeles just where we wanted 'em. That's what I'll be remembered for. And just think, I was within a hair's breadth of losing it all, and having that Mary Martin laughing at me through all eternity, just through being taken in by your friend Étienne de Sevenac!

'Well, well, well!' she said, cosily, finishing her story. 'I guess we're all fools once in our lives.'

She put her hand out to her glass, drank the last drop in it, set it aside, turned to her triple mirror and began to powder her face and neck with a great puff, looking over her shoulder to ask, without shyness, with an air of disinterested curiosity, 'You knowing the fella and all, can you believe it?'

'Knowing Étienne?' I murmured. 'Oh, yes . . . Oh, yes . . .'

But Nancy Sarle had stiffened as she sat before the triple mirror, was holding her great puff in mid-air. And it was not her own reflexion that had startled her. Kindly, regretfully, she said to me, 'Here, what've you been letting me say to you that's made you so blue?'

I shook my head. 'Nothing,' I said, but for a millionth of a second, before the censor we all carry within us who respects society had pulled me together, I looked past her at a reflexion that was my own, and that was utterly desolate.

I told you that there was no conversation; that no one listens to what the other one says. But it appears that the inter-silence of the universe is more profound even than this. It appears that even the different parts of the same person do not converse among themselves, do not succeed in learning from each other what are their desires and their intentions. The part of me that had had in hand the detective work on Nancy Sarle had pretended that it was taking all this trouble just for amusement. As I have said, I adore strong feeling, having myself a heart that paints exquisitely but only in water colours. It shows how temperate I am, and how likely to have this dilettante passion for violent emotion, that I should feel this cool, kind, amused interest in Étienne, of all people in the world. For the very minute after I had seen myself in the mirror hunched in desolation and had pulled myself together I was presenting a picture shaped by the nicest feeling towards him. I was smiling sadly because I had remembered a remark Étienne had made to me some years before, one of the first of many remarks he made to me which had sent a searchlight into the uncomprehended parts of his soul and shown them a desert. 'It always puts a woman at a disadvantage,' he had said, 'if when she reproaches you for not loving her you say very solemnly, "My dear, I have always cared for you far more than you have cared for me." She cannot possibly dispute that, you see, so she feels foolish, she flounders, she loses her bearings, one can make her cry then quite easily, and it is all over.' Poor Étienne, he had paid so heavily for not having made this remark on the one occasion when it was more or less true! I smiled, because obviously that is funny, but I smiled sadly, because even a wolfish mechanism of crafty, busy hungers has its right to pity, since it is human.

Yet what the mirror had first shown me was the truth. I was utterly desolate, because of a cry from my heart, which was not reasonable, and had not been understood by the rest of me, which is governed by reason. I have told you that I am happy with my husband and with my daughters, that they do not dwell in the desert, that they live without cruelty and treacheries, that they are the inheritors of beautiful traditions and will themselves leave such as well as their bones to those who come after them. Yet I had opened my windows and was leaning out into the desert, where once I wandered for a long time and nearly met with death, almost as if I would like to wander there again. At least I was feeling as if it were an important part of my life, of which I was anxious to receive news, so that I might think of it as something other than a bad dream, an accident, a disaster which I ought to forget as absolutely as I can. I had pried into Nancy Sarle's story because I had believed that she had done what she did as a consequence of love; and I had longed for her to describe and justify that love so that it would sanctify my days in the desert. I had wanted her to tell me that she too had found it possible to love a cad. I had wanted her to disclose some detail, such as had not been apparent but must be latent in my own story, which would prove that it may be inevitable for a woman to love a cad. I had wanted her to lay something before me which I realized I had never ceased to seek, something which would make it right and reasonable that I should have spent ten years of my life with my first husband, who was Étienne de Sevenac, enduring unfathomable agony, sustained by unsurpassable pleasure, until I was overcome by a fatigue that seemed like the judgement of a third person; adding up with equal frenzy the reasons why I should leave him and the reasons why I should stay, while the same third person within me who was responsible for my fatigue presented me with ultimatum after ultimatum, which I filed in my brain as one sticks bills on the mantelpiece, knowing quite well that they must be ascending some scale of urgency, but not doing anything about them, until there came the one that had the finality and potency of a summons. I had hoped to get from her some argument to prove that I am right in my feelings, which I never admit because it is a disloyalty to my present life yet which makes my present life seem a disloyalty, that some circumstance connected with this anguished sacrifice of my best years to a cheap and empty man made all of it worth while. Actually an insane part of me feels that there is a sanction for my life in that miserable and fruitless time, if I could only lay my hand on it, which transcends all the claims that I can make for myself because of these later years when I have been building up a tranquil home for people who are among the salt of the earth. That insane part of me had been listening to her story as for a miracle, which would have proved it sane. Yet what I said at the beginning was true. I have no feeling left whatsoever for Étienne de Sevenac. I do not even like him. I am so tired of him that when I see him I feel ill, I can only tolerate his society by studying the absurdities of his fight against age, which I can do quite easily without pity.

'I've made you blue!' murmured Nancy: and her eyes were less like coarse china because of their kind concern for me.

I rose and patted her on the broad, long, Sealyham, satin back. 'Nothing you could ever tell me could make me blue,' I told her, 'I think you're simply splendid.'

In the mirror our eyes met and smiled. She murmured, 'You're quite sure I haven't done anything, said anything?' I shook my head. 'Swell,' she said. 'Now let's have some more of that Tokay, before we get downstairs. That crowd'll be ripping up the floor-boards if I don't get back to 'em.' We each drank a glass. I had never noticed before what a strong malty taste there is at the back of Tokay. 'Funny things, fellahs,' she chuckled, putting down her glass. 'Very funny,' I laughed back. Then she wriggled her toes into the gold slippers, shook herself, and was a hostess again. As we walked through the long corridors, past the tall-boys and tapestries, with her hand on my arm, I regretted the greater geniality of our march up to her bedroom. I did not suppose we would ever recapture that glow of friendship, for I could feel that some part of me would never let me like her as I had liked her before, now that I knew that she had ruined Étienne not out of love but out of indifference. Yet Étienne means nothing to me. He means nothing at all to me.

THE SALT OF THE EARTH

THE SALT OF THE EARTH

I

ALICE PEMBERTON had not expected to enjoy the motor-drive home, since because of it, the previous afternoon, she had received a bitter hurt. She had gone into the drawing-room to tell her mother that one of the young men who had been coming in for tennis so much of late, was very pleased indeed to give her a lift to Camelheath. With her invariable consideration she had been careful to mention the proposal nonchalantly, though she knew she would enjoy the drive through the spring countryside, and would find the society of the obviously admiring young man just such a gratification as a woman of forty needs from time to time. There could be no getting away from the fact that this meant her leaving her mother two days earlier than had been planned, and she was never one to take family duties lightly. But before she could well get the sentence out of her mouth there had flashed into her mother's eyes a look which nobody in the world could mistake for anything but an expression of intense, almost hilarious relief.

'It ought to be lovely for you!' Mrs Anglesey had exclaimed. 'You'll go through the New Forest, I expect. It'll be at its best with all the trees coming out.'

'Very well, mother dear,' Alice had said quietly, and had gone out of the dark drawing-room into the sunlit garden. Though she was reassured by the sight of the young man in white flannels, plainly eager to hear her decision, she could hardly still the trembling of her upper lip.

'Not, my dear, that I shan't be terribly sorry to lose you!' her mother had called after her, but a second too late, a semitone too high pitched.

That night she lay awake for quite a long time wondering why it was that her mother had always had such a curious attitude to her. It was not that she did not care for her. Alice knew that quite well. When she had had diphtheria as a girl at school, when she had been operated on for appendicitis, the extremely passionate quality of her mother's anguish and relief had been as recognizable as the brilliance of lightning. Nevertheless she could not help seeing that in the ordinary intercourse of life Mrs Anglesey felt her as a burden. She had sometimes suspected that her mother had hurried on her marriage to Jimmy not only because as she had so often said at the time, long engagements dragged young romance past its proper time of ripening, but because she wanted her out of the house; and she had had to do more than suspect, she had often to record in black and white on the pages of her diary, that when her mother came to stay with her her visits were apt to be far briefer than those she paid to Madge or Leo.

'Of course there may be some reason for it,' Alice pondered, determined to be broad-minded and generous. 'I am the eldest of the three, I was born very soon after she married. Perhaps I came too soon, before she was reconciled to giving up all her pleasures for her babies, and she may have felt a grudge against me that she has never lived down.'

But she could not help thinking that her mother ought to have lived it down if she had any sense of gratitude. For neither Madge nor Leo had done anything like as much for their mother as she had, and she had been willing to make even greater sacrifices, had they been accepted. Though she and Jimmy had loved each other so much, she had been quite willing to face a long engagement, simply because she hated to imagine what home would be like without her. Since her father's death she had done what she could to replace his influence. She had kept Madge and Leo from getting out of hand as fatherless children notoriously do, she had tried to prevent her mother from giving way to that strain of fecklessness and untidiness which her most fervent admirers had to admit existed alongside her charm and vividness. Well, all that hadn't been appreciated. Alice remembered, and it was as if a pin had stuck into her, how Mrs Anglesey had grown gay and gayer as the wedding-day approached, and at the actual ceremony had shone with a radiance quite unlike the melancholy conventionally ascribed to the bride's mother. She rolled over in bed, rubbing her face angrily against the sheets.

Anyway, even if her mother had not valued her properly then, she ought to have learned to do so, in the last few years of her age and mellowness. Hadn't she noticed what her daugher had done for her during this visit? Alice had put out of doors the horrible gipsyish old dressing-gowny tea-gowns her mother had loved to shuffle about in for the evenings, and had bought her some nice old-lady dresses from quite a good shop, in the proper colours, dove-grey and dark brown. She had gone over the housekeeping books and saved pounds by changing several of the shops, and had put an end to the custom by which cook had brought in the menu-book last thing at night and launched out into what proved simply to be shockingly familiar gossip. One can't get on those terms with one's servants. She had hired a car, too, and taken her mother round calling on all the nice people with whom she had lost touch, and when her mother had insisted on calling on the Duchess, and had settled down to chat as if they were two old cronies, she had been firm and just taken her home, for it does not do to presume on one's acquaintance with people like that. It had all been a lot of trouble, too, particularly when she was still feeling so weak. But it had all gone for nothing. And so, too, she suspected, had all she had done for Madge and Leo. They hardly ever seemed to realize any of her kindnesses to them, and sometimes they were quite rude. And Leo's wife, Evie, was almost worse.

But perhaps this was the price she had to pay for her perfect marriage. At least Jimmy adored her. 'My dear husband!' she sighed, and presently went off to sleep, but not, as it appeared, to rest. For there began to hover about her a terror which she had met before in her sleep, and she stood helpless while it circled closer and closer, unable to move hand or foot, able only to shriek. Able to shriek, it appeared, not only in her dream, for she opened her eyes and found her mother leaning over her and trying to shake her, although she herself was shaking so that there was very little strength in her hands.

'Oh, mother darling!' said Alice. 'These wretched nightmares! I wish I didn't have them so often!'

Mrs Anglesey sat back, still shaking, her grey hair wild about her.

'Oh, my poor little girl,' she gasped. 'My poor little girl! What can it be that frightens you so?'

The immediate preludes to the motor-drive, therefore, were not auspicious. Alice had a headache when she woke in the morning, and on the young man's arrival her mother proved uncommonly tiresome. She insisted on getting up to say good-bye to her daughter, and when she presented herself on the front lawn Alice realized that a ruby velveteen morning gown, adorned with moulting marabout of a fawn shade that owed more to time than to the dyer, had somehow got back from the dust-bin to which she thought she had sent it. The young man was very nice about it, even affecting interest when Mrs Anglesey insisted on telling him the story of the time when she met Edward the Seventh at Monte Carlo; and he dissembled what must have been his emotions when, after he had started his engine, a shriek from her made him stop again.

'Alice! Have you remembered to send them a telegram to say you're coming?'

'No. I don't want to. It'll be a lovely surprise for Jimmy. And I like walking in on servants unexpectedly. It does them good.'

The engine birred again. There was another shriek. ' – and Alice!'

'Oh, mother dear!'

'Be sure you look in the kitchen for the copper pan. It's no use your laughing, my dear, it might be that – ' she had her arm over the side of the car and they had to let her go on talking – 'you know, Mr – Mr? – Mr Acland, is it? – my daughter came here for a little sea air after she's been terribly ill, and my doctor says that though he didn't see her during one of the attacks he thinks it sounds like irritant poisoning. Anything gastric he says wouldn't have been cured so soon. And we can't account for it any way except that I say it is one of the copper pans I gave her for her wedding that they've forgotten to have re-coppered. That's dreadfully dangerous, you know. The Duchess's sister Jane died of it somewhere abroad. So I tell Alice she must look most carefully when she gets home. Oh, my dear Mr Acland, you don't know how ill she was, yellow as a guinea, and such vomiting and diarrhoea . . .'

These are not words one wants shouted to the winds as one drives off, looking one's best, beside a young man of twenty-three who believes one to be very nearly his contemporary, for a journey through the springtime. But the day went very well indeed. They got out of the town very soon and cut up through pinewoods to the heathy hills, presently turning and looking their last on the Channel, where immense pillars of light and darkness marched and countermarched on a beaten silver floor against a back-cloth of distant storm. Not long after they were in the New Forest, where the new grass blades were springing up like green fire through the dark, tough matting of heather, and in the same plantations the black ashes affirmed it was still winter, the elms went no farther than to show a few purple flowers, the oaks made their recurring confusion between spring and autumn and were ablaze with red young leaves, and the birches and hawthorns were comfortably emerald.

Up there, as the morning got along, they had their lunch, sitting by a stream that reflected a bank of primroses. Mr Acland told Alice many things. Helping in his father's factory seemed rather grim after Oxford. It was terribly hard work, and no chance of success, only the hope of staving off failure. Life was awfully difficult just now, particularly if you were young. When, for example, was he likely to be able to afford to marry? And he would like to marry. Not that he knew anybody at the moment that he wanted to marry. There had been somebody . . . but that had proved to be a mistake. He supposed he wasn't quite like other people, but he wanted something more than mere prettiness. He wanted ideas . . . broadmindedness . . . sympathy . . . .

He kept his eyes on Alice as he spoke, and that was very natural, for she was very nearly a perfect specimen of her type, and time had done almost nothing to spoil her. A touch of silver gave her golden hair a peculiar etherealized burnish, and the oval of her chin was still firm. She had neither crowsfeet nor lines round her mouth, perhaps because she habitually wore an expression of child-like wonder, which kept her blue-grey eyes wide open and her lips parted. She did in actual fact look under thirty, and what was more than that, she looked benevolent, candid, trustworthy, all in terms of grace. Her acts of kindness, her own resolutions of honesty, her Spartan guardianship of secrets, would all, one felt confident, be transacted so that the whole of life would take a more romantic form for evermore. It was no wonder that Mr Acland felt the liveliest satisfaction at her appearance.

His own, however, did not satisfy her nearly so well. She realized this when, speaking as earnestly as he had done, and encouraging him to seek for the perfect mate by relating her own story, she fixed her eyes on his face. Proudly yet modestly she described how she had lived all her life in Camelheath, and admitted that many people might pity her for this, since it would be idle to deny that it was quite the dullest town that could be found within fifty miles of London, but she claimed that nobody in the world could have lived a richer and fuller life than she had, thanks to the circumstance that when she was nineteen the leading solicitor in the town had sent for his nephew to come and be his junior partner, and that the boy had immediately fallen in love with her. 'We have been married nineteen years, and we are as much in love as ever,' she said. The sound of her own words made Jimmy's face appear before her, and she realized with an almost shuddering intensity how much she would rather be looking at him than at Mr Acland. This was no vague, sentimental preference. There was some particular feature in Jimmy's face that gave her deep and delicious pleasure; yet she could not think what it was. Academically, she acknowledged, Mr Acland's broad-browed fairness was more likely to earn points than Jimmy's retiring, quickly-smiling darkness, but that was irrelevant to the intense joy he gave her by this quality which, just for the moment, though she would have liked to tell the boy about it, she could not name.

After she had told her story they got back into the car, feeling very warm and intimate but a little solemn and silent; and about half-past three they stopped in front of the Georgian house at Camelheath which was her home.

'It's a very pretty house,' said Mr Acland.

'We've done a great deal to it,' said Alice.

She rang. Though she always carried a key she hardly ever used it, for she liked to keep Ethel on the alert about door-opening; and this technique had evidently paid, for Ethel confronted them before a minute had passed.

'Why, it's the mistress! And looking so well, too! Why, I never did expect to see you looking so well, ever again mum! Well, the master will be pleased ...'

Cook, who had been waddling upstairs when the door opened, leaned over the banisters and joined in.

'Well, mum, it's no need to ask if you're feeling better! I didn't never see anybody so far gone come right up again! You're the proper picture of health, now, you are, mum ...'

She beamed at them while they ran on, regretting that Mr Pemberton wouldn't be able to run over from his office that very minute, because old Mr Bates up at Stickyback

Farm had died three days ago, and he had had to go to his funeral this afternoon, assuring her that Mr Pemberton had missed her ever so, that when Ethel had taken him up his blacks for him to change into after lunch he had said, 'Well, thank goodness, we'll be having your mistress with us very soon.' Of course the servants adored her. Well, so they might. She knew she had an almost perfect manner with subordinates, and she really took trouble over training them and thinking out devices for ridding them of their little faults. She would never need to part with her servants, if it was not for the curious vein of madness running through all women of that class, which invariably came out sooner or later in some wild attack of causeless rage. Well, there was some ground for hoping that these two were superior to the rest of their kind. Cook had been with her eighteen months, Ethel nearly three years. Perhaps at last all her kindly efforts were going to be given their reward.

Graciously smiling, she dismissed them and took Mr Acland into the drawing-room. But he would not stay for tea. He had to admit, with some nervous laughter and blushes, that his home was not quite in the direction he had led her to suppose: that, in fact, he had made quite a preposterous detour to drop her at Camelheath, and that he would have to keep quite good time for the rest of his drive to get back for dinner.

'But it's been wonderful to see where you live,' he said, looking round with admiration. Alice was leaning on the Adam mantelpiece, her brilliant fairness and her quiet, good beige suit harmonizing with the pale golden marble. On the fine Chippendale furniture, polished till amber light seemed to well up from the depths of the wood, were bowls of daffodils and early tulips; and between the mellow green brocade curtains a garden tidy to the last leaf showed spring flowers against the definite fine-grained darkness of hoed earth, a quaintly planned rose-garden here and there ruddy with new shoots, and orchard boughs rising frosted with blossom above black yew hedges.

'It's lovely, of course. But can you find people fit to be your friends in this little town?'

'I don't ask for very much, you know,' said Alice bravely, 'and I'm the centre of quite a little world here. Do you see that house over the fields, standing among the elms? My sister, Mrs Walter Fletcher, lives there.'

'It looks as if it was a lovely house, too.'

'It might be. But poor Madge is a funny girl. She isn't a very good manager.' She paused and sighed. 'Then, as you drive out of town, you'll pass a big modern villa just by a fork in the road. That's where my little brother lives. At least he isn't little at all now, in fact he's the local doctor, as our father was before him. But I always think of him as my little brother. I had so much to do with him as a baby, you see, and then I haven't been able to see so much of him in later years. He made a marriage that from some points of view hasn't been a success.' She looked into the distance for a minute and then said simply, 'You know, I used to mind terribly not having any children. But I realize that if I had I wouldn't have been able to do a whole lot of things for others that badly needed doing.'

'I'm sure that's true,' said Mr Acland gravely, 'there aren't enough people like you to go round.'

Soon after that he went. Alice was quite glad, for it would have been an anti-climax for him to have stayed any longer now that they had established this peculiarly deep and reticent sympathy. She walked out with him through the front garden, pausing sometimes to show him her collection of old-fashioned English herbs. 'They have such lovely names,' she said, 'rosemary . . . thyme . . . musk . . . herb-of-grace . . . and dear old lavender. They give one the feeling of an age I believe I would have liked better than this horrid, hustling present day.'

When they said good-bye he held her hand a minute longer than was necessary. 'I wish you'd promise me not to do too many things for other people,' he said. 'I expect that's how you got ill.'

'I'll try and be more sensible,' she smiled.

As soon as she got back to the house she started on a tour of inspection. There was a pile of visiting-cards on the tray on the hall table – odd how many people had called while she was away – and lifted them to see if there was much dust underneath. But there was none there, nor anywhere in the drawing-room, nor in the dining-room, nor in the little library. Everywhere the flowers were fresh, and the water in the vases had been changed that morning, the ash trays had been emptied and polished, and the oak floors shone like brown glass. She went upstairs, running her hand along the fluting of the banisters. When she reached the landing she paused and examined her fingers, but they were still pink and clean.

There was nothing wrong in her bedroom, either. The billows of glazed chintz, biscuit-coloured and sprigged with rosebuds, had evidently just been put up again after a visit to the cleaner's. The silver toilet set on the dressing-table caught the afternoon sun with its brightness; and on the top of the tall-boy the pot-pourri bowl of blue and white porcelain shone with the proper clean milky radiance. She felt a great relief at getting back to her own house, so airy and light and spacious, so austerely empty of anything that was not carefully chosen and fine and mellow, after her mother's cluttered rooms. But she did not linger any longer, though this was perhaps her favourite room in the house, but opened the door into her husband's dressing-room. Perhaps Ethel had let herself be careless there.

Everything was all right there, too, however. There were too many books on the table beside the bed; its Sheraton legs quivered under the strain if one added the weight of a finger tip. She took an armful and put them back on the shelves on the wall, marvelling at the kind of book her quiet Jimmy liked to read: crude, violent tales about tramps, sailors before the mast, trappers of wild animals. But there was nothing else in the room that she could have wished different. The brushes and combs lay in front of his swinging mirror, gleaming and symmetrical; even the sock and handkerchief drawer was in perfect order; and the photograph frames along the mantelpiece almost gave her what she wanted, for it seemed impossible that Ethel could have got them quite as bright as this without neglecting some of her other duties. But as she turned away, her eye was caught by something about the largest photograph, the one standing in the middle of the mantelpiece, which showed her as a bride looking with wide eyes and parted lips over her sheaf of lilies. There was a hair running half across it, under the glass. She took up the frame and slipped out the photograph and then paused in surprise. There was no hair on the glass; but the photograph had been torn almost in two.

'Ethel!' she said angrily, and stretched her hand towards the bell. But she perceived that this damage must have been done long ago. Somebody had tried their best to repair it by pasting the torn edges to a piece of paper beneath, and had made a very neat job of it. It had only become visible now because the paste had shrunk and hardened with age and the torn edges were gaping again. One of Ethel's predecessors must have done it during the frenzies of spring cleaning. 'It must have been Lilian Hall,' thought Alice bitterly. She could remember the names of all her many hated servants. What a pack they were! One could not trust any of them. She peered eagerly into her husband's wardrobe, for she knew that her careful supervision of his valeting had given him such confidence that he never looked at his clothes or shoes. But the suits hung sleekly pressed and completely buttoned from the hangers, and down at the bottom black shoes looked inky, brown shoes glowed with their cornelian tints.

When she saw the grey tweeds she felt a little startled, for he always wore them at the office, until she remembered he had had to change to go to a funeral. The sight of his everyday suit brought him vividly before her, with his dark, thoroughly pleasant but not excessive good looks, his slouch that seemed not so much slackness as a modest retreat from notice, the curious thrilling sense of expectation which, in spite of his quietness, he still gave her after their nineteen years of marriage. She put out her hand and stroked the suit affectionately, and then paused, puzzled because she had felt through the tweed something hard of an odd shape. It was lying along the bottom of his right hand inside breast pocket, and when she fished it out she saw that it was a cylindrical tube of very thick glass fitted with a screw-top, and two-thirds full of white powder.

'Why is Jimmy carrying medicine about with him? Can he be imagining he's ill again?' She wondered not for the first time, why she should be the only perfectly normal person, who never said she was ill except when she was ill, in a family of hypochondriacs. Then her heart contracted. 'Perhaps he really is ill!' She remembered what her mother had suggested, that there might be a faulty cooking vessel in the kitchen which was tainting the food with mineral poison, and she hoped that poor Jimmy had not been keeping from her the news that he had had an attack like hers. To see what the medicine might be, she put her finger in the white powder, and sucked it; but though the haunting bitterness of its taste reminded her of something, she could not put a name to it. But she recognized the container. Old Dr Godstone, who had looked after the local practice during the period after her father had died and before her brother had been ready to take it over, had used these funny glass containers for some of his drugs. How like Jimmy to go on using something made up by that silly old man, which had probably lost whatever virtues it ever had through the lapse of time, instead of going along to Leo and having something really up to date made up! What would Jimmy do without her?

She went down the stairs humming with satisfaction and looked down on the top of Ethel's head in the hall, as she bent over her mistress's suitcase. Then it flashed over her why the house was so tidy. Mrs Anglesey had rung up after all and warned them she was coming back. That had happened once before, shortly after Ethel had first come to her. She had come back and found the house a whirlwind of plate-powder and blacking-brushes with the girl's attempts to catch up with her neglected work. What a talking-to she had given her! The silly girl had cried her eyes out, and would probably have left if her mother hadn't been so ill. Of course she had greatly improved since then, and no doubt she had allowed less to fall in arrears this time, but only some such warning would account for the exquisite order she had found everywhere.

'Ethel!' she called, in a coolly humorous tone.

The girl's sleek head cocked up. 'Yes, mum.'

'The house is beautifully tidy.'

'I'm so glad you found it right, mum.'

'So tidy,' said Alice, who had got down to the hall and was standing with her head lowered so that she could look searchingly into Ethel's doe eyes, while a whimsical little smile played round her lips, 'that I was wondering if Mrs Anglesey hadn't telephoned this morning to warn you I was coming back.'

The girl grew pale and caught her breath for a second, then banged the suitcase down on the floor. 'No, she didn't,' she said. 'The house has been this way all the time you've been away, and would have stayed so if you'd been away twice as long. And if you don't believe me you can call up the Post Office and see if there's been any but local calls put through here all day.'

'Oh, very well, very well,' said Alice, 'but such things have been known to happen, haven't they, before now?'

The girl's eyes blazed. She picked up the suitcase and went up the stairs with it. As she went by her resentment was as tangible as a hot wind.

'What tempers they all have!' thought Alice. 'And how tiresome it is just when I've got home! I wonder if anyone realizes just how much it costs me to run this house in self-restraint and patience.' She sighed as it occurred to her that her own household was only one of her responsibilities, and looked at her wrist-watch. It was improbable that Jimmy would be in before five, she might just as well go over and see how Madge and Leo were getting on, and what new problems she would have to cope with in their households. 'Ah, if I only keep my health!' she said, looking at herself very gravely in the glass over the hall table. It often struck her that there was something terrifying in the way the happiness of so many people, Jimmy, Madge, Walter, and their two children, Leo, Evie, and their four, all depended on her physically fragile self.

She liked the little walk across the fields to Madge's house; every corner of the district was dear to her, for she was one of those people who feel that they live in the nicest house in the nicest town in the nicest county of the nicest country. But she was not so happy when she was inside Madge's garden. If it looked as wild as this in the spring, what would it be like in autumn? She knew Walter had turned off one of the gardeners, but it shouldn't have been necessary to do that, considering his income, if only Madge had been a better manager. It was really impossible to guess what she did with all her money. And if one did have to turn away a gardener, surely one tried to repair the damage by taking on as much of his work as possible. But she wasn't in the least surprised to find Madge lying on the sofa in the drawing-room, wearing an invalidish kind of tea-gown that suggested she had been sticking in the house all day. She looked a very bad pasty colour. It was really dreadful, the way she was letting herself go.

But she jumped up and kissed her sister with quite a show of animation. 'Why, Alice, how marvellous you look! But I thought you weren't coming back till Friday?'

'That's what I had planned, but a young man gave me a lift in his car,' answered Alice. 'We had such a lovely drive across the New Forest. It's been the most glorious day. Haven't you been out at all, dear?'

'As it happens, I haven't.'

'My dear, you ought to make some effort to get over this

tendency to lie about. It isn't good for you. You're a most dreadful colour . . .'

'Am I?' asked Madge, with a curious, distressed urgency. She sat up on her cushions and stared at herself in a mirror on the other side of the room.

'Yes, you are,' said Alice, 'most earthy and unwholesome. And it's all because you don't take enough exercise. Look at me!' She laid a finger against her perfect cheek. 'I'm out in all weathers. Really, dear, you must be careful. You know you're five years younger than me, and you look at least five years older.'

'I dare say you're right,' said Madge listlessly. 'But you, dear? Are you quite better? You haven't had any more of those terrible attacks?'

'Not a trace of them. Mother's doctor thought they might have come from some pan in the kitchen that we hadn't had re-coppered. I'm going to look. I certainly hadn't a suspicion of a recurrence while I was away. But I did have another of those awful nightmares, you know. I suppose it's all the worry that weighs down on me.'

'What worry?' asked Madge, rather petulantly.

Alice smiled to herself, but the smile was a little sad. Didn't Madge really know even now how much of her happiness she owed to her sister's readiness to take on what most people would have pushed away as unnecessary worries? How Alice worked over her when she was a girl, always saying to her just as they went into the ball-room, 'Now do hold yourself properly and try to hide those dreadful elbows,' and keeping near her to see that she was behaving properly and saying the right things to her partners, and on the way home telling her all the things she had done wrong! And then, since Madge's marriage to Walter, Alice had been on hand day in, day out, always ready to point out faults in her housekeeping, to explain just why her parties had not been successful, to suggest where she was going wrong in bringing up her children. There was no use pretending it had always been an easy task. Madge had a childish intolerance of criticism, she sometimes became quite rude.

'Well, Madge,' Alice began quietly, but Madge was asking, 'How did you leave mother?'

'Oh, mother's all right,' said Alice indulgently, 'it's funny how she's quite happy muddling along.'

'I don't see that she does much muddling,' said Madge. 'She knows how she likes to live, and she lives that way.'

'Oh, my dear!' exclaimed Alice. 'I call it a terrible muddle. Just think what I found her doing . . .' But Madge cut in quickly, 'Here are the children coming in from their walk, and please, please, don't encourage Betty!'

'My dear, I think you're so wrong about Betty,' Alice started to explain, but the children were with them. Little Godfrey ran straight to his mother; there was really something very morbid and effeminate about the way he always clung to her, and he ought to have been told to be polite and run and kiss his aunt instead of staring at her with great vacant eyes. But Betty went at once to Alice, who held out her arms. The child had a touch of her own brilliant fairness and neatness and decision, which was urgently needed in this dingy, feckless household. It was really very strange, the way that Madge did not seem to appreciate having such an attractive little girl. She supposed that it was just such an unreasonable aversion, probably springing from some odd pre-natal cause, as her own mother felt towards her. Every now and then she gave Betty a little smile, to show that there was a special understanding between them; but really she regretted having done it before long, for the poor child began to make confidences to her, which seemed to exasperate Madge. When Betty said that she had been sure her aunt would get better, because she had prayed for her every night, Madge had been visibly annoyed; and when Betty carried on the conversation along these lines to the point of describing a lecture on Indian missions that had been given at their local school and expressing a hope that she herself might become a missionary some day, Madge called sharply, 'Annie, Annie!'

The nursemaid hurried in from the hall.

'Take the children straight up to the nursery,' Madge told her, and leaned back on the cushions with her eyes shut until the din of protest had died, and she was alone with her sister again. 'I asked you not to encourage Betty,' she said. 'I really don't see why you should come here and make my family talk the idiom of very old volumes of *The Quiver*.'

'My dear, I never heard such nonsense,' Alice objected. 'If modern ideas have come to such a pass that a little girl of ten can't show a nice healthy interest in religion . . .'

'Betty's interest in religion isn't nice or healthy,' said Madge. 'It's sheer priggishness and exhibitionism.'

'If you used shorter words and didn't try to be so scientific, and looked after your children in an old-fashioned way, it might be better. Must you have that untidy girl from the village as a nursemaid? I refused to let her come in and help Ethel last winter, she's so slatternly.'

'We know she's not ideal. But we can't afford anyone better.'

'But, my dear, why can't you? Your money seems just to run through your fingers. It isn't fair to Walter, and it's simply cruel to the children. They ought to have a nice, well-trained woman to look after them and teach them pretty manners.'

She waited for any defence that might be forthcoming, but Madge had fallen into one of her sulky silences. 'Well,' said Alice at last, 'you're a funny set, you new-fashioned mothers, I must say. Goodness knows what I shall find when I get to Leo's.'

'Oh, are you going to Leo's?' said Madge. 'I'll go down the avenue with you if you like.' She was on her feet at once and moving towards the door, while Alice thought in amazement, 'Why, I believe she's trying to get me out of the house, and I haven't been here for much more than half an hour! How queer and . . . petty!'

But she tried to conceal her feelings as they walked under the trees to the high road. 'Nobody can say I am tactless,' she thought, as she passed by the patches of rough grass and weeds without pointing them out to her sister. 'And I'm not saying anything about how absurd it is that she should be wearing those trailing things that she has to hold up round her when she gets a breath of fresh air, instead of being out and about in sensible country clothes. I'll just give her a word about pulling herself together when we part.' But when they came to the gate she forgot, for Madge let her skirts fall and put both her arms round her giving her a hug as if they were children again.

'Dear Alice, I'm so glad you are better,' she said, and stood with her head on one side for a minute admiring her. 'I love to see you looking so young and pretty. It was horrid when you were ill. You ought always to be well and happy.'

'You're crushing my coat,' said Alice; but she was pleased. 'I think she is really grateful, though she's so odd and ungracious,' she said to herself as she hurried along to Leo's house. 'Well, it's encouraging.'

She received no such encouragement when she arrived there. The front door was open, and when she passed into the hall she saw Colin, the eldest boy, walking up the staircase in the undisciplined manner of the bookish young, taking an immense time to mount from step to step because he had his nose deep in an open book.

'Colin!' she called.

He turned round, but did not answer the greeting. For a minute he stared blankly at her, his black forelock falling over his brows – heaven knew why Evie let her children go about with their hair that length – and his mouth stupidly open. Then a look of consternation spread over his face, he slammed the open book, and without saying a word rushed upstairs two steps at a time.

'Well, of all the manners!' breathed Alice. She heard her brother's short, dry, tired cough from the surgery, farther down the passage, and made a step in that direction. 'Leo really ought to be told,' she thought furiously. But just then her sister-in-law came to the top of the stairs. She stared down on Alice incredulously, turned and whispered, 'Hush!' as if she were quelling a tumult in the shadows behind her, and then ran downstairs saying, 'Well, Alice, this is a surprise! We thought you weren't to be with us till Friday!'

How hopelessly odd she was, how neurotic and unstable, the very last person to be a doctor's wife. She was trembling and breathless as if she had had a severe shock instead of merely receiving a visit from a sister-in-law. It was no wonder the children were such unattractive little savages.

'A young man gave me a lift in his motor-car,' said Alice, trying to pass things off lightly, 'and I thought I'd come along and see how you all were. How are you, Evie? That's right. And Leo? No symptoms, I hope?'

'None,' said Evie, 'absolutely none.' She said everything with such odd over-emphasis that it really made one feel uncomfortable.

'Can I see him?' said Alice, moving towards the surgery.

'No, you can't,' said Evie, stepping between her and the surgery door. 'He's out. He's gone to Cadeford for a consultation.'

There was a minute's silence.

'Has he, Evie?' asked Alice, raising her eyebrows and smiling.

Again there came the sound of Leo's high, dry, tired cough.

'I'll come some other day,' said Alice, turning to the front door, 'when I'm not in the way.'

Evie put out a weak, shaking hand. 'It's only that he's so busy . . .'

'Oh, my dear, I understand,' said Alice. 'It's a wife's duty to protect her husband. And anyway you of all people must know by this time that I'm not one of those people that bear grudges.'

With a frank smile she held out her hand and after Evie
had gripped and released it she let it rest for a minute on a
half-inch of gaping seam in the other's jumper. 'I wish
you'd let me send you my little sewing-woman one day.
Let me ring up and find out what day would be convenient.
It would be a real pleasure if you'd let me treat you to that.
I always think one feels much calmer and happier when
one's really neat and tidy.'

She found herself walking back to her house at a swinging
pace. 'I mustn't be angry with her,' she kept on telling
herself. 'I know there's nothing the matter with the woman
but jealousy, and it's a shame that Leo's children should be
brought up as ill-mannered little gutter-snipes, but I must
remember that she can't help being what she is. It's only by
chance that I was born what I am instead of like her.' When
a turn of the road brought her house in sight tears of
relief stood in her eyes. There, in her beautiful, orderly
spacious rooms, she could shut out all these awful people
who loved quarrelling and unkindness. Already the afternoon sun was low over the fields, and it would soon be time
to turn on the lights. She liked to think of that, because it
had occurred to her once, when she had driven home later
and seen from far off the rosy glow of her curtained windows, how fortunate, how right it was that her house could
send brightness shining out into the dark, but that the dark
could not come into her house and dim the brightness. In
one's own home one was safe. She would take off her suit
the minute she got in and put on a soft, lacy dressing-gown
and put eau-de-Cologne on her forehead, and lie down on the
couch in her bedroom till Jimmy came.

But when she got home she was waylaid by the cook.
'Might I speak to you, mum?'

She followed her into the big, clean, airy, blue-and-
white kitchen. 'Well?' she said, looking round. 'I'm sure
you've nothing to grumble about in your kitchen, Cook!
It's really a picture. Everything you could possibly want...'

'Yes, indeed, mum,' said Cook. 'But I was going to tell

you we'd forgotten to say Mr Robert Norman's coming to dinner with the master, and I wanted to ask you if I should cook something special for you, or if you'd have what they do.'

'What are you giving them?'

'Artichoke soup, cod, saddle of mutton, and apple dumpling, and welsh rarebit.'

'Oh, Cook,' said Alice, 'what a dreadful dinner! So dull and so heavy! After all the trouble I've taken working out menus with you, you really shouldn't give the master dinners like that just because you think I'm going to be out of the way.'

'I wouldn't do no such thing,' answered Cook, with her colour rising, 'the master's eaten full as dainty every night you been away as when you was here. But Mr Robert Norman likes to eat when he eats, and it was for him the master ordered this very dinner. I ain't nothing to do with it, 'cept cook it best I can.'

'I can't think he really wanted this awful dinner,' said Alice. 'Are you sure you haven't made a mistake? Such things have been known to happen, you know, Cook. We're none of us perfect. Do you remember when just after you came you sent up a rice pudding at a dinner party when I ordered ice pudding? That was funny. Fortunately they were all very nice about it. Oh, don't be offended, Cook. We all make mistakes sometimes.'

'We do, mum,' said Cook. 'And shall I cook you anything separate?'

'Well, I certainly won't be able to eat much of this terrible meal,' smiled Alice. 'But I'll try to get along on the cod and some of the apples out of the dumpling. And then before I go to bed I'll have my usual glass of hot chocolate malted milk.'

'I've got a new brand of that for you,' said Cook. '"The Devon Dairymaid", instead of Harrison & Cooper's. The man at the stores told me he had it, and I ordered a small tin to try.'

'Oh, Cook, why did you do that? Haven't you a tin of the old sort left?'

'No, mum. It was all finished when you left. But it was twice you complained that the old kind tasted bitter.'

'Yes, but I've tried this new kind when I was staying with Mrs Anglesey, and it's horrid. It's just as dark as the other, but it has hardly any chocolate flavour, and you know I can only get down the malted milk if I don't taste it. I do think it's a pity you did that without asking me.'

'Well, I'll get a tin of the old in the morning.'

'Yes, but there's the new tin wasted, and every penny counts nowadays. And there's to-night. I'll have to do without one of the very few things I enjoy. But send it up just the same. Now do remember not to do this sort of thing. The times when you should show initiative you never do, giving people the same dreadful dinners I've taught you not to do, and then you go and make a perfectly unnecessary purchase like this. It's heartbreaking, Cook.' She repeated, 'Yes, it's simply heartbreaking'; but Cook made no answer, so she moved towards the door, but was plucked back by a recollection.

'Oh, by the way, Cook, are you sure that there's none of the copper pans that need re-coppering?'

'Quite sure, mum. We had the man to look at them only a few months ago. And anyway I'm cooking more and more in the fireproof and the aluminium.'

'That can't be it, then. You know, Mrs Anglesey's doctor thought that my attacks might have been not gastric at all, but due to irritant poisoning. And the only way we could think that I could have been poisoned was through some of the copper vessels having worn out. I can't think of any other way, can you, Cook?'

'No, mum, I can't. If you was a lady with a nagging tongue, always finding fault with everything, and making trouble where there's only kindness meant, then I suppose we might all be wanting to drop poison in your food. But you aren't like that, are you, mum?'

Alice's heart nearly stopped. Cook's face was bland, but her tone was unmistakably insolent. What was the reason for this madness that afflicted one and all of the servant class?

'We'd better talk about this to-morrow, Cook,' she said quietly, and left the kitchen. She supposed that they would both be going now, Ethel as well as Cook. How could they be so causelessly malevolent as to do this when she had just come home? The tears were rising in her eyes and she was going blindly towards the staircase when she heard an exclamation, and turned to see that the front door had opened and Jimmy was standing on the step outside, paralysed with amazement in the act of pulling off his gloves.

She ran to him and stretched her arms up his tallness. 'Yes, I'm back two whole days too early! But a nice young man gave me a lift in his car!' Under her lips his face felt worn and cold; but clients' funerals were always trying. 'Oh, my dear, I'm so much better!'

'I'm glad of that,' said Jimmy. 'I'm very glad of that.'

'And, oh, I'm so pleased you've come in!' she cried. 'It's been so horrid ever since I got back. Madge was horrid to me except for a little bit at the end, and Evie was horrid, and Colin was a hateful little beast, and Ethel was horrid, and now Cook's been horrid. Why does nobody but me want to be happy and live in peace?'

Jimmy put his arm round her shoulder and led her into the house, looking down on her tenderly as one might on a crippled child. 'Poor little Alice,' he said, 'Poor little Alice.'

II

ETHEL had lit the log-fire in the drawing-room, and it spat at them playfully while they crouched on the rug, Jimmy stretching out one hand to the warmth while Alice rubbed the other.

'It'll be a glorious blaze in a minute,' said Alice, 'and just as well, for you're simply icy, my darling. Was it too dreadful at the funeral?'

'No, not really,' said Jimmy. 'It wasn't too cold, or too harrowing, even. They'd all been expecting the old chap to go for ages so nobody felt it as a great shock.'

'I like the younger son best, I hope he stays on at the farm, he's an awfully nice boy. Oh, Jimmy, the young man who brought me home was so nice. And it was miles out of his way really. He's coming to see us some day, you will like him. He was so sweet and patient with Mother, too. Just think, she would not let us get off this morning until she'd told him the whole of that interminable story about how she met King Edward at Monte Carlo.'

'But perhaps he liked hearing it.'

'Oh, my dear, who could? Who cares about such things nowadays. Besides, it's rather vulgar, I always think. But, darling, I do appreciate the way you turn a blind eye to my family's failings. I know perfectly well they're awful...'

'But, Alice, I don't think your family's awful.'

'You chivalrous darling, you know it is. Anyway Madge and Evie were pretty awful this afternoon, I can tell you.'

'What did they do?'

'Oh, Madge was lying on the sofa looking horribly pasty and unwholesome. She hadn't put her foot outside the house all day. I can't understand why she's letting herself go. And then she's so silly about Betty. Just because the child's got a natural leaning to religion...'

'But, Alice, it's Madge's foot and Madge's house. If she doesn't want to put the one outside the other, surely it's her business. And surely Betty's her child and her business too?'

'But, Jimmy dear, Madge is my sister. You haven't any family feeling. You don't understand that I can't watch my sister doing everything wrong and just let her do it.'

'Why not? She's thirty-five, darling. Time she learned to save her own soul.'

'Nonsense, dear. You'd never have any civilization at all

if you didn't have the people who knew best teaching all the others what to do.'

'Oh, Alice, dear!'

'Well, it's true, darling. And that's why I won't give up going to Leo's house, however rude that woman is. Do you know what she did this evening? She looked me straight in the face and told me that Leo was out, when I could hear him coughing in the surgery! Did you ever hear of a wife being so jealous of her husband's sister? But I'm not going to give up. I've got a duty to that household. I must see the children get some sort of upbringing. That Colin's a perfect little savage.'

Jimmy had got up and was standing above her, lighting his pipe. 'Alice, Colin belongs to Leo and Evie, not to you.'

'But, darling, you don't understand! If they can't look after him properly then I must do what I can,' she answered absently. She loved the look of his face, lit red by the flame.

He sat down in the arm-chair and beckoned her to come and sit on his knee. 'Alice, I wish you'd promise me something. It would really do a lot to make me happy. Will you do it?'

'I'll do anything for you, darling.'

'Then promise me to leave Madge and Walter, and Leo and Evie alone for a bit. Don't visit them unless they ask you. Don't try to manage their affairs.'

Alice stood up. 'Jimmy, how absurd you are!' she exclaimed. 'I've never heard you say anything so silly before! Anyone would think I was tactless or interfering.'

'That's what I want you to promise.'

She stared at him with eyes made immense by tears. 'Jimmy, you don't think I'm tactless and interfering, do you? Because I couldn't bear to think you so completely misunderstood my character! As for being tactless, that is absurd, because if there is one good quality that I've got, it's tact. I've always been able to handle people without hurting their feelings. And as for interfering, I simply loathe it. But after all Madge and Leo are my sister and brother, and the trouble is that since they were babies they've depended on me for everything, and they'd never get anywhere if I didn't push them.' She suddenly dropped on her knees and looked up into his face with an expression of panic. 'They don't think I'm tactless and interfering, do they? Because I couldn't bear that, it would be so ungrateful of them! And you know I've thought of them, all my life long, far more than I've thought of myself.'

Sobs began to shake her. 'Oh, you poor child!' said Jimmy, and drew her close to him. 'I know you have. But people are funny after they've grown up and married and got children. They like to be left alone.'

'But they couldn't think that,' said Alice, the tears running down her cheeks, 'unless they'd stopped loving me.'

'My dear, I'm sure they haven't. But I want you to make that promise all the same. Just humour them. Just let them be silly. To save your nerves.'

'I'd rather do what was right than save my nerves.'

'To please me, then,' said Jimmy. He took her by the shoulders and smiled into her eyes, his dark, secret smile. 'I might beat you if you didn't,' he told her gravely.

He always made her laugh when he said that. 'Silly!' she giggled, and he crushed her suddenly in his arms. 'I promise!' she whispered in his ear, and disentangled herself just as Ethel brought in tea. 'But all the same,' she said, to cover her embarrassment because she knew her hair was rumpled, 'I think they're preposterous if they are offended.'

For tea there was a whole jarful of strawberry jam, which neither of them liked very much, and only a little cherry jam, which they both liked so well that the household supply rarely lasted thus late into the spring. It might have been thought there was enough of this for two, but she knew how thick he liked to pile it on his buttered toast, so she gave it all to him, and took the precaution of spreading it for him and putting it on his plate, so that he had no chance to be unselfish. Then, when the tea had been cleared away, she went and sat on his knee again and they were both silent, looking into the blazing wood.

'Lovely your hair is,' he said at last. 'You're a lovely child, and capable of being noble, even about cherry jam.'

She leaned farther back, putting her face close to his. 'Yet you haven't kissed me properly yet,' she said.

'Haven't I?'

'No. You let me kiss you in the hall. But you haven't kissed me.'

He murmured something under his breath and bent his lips towards her. But she twisted out of his grasp.

'Why did you say that under your breath?'

'What did I say?'

'You know perfectly well what you said. You said, "Forgive me". Why should I forgive you? Oh, Jimmy, what have you been doing?'

'Nothing. I didn't mean anything. They were just words that passed through my mind. Something I've been reading.'

'Jimmy, really? Is that really true? You haven't been unfaithful to me?'

He shook his head. 'No. I couldn't have done that, even if I'd wanted to. I've thought of you continually nearly all the time you've been away. No husband ever was haunted more steadily by the presence of his absent wife.'

Her storm of suspicion weakened. 'Is that true?' she asked piteously. 'Are you sure? But then what did you want me to forgive you for?'

'I wanted you to forgive me for being me,' he said, 'and having to be what I am, and do what I have done.' A smile passed over his lips. 'Just as you might ask me to forgive you for being you.'

She laughed happily at the idea, and settled down in his arms again, to receive his embrace. After his mouth had left hers she nodded her head wisely. 'Yes, you love me. But how tired you are.'

He muttered, lying quite relaxed, his head against her breast. 'Yes, that's just it. I love you. But I'm so tired that I don't know what to do . . . I don't know how to carry on . . .'

'My poor darling, there's nothing worrying you in your business, is there?'

'Nothing.' She could hardly hear his voice, he was evidently just dropping off to sleep.

'Well, everything else will be all right now I'm home.'

'I hope so . . . I hope so . . .' She saw his hand drowsily groping for the table beside the chair, to touch wood.

They sat thus, with the twilight deepening on them to darkness, the firelight showing redder and more comforting. Sometimes they sighed in contentment, sometimes one or the other began to murmur a phrase of endearment, but did not finish it, sometimes they slept. Then all of a sudden, the room was flooded with light and Ethel was saying, 'It's seven o'clock, and time you were dressing, because Mr Norman do come early and no mistake. And I'd like you to have a look at the table, mum, to see if you think I did it right.'

She spoke with the benignity of conscious pride, which they understood when they stood in the dining-room and saw the shining glory she had made.

'I put the tall daffies at the corner,' Ethel told them expansively. 'Nobody else done a table that way, that I ever see, but it gives you the good of them without you having to crane your necks to see who you're eating opposite. And I put the little dwarf daffies in the middle.'

'My word, you've made a lovely thing of it, Ethel,' said Jimmy. 'The flowers aren't so many that the table looks crowded, but it's a grand show.'

Alice said, 'Wait a minute,' moved a fork a little to the left, leaned over and shifted the linen centrepiece under the dwarf daffodils a fraction of an inch, then moved back and surveyed the table with great satisfaction. 'Yes, that's very nice.'

Jimmy sighed, very deeply. He seemed to be terribly over-tired.

Ethel, blossoming under the warmth of praise, continued, 'There's so many daffodils out now that even old Wray can't be stingy about bringing them up to the house, though he'd do anything to keep all his flowers to hisself in the garden.'

Alice said stiffly, 'Well, Ethel, we've all of us so many faults that I don't think it becomes any of us to make fun of others.'

There was a minute's silence, before Ethel swung round and went out of the room. 'I say, I don't think you need have said that,' said Jimmy. 'She didn't mean to be ill-natured. She just said it as you or I might have said it.' He had dropped into a chair and looked very white and lined.

'Nonsense, darling,' said Alice, 'you can't have servants talking against each other. But, oh, Jimmy, you do look tired. I wish this old man wasn't coming.'

'Oh, I like old Norman. We get on awfully well together. He's been in a lot while you've been away. The nurse who looks after his imbecile child isn't well, and Mrs Norman has to take charge in the evenings a good deal. So he's been glad to come along and have something to eat, and play a bit of two-handed bridge.'

'Funny darlings you must have been together,' said Alice. 'Let's go and dress.'

It was quite a successful dinner, Alice thought. She put on the new turquoise dress she had bought when she was staying with her mother, and the old man's eyes had brightened when he saw her. He was a gentleman farmer, the wealthiest and most important of his kind in the district, and there was some seignorial dignity about him, as well as the ashes of romantic charm, for, till he had been sobered by the tragic issue of his marriage, he had been a famous beau and blood. Even now that he was silver-haired, he made every woman he spoke to feel a little better-looking than she really was, and Alice found herself glowing as she entertained him, and forgetting to be sorry that she and Jimmy were not alone. But Mr Norman seemed to tire very soon. His frosty grey eyes stopped sparkling and grew heavy, he talked less and less, and though they had started bridge he rose and left at twenty minutes to ten.

'What a handsome old thing he is, in his weatherbeaten way,' said Alice, when Jimmy came back from seeing him out. 'But does he always leave so early?'

Jimmy went over to the fire and kicked a log down with his heel. 'No, I've known him stay quite late.'

'I expect that dreadful heavy dinner made him sleepy,' said Alice. 'I was sure when I heard what you'd ordered that it was a mistake.'

Jimmy sat down in an arm-chair, and stared into the fire. 'No, I don't think it was the dinner. But I think it was a pity you tried to teach him those new Culbertson rules. He's an old man, and he'd probably been out on horseback since eight o'clock this morning, and he just wanted to fiddle round with the cards a bit.'

'Oh, my dear, he can't have found that a strain! And anyway, what's the use of doing anything if you don't do it well? Still I probably was wrong. But you forget, when you've been away, what clods the best of these people are.'

'Yes, clods,' said Jimmy, 'without brains, without feelings, without sensitiveness. I think it was a pity too that you told him he ought to take his child to that brain surgeon at Geneva.'

'Well, why shouldn't I? He's a wonderful man. Mother knows somebody who told her about the most marvellous cure ...'

'I dare say,' said Jimmy, 'but you see Norman and his wife took the child there six years ago, and it wasn't any good.'

'But why didn't he tell me so? What an extraordinary thing of him to do, to let me go on talking about it and never say a thing!'

'I expect he likes so little hearing the child talked about that when people start he just lets them say what they have to say and finish, and doesn't prolong it by getting up an argument.'

'Well, if he feels like that even when people are trying to help him, I can't help it,' said Alice, 'but I must say I'm disappointed to think the old man's so ungracious.'

'And I think it was a pity, too,' said Jimmy, 'that you told him so much of the ways you've reformed me since we were married, the way I naturally forget everything and lose everything unless you look after me. You see, he's thinking of handing over all his business to me, because he isn't satisfied with the firm of solicitors at Rosford that have handled his affairs up till now. The old partners are too old, and the young partners are too young, and he thinks I'm about right.'

'Well, my dear, nothing I said can have made much difference. He can't have taken it as seriously as all that. And I did say I'd got you over all those things.'

'Oh, I don't think he thought I really do lose and forget things more than most people,' said Jimmy, 'but I think he thought that a man whose wife talked about him like that couldn't be very good stuff.'

'What a funny, old-fashioned point of view!' laughed Alice. 'But I wish you'd dropped me a hint of all this. I might have said a few things that would just have turned the scales.'

'I know. I was afraid of that,' said Jimmy. 'I think he might not have liked having his mind made up for him.'

'If he's such a hopeless old crotchet as that,' said Alice, 'I wonder you want to have anything to do with him.'

'Well, for one thing, I really do want some new business,' said Jimmy. 'It's odd how people don't come to me. It's almost as if one or other of us were unpopular in the county. And for another thing, I'm fond of old Norman, and I'd like him to feel confidence in me for his own sake. It's worrying for an old man to have a wife thirty years younger than himself, with a big estate and the responsibility of the child, and not feel that he's put some reliable person to look after her. I wanted to do that for him.'

'Well, my dear, it's certain to come all right,' said Alice. 'We must just have him to dinner again, and I shall be specially nice to him. Are you coming to bed now, dear?'

'No, dear,' said Jimmy, 'not at once. I want to stay down here for five minutes and think something out.'

He looked so boyish and pathetic, as he lay back in the chair with his long legs stretching out in front of him and his dark hair rumpled, and his perplexed eyes staring into the fire, that she had to bend over and kiss him as she passed. 'Poor little boy!' she murmured in his ear. 'You're sure you've got no special business worries? You will tell me if you have, won't you? If you've got into a muddle, it's quite likely I shall be able to think of some way out.'

'Thank you, dear,' said Jimmy, 'there's nothing special. It's only that I'm living under a strain, and I've got to make up my mind to bear that strain.'

'But what strain, darling?'

'Oh, just these difficult times, these difficult times.'

She kissed the top of his head. 'Poor little overwrought fellow!' she crooned, then straightened herself. 'Don't be too long coming up to bed.'

She enjoyed undressing in her own lovely room after having been away so long. Humming to herself she kicked off her satin shoes and peeled off her stockings, and stood on the rug in front of the fire, digging her bare toes into the clean, smooth, clipped lamb's pelt, as she cast her several skins of silk. She liked the mountainous softness of her bed, with its fluffy apricot blankets and honey-coloured taffeta quilt, and the secret, sacred look the hangings gave the shadowed pillows, and the rosy, lacy nightgown they had spread out for her. In her mind's eye she saw her gaunt, voluble, wild-haired mother pacing her utilitarian room where there was a mahogany bed and a big round table with a reading lamp and many books on it, and she shuddered. 'Will I ever get old?' she thought, 'and stop matching my lovely room? I suppose I will some day, and quite soon too, for I am not young. It will be awful. But Jimmy will be nice to me, he will somehow spare me the worst of it. He always tries to spare me things, he is always kind. I thought he was a little fault-finding this evening, but that was only because he was tired. Oh, I am a lucky woman, I ought to be very kind to other people out of gratitude.' Grave with this reflexion she went into the bathroom, and as she lay in the warm waters a way she could be kind occurred to her. It was such a good plan that she longed to work it out at once, and a pricking urge to activity swept through her body, so that she had to jump out of the bath almost at once and rub herself with hot towels. Then she heard Jimmy go into the bedroom, and she flung on her dressing-gown and hurried in to tell him the news.

'Jimmy,' she said, sitting down on the long stool in front of the dressing-table and brushing her hair with long, vigorous strokes, because her inspiration had filled her with vigour. 'I've had an idea.'

He had opened the dressing-room door, but he turned. 'Well, it suits you, darling,' he said, and came and stood by her, smiling as he watched her glowing face in the mirror, the flash of her arm as she passed the brush to and fro, and the changing lights in her hair.

'Listen,' she explained, 'I've been thinking over Madge. She can't go on as she's doing. I can't stand by and see my sister turning into a dowdy, middle-aged frump years before her time. Darling, do you realize she's a whole five years younger than I am? I must do something about it, and to-morrow morning I will. I'm going straight to Walter, and I'm going to suggest that he sends Madge for a month to that wonderful sanatorium near Dresden where they did Mrs Lennox so much good. It's just what she wants. They give you massage and baths, and above all they won't let you be soft. They get you out of bed at seven o'clock and make you do exercises in the pinewoods in a bathing dress, no matter how cold it is. She'll come back a different person. And while she's away I'll take on Betty and Godfrey – I am sure I could bring out Betty quite a lot, they don't understand her – and maybe I could look into the house-keeping books and see where the waste is, why there's always this air of pinching and scraping where there's ample money. Don't you think it's a grand idea?'

Jimmy sat down beside her on the stool. He took the hairbrush from her and laid it down on the dressing-table, then gripped both her hands with his. 'Alice,' he said. 'Have you forgotten the promise you gave me this evening, in front of the fire? Didn't you give me your word you wouldn't interfere with Madge and Walter, or Leo and Evie any more?'

'But, heavens alive, this isn't interference!'

'My darling, what else is it?'

'Oh, it may be interference, strictly speaking, but you must admit that sometimes one just has to interfere. If Madge fell down in the road and there was a car coming along, surely you'd let me drag her out of the way?'

'Alice, won't you stop doing this thing if I tell you I'd rather you didn't?'

'No, I don't think I will. I hate the way you've suddenly started objecting to everything I do that's kind. And any-way I don't think it would be fair to Madge not to do it.'

'Then,' said Jimmy, 'I'll have to tell you a whole lot of things that we all rather wanted to keep from you.' He got up and walked to the fire and stood on the hearth, looking down on her intently. 'Alice, you're all wrong about Madge and Walter. If you went to Walter to-morrow and told him that Madge ought to go to a sanatorium in Dresden, it would be monstrously cruel of you. Because he couldn't afford it.'

'But, darling, it wouldn't cost much more than a hundred pounds.'

'Walter hasn't got a hundred pounds.'

'What do you mean, Jimmy? You must be mad. You know perfectly well they've at least three thousand pounds a year.'

'They had, Alice. They haven't now. We live in bad times, and the worst of it is we've come straight to them out of times that were too good. About six years ago, when prices were rocketing, Walter sold out all his safe stuff, his gilt-edged, and bought things like steel and oil. They aren't worth a tenth of what they were. I tell you Walter hasn't got a hundred pounds. He owes quite a number of hundred pounds to the banks and the income-tax people.'

'But, Jimmy, Walter must have been atrociously reckless. I do think when he had a wife and children he ought to have been more careful. I do think someone ought to speak to him . . .'

'Anyone who spoke to him would be a meddling fool that likes to kick a man when he's down. The whole world did what he did. It seemed the only sensible thing to do at the time. I'm sorry, Alice, but there isn't a single way of looking at the situation which affords one the slightest justification for feeling superior to Walter.'

'Well, goodness knows, one wouldn't want that. Oh, I am sorry for them. But I do hope Madge is doing everything she can . . .'

'She's doing marvels. I've been over all the books. There isn't a woman living who could have been pluckier and more sensible. Madge is all right.'

'I'm glad. Dear little Madge. But what I don't understand is why they didn't tell me? It seems a little cold and inconsiderate, when they know how fond I am of them. I can't help feeling just a weeny bit hurt . . .'

'They're hurt themselves, Alice. Walter's a proud man, and he cares for his family. He wanted to give them the best of everything, and leave them to carry on the life his stock have always lived, in the house where they've been for a couple of centuries. Now he can't give them anything but the bare necessities, they may not be able to go on living in that house. They're struggling nobly, but they may be beaten yet. While they're struggling they don't want anyone to talk to them about the tragedy, to suggest that if they had acted differently it needn't have happened, that they aren't taking it as sensibly as they might, that this and that little treat they give themselves when they're at breaking-point is an unjustifiable extravagance. That would just put the lid on their torture.'

'Yes, but I obviously wouldn't be that someone. I only would have tried to help. Well, I am sorry!' She sighed and took up her hairbrush again.

Jimmy came back and sat beside her. He put his arm round her body, and kissed her ear, and she rested her cheek against his. He whispered to her and she said, 'What, darling?' but then recoiled from him with annoyance, exclaiming. 'No, of course I won't speak about it to them. I wouldn't care to, since they haven't chosen to tell me themselves.'

'That's a good girl,' said Jimmy.

Alice went on brushing her hair, and presently she smiled at the dark face she saw smiling at her in the mirror. 'Aren't we lucky to have no worries?' she said. 'Really, we couldn't be more at peace with ourselves and the world. But I suppose that's partly our own doing. We might have had lots of worries if we'd given way to them. I think I shall say something to Madge, you know. That's what she's doing, giving way to her troubles. Just because Walter's lost some money and she has to be careful, she needn't lie about on sofas looking dowdy and listless – Jimmy, Jimmy, what are you doing? Let go my wrist!'

'Alice, won't you please take it from me that there isn't any necessity to say anything at all to Madge, that she's one of the finest women who ever lived, and that she doesn't need any advice at all?'

'No, I can't take it from you, because I can see with my own eyes, and – Jimmy, you're hurting!'

He got up and went back to his place on the hearthrug,

and looked down on her again with that queer, intent look.

'Jimmy, what's the matter with you? Your eyes are blazing! And you haven't said you're sorry!'

He did not seem to hear. 'Alice,' he said, 'have you ever read a fairy story where the princess lived in a beautiful palace, with a beautiful garden, and was warned by her fairy godmother that she could enjoy all this happiness for ever only if she didn't pick one particular flower, or eat one particular fruit? If she ignores that prohibition, she loses the whole thing. Out palace, out garden, out princess. It's quite an important story. You'll even find it in the Bible. And you sometimes find it coming true in real life.'

'Jimmy, what are you talking about?'

'The point is that the fairy godmother's perfectly right, though there's no reason on the surface to show that she is. When the princess picks that flower or eats that fruit, the whole thing really does fall to pieces. If I ask you to take me as a fairy godmother, and ask you not to speak to Madge about being listless, will you remember and grant me this favour? Do it, do it, darling. Let's pretend we're people in a fairy-tale.'

Alice turned her back on him and stared into the mirror, and presently saw him reflected just behind her. 'Well,' she began, but he said, 'No. You needn't make any promise or half-promise. I can see from your face that you'd speak to Madge, if I went down on my knees, if the heavens opened. You couldn't possibly give up such a good opportunity of ordering somebody about, of making them feel inferior to you, of making their destiny seem so that if it worked out well they'd have to thank you for it, and not themselves.'

'Jimmy!'

'Now listen. Madge doesn't lie on sofas and look dowdy because she's a sloven. She does it because she's ill. So ill that it's an effort for her to walk, to put on her clothes.'

'Jimmy, you're dreaming! Madge has always made a fuss about little ailments, but she's as strong as a horse.'

'Alice, Leo arranged for her to see a specialist six months

ago, and I sneaked up to town to go with them. He said there wasn't any doubt. She's got pernicious anaemia.'

'Oh, my dear, I know all about that. There's a wonderful new treatment for pernicious anaemia. I'll soon see to it that ...'

'Alice, there isn't anything you can see to. There is a wonderful new treatment for pernicious anaemia, which cures everybody except two or three people out of every hundred. And the trouble is that Madge seems to be one of those two or three people. She's persevering with the treatment, and the tide may turn at any moment, but up till now she's been getting worse and worse. Do you understand? She's very, very ill.'

Alice stood up. Her hairbrush slipped from her hand to the floor. 'Oh, poor little Madge! My poor little Madge!' she whispered.

Jimmy gathered her into his arms. 'I knew you'd feel pretty bad when you heard that,' he said. 'I've always known you really cared for her a lot. Cry if you want to, dear.'

But she swallowed her tears and drew away from him briskly, saying, 'But we ought to do something! What can we do for her?'

'Heaven's alive, why should we have to do anything? Why must you always try to be omnipotent, and shove things about? Tragic things happen sometimes that we just have to submit to. We can't do anything in this particular case except stand by and be sorry for little Madge, and hope that the tide will turn, and give her as many presents and treats as we can. And above all we mustn't ever talk of it again. We mustn't even think of it, in case it shows in our talk, because Walter doesn't know.'

'Walter doesn't know! But that's absurd. He ought to be told.'

'Dear, he's having a hard struggle. Madge doesn't want him to be worried by knowing that she's dangerously ill. Particularly when the danger might pass and he'd have had the worry all for nothing. Besides, it's Madge's husband, and it's Madge's secret, and it's for Madge to decide whether he shall be told.'

'But, really, Jimmy, I think you're wrong. Walter ought to be told. It's only fair to him. You know how irritable he is. I've often heard him say things to her lately that he wouldn't have said if he'd known how ill she was.'

'Alice, I think I'll kill you if you don't promise not to tell Walter.'

'Jimmy! What a queer, exaggerated thing to say! What's the matter with you to-night, Jimmy? I've never known you like this.'

'Stop staring into that mirror. Put down that hairbrush. Turn round and look at me.'

She wriggled round on the stool, her lip quivering. 'It was your face I was looking at in the mirror, Jimmy.'

'Listen,' he said, 'because I'm going to tell you the truth ...'

'Don't tell me anything to-night. I'm tired and you're tired ...'

'I'm going to tell you the truth about yourself, and I'm going to do it now, because it may be too late to-morrow. Alice, you're the salt of the earth. In all the twenty years I've known you I've never seen you fail once in honesty or courage or generosity. You wouldn't tell a lie if you were to gain a million pounds by it. You'd hold your hand in the fire to save a person or a principle you valued. You'd give away your last crust to anyone you felt as kin. I know perfectly well that now you've learned Madge is hard up you'll cover her with presents, even if it means you have to go without things yourself. And besides that, you've got a kind of touching, childish quality – a kind of – a kind of ...'

'Jimmy, what's the matter with you? Why, you're almost crying! What's the ...'

'Well, we'll leave that. The point is that nobody likes having salt rubbed into their wounds, even if it is the salt of the earth.'

He bent over her like a boxer, peering at a recumbent adversary to see how his blow had told; but her blue gaze returned his steadily. 'I'm afraid I'm not clever enough for all this,' she said. 'I haven't the vaguest notion of what you're driving at.'

'I'm trying to tell you that you hurt people. You hurt them continually and intolerably. You find out everybody's vulnerable point and you shoot arrows at it, sharp, venomed arrows. They stick, and from time to time you give them a twist.'

'Jimmy . . .'

'I know why you want to talk to Walter. You'll point out to him that he's been sharp to Madge several times lately, and that she's probably a dying woman. That'll harrow him. It'll add remorse to the agony he'll be filled with by the dread of losing her. It'll turn a simple, honourable grief to something shameful and humiliating. But it'll do worse than that. Walter's a man who lives on his temper. He can't find his way in action unless he lets himself go. When something happens he's quite incapable of thinking it out quietly. He has to swear and storm and stamp about, and at the end of all the fuss some definite plan has crystallized in his mind, and he can get on with it. Madge doesn't care when he snaps at her, she knows perfectly well that at the bottom of his heart he hasn't a thought except for her and the children. But if you pretend to him that what he did in temper was of deadly importance, then you break his mainspring. He'll go about cowed and broken, he won't be able to stand up to life. That's the worst of you, Alice. You find out what people live by, and you kill it.'

Alice said gravely, 'Jimmy, I don't understand this. Are you telling me that Madge and Walter have been talking against me? I've sometimes thought Madge wasn't quite loyal.'

'Oh, stop talking nonsense.'

'But you're being rude!'

'No loyalty can live near you. You are disloyalty itself.

Of course we talk against you behind your back. We have to protect ourselves. You're out to kill your nearest and dearest. No, sit still. I've got a whole lot more to tell you. Do you want to know the real reason why you aren't welcome in Leo's house? You think it's because Evie's jealous of you. That is the most utter rubbish. The trouble about Evie, if there is any trouble about Evie, is that she's over-trained. She's had every instinctive naughtiness like jealousy educated out of her. If she thought your brother was fonder of you than of her she'd set her teeth and invite you to lunch, tea, and dinner, at her house for every day in the week. But she knows that Leo can't bear you. Oh, he loves you, as we all do, because we know that apart from this devilish cruelty you're an angel, and because you've got this queer power of seeming a pitiful child that one can't help loving. But you frighten Leo. You see, he came back from the war after he'd been gassed, and forgot it. He felt splendid, and he married Evie, and they had four children. Then he had to remember he'd been gassed. He had that attack of pneumonia, and that slow recovery. And every day when he was getting better you went and saw him, and you sat and looked at him with those round eyes and asked, with an air of prudence and helpfulness that meant damn-all, "But what are you going to do, Leo, if you have a breakdown and have to give up your practice?"'

'Well,' said Alice, 'if a sister can't express her concern when her only brother's ill, I really don't know what we're coming to.'

'Darling, don't you see what you were doing? You were up to your murderous tricks again. You were killing the thing by which he lived. He knows his number's up. He knows that one winter's day he'll get pneumonia, and then he'll die. And he doesn't want to die. He doesn't want to leave Evie. He adores her wit and her carelessness and her funny offhand way of treating everything as if it were a joke. People do, you know. Leo and Evie have a lot more friends than we have, you know. He doesn't want to leave his children either. And especially he doesn't want to leave Evie and the children deadly hard-up as he knows he will. So the only way he can get on from day to day is to forget that he's ill and going to die. But every time you come near him you remind him of it. "How's the cough to-day?" you say. "Oh, Leo, you ought to be careful." My God, if you knew how often Evie's telephoned me, "He's feeling low to-day, for God's sake keep her away . . . "'

'Jimmy,' said Alice, 'are you admitting to me that behind my back you've entered into a conspiracy against me with that woman?'

'But don't you understand that I'm telling you something real and true that you've got to listen to? This is something that you've done and mustn't go on doing. You've tortured Leo. Don't you realize that's why the eldest boy hates you so? Colin adores his father and he knows that every time you go to the house you leave him fit to cut his throat with depression. Naturally he gets black in the face when he sees you. But you're wrong when you hate him just as you're wrong when you like that abominable little pest Betty. She's becoming practically what they call a problem child. Just about her age children often start imitating some particular person in their surroundings, and somewhere in Betty's surroundings she seems to have found somebody who is an aggressive prig and public nuisance, who spends the whole of her forcible personality in proving everybody else her inferior. I can't think who it can be, of course. But anyway, she's almost driving the family mad. Will you try and realize in future when you try to stir up trouble against Colin that you do it because the boy comes between you and somebody you're trying to hurt, and when you encourage Betty it's because you scent she's going to be as cruel as yourself?'

Alice turned round on the stool and began to brush her hair again. 'You're simply being rude,' she said icily. 'I think you'd better sleep in the dressing-room to-night.'

'Oh, for God's sake listen to me and try to understand! Don't you realize that there's something wrong in this household and that we've got to alter it? Hasn't it struck you as odd that we've got no friends? People come here to formal dinner-parties and they ask us back, but they keep at arm's length. They're afraid of us. They're afraid of you. Look how you got old Norman on the hip to-night. Look how we can't keep our servants. And look how your own mother had to pack up and leave the town where she was born because she couldn't bear your tongue . . .'

'Oh, Jimmy, Jimmy, you mustn't say that!'

'It's true. You couldn't bear to admit her qualities, that she was brilliant and erratic and a marvellous story-teller. You built up a pretence that she was silly and untidy and garrulous. Didn't you tell me to-day what a shame it was that she'd made the young man who brought you here listen to the story of how she met Edward VII at Monte Carlo? Well, you're no fool. You ought to see that that's one of the funniest stories in the world, that she tells it superbly, and that the whelp, whoever he was, was damn lucky to have the chance of hearing it. But you don't see that because you want to make her out senile and worthless. Well, she knew that perfectly. She went to Madge and Leo crying and said that she hated leaving them, but that you made her feel she ought to be either in her coffin or in a home for the aged . . .'

'Stop, Jimmy, stop! I know that's true!' She was crying now, with the deep, painful, interminable sobs of a child, with their overtone of rebellion against wrong.

'Oh, my poor little girl, don't cry!' He had taken her into his arms, he was pulling out his big handkerchief. 'You don't know how I've hated saying all this.'

'But it's true about mother. I know that it's true about mother. She was so horrid to me.'

'Horrid to you? But she was crazy with anxiety when – when you were ill, and she wrote again and again saying how much she wanted you to come down and have your convalescence with her. Don't think she doesn't love you. We all love you – only . . .'

'No. No. She doesn't love me. She was horrid to me last night. I did everything I could to be nice to her, I helped her in all sorts of little ways. But when I told her that I was going home two days earlier than I had meant, she was glad. She gave an awful look of relief that I'll never forget.' She rubbed her weeping face against his coat-collar, but raised it to accuse him with miserable puzzled eyes. 'Of course mother's always been horrid about me underneath, and of course we haven't any friends. People have always loved being nasty to me all my life. The girls at school gave me a most horrible time. And I've always minded it so because I do so like people to like me.' Sobs choked her. 'That young man – who brought me home in his car – he liked me.'

'I'm glad of that,' said Jimmy. 'Poor little Alice, I'm glad of that.'

For a minute her memory blotted out this hot room full of quarrelling, and built round her the fresh morning on the moors, with its background of sooty branches and sharp green buds, its music of birds singing high in blue, shower-washed space, its foreground of forget-me-nots bending all one way under a glassy grey current. She remembered how gravely the boy's eyes had rested on her face, how gravely he had said good-bye. Then her face was contorted with a fresh spasm of weeping. 'People are always so nice to me at first,' she murmured, 'but afterwards when I get to know them something hateful happens to them and they turn round and are cruel to me. But what I can't under-stand is why quite suddenly you've taken sides with them against me.'

He gently pushed her away from him and took her face between his hands. 'Alice, is that really all that I've been saying has meant to you? Haven't I made you feel the slightest suspicion that maybe you do things to people which they think horrid?'

'You've been talking a terrible lot of nonsense,' said Alice. 'What's the use of pretending that a dreadful boy like Colin, who sticks out his underlip when he sees you and looks awful and hasn't any manners, is a nice child, and that a charming little girl like Betty, who's always polite and clean and well-behaved, is for some obscure reason a little horror? And as for the rest, I think I understand only too well, thank you. For one thing it's perfectly plain that you've been listening to Evie. She's apparently made some wonderful story out of the simple fact that, being fond of my only brother, I've guessed that there's something wrong with his health, and shown a very natural anxiety. And as for Madge, I can see she's been disloyal. But sisters often are, and I never thought poor Madge was perfect, and I won't let it make a bit of difference. What worries me is that you should have listened to all these people when they were being spiteful about me.'

'But, Alice, hasn't what I've said made any difference to you at all? Don't you feel that you've been doing some things that maybe, after what you've heard, you'd better stop doing?'

'No, I don't', said Alice. 'It seems to me that what you've been attacking me about, thanks to all this nonsense you've been listening to, is just what you have to do when you're one of a family. I can't suddenly pretend that I haven't got any relations. Why, they'd be the first to be hurt. If I stopped going round to Evie's and helping her to clear up the messes she's always getting into, there'd be no end to her complaints.'

'Sometimes,' said Jimmy, 'you don't strike me as a grown-up, wicked person at all. You strike me as a child who for some extraordinary reason wants to be punished, and who goes on behaving worse and worse so that she'll compel somebody or other to punish her. Do you really mean to go on just the same?'

'Yes, I think so. If there's anything particularly you object to, I might...'

'Do you mean, for instance, to speak to Walter about Madge?'

She sat down on the stool again, and stretched behind her for the hairbrush with an enchanting gesture. 'As a matter of fact, I do.'

'Alice!'

'You see, I must.' She squared her jaw and looked like an exquisitely beautiful, tear-stained little bull-dog.

'Why?'

'I happen to know something about Walter that makes it necessary.'

'What's that?'

'Walter hasn't always been the husband to Madge that he ought to be.'

'You mean he's been unfaithful to her? Ah, that little blonde slut at Cadeford.'

'And he'd better be warned that this is no time for that sort of thing.'

Jimmy whistled. 'You could have a whole lot of fun out of that, couldn't you?' he said. 'You might even get poor Walter into such a state of dither that he confessed everything to Madge, and that would kill her outright. She doesn't understand that sort of thing, God bless her. Really, this is a find of yours, Alice. With your peculiar gift there's no end to what you might be able to make of it.'

He slid to the floor at her feet so suddenly, and in so limp a heap that she thought he had fainted, and was about to scream when he gripped her knees, laid his head on her lap, and spoke softly, 'Alice, remember what I said to you. About the unreasonable requests in the fairy-tale, and how the threats came true. That if the flower was eaten, the fruit plucked, the castle falls to pieces. I'm going to make another of those unreasonable requests.'

'My dear, I'm tired. This is my first night home, and I'd hoped for something rather different. What is it?'

He raised his head and his eyes implored her. 'Let me sell the business. Let's sell this house. Let's go abroad. Let's stop bothering about Madge and Walter, and Leo and Evie, and just be ourselves. We wouldn't be rich, but with what Father left me, we'd have enough for comfort. Please, Alice. Please.'

'Jimmy, I can't fathom you to-night. Do you really mean this?'

'I mean it more seriously than I've ever meant anything in my life.'

'You seriously mean that for no reason you want us to sell all our beautiful things and give up my family and my friends, and wander about as if we'd done something awful and had to live abroad? Jimmy, I really think you're mad.'

His head dropped back in her lap. It felt as heavy as a lump of lead, as if he were asleep. Then he looked up, and she saw with a kind of faint disgust, for she hated emotional displays in men, that the tears were thick on his lashes. 'Forgive me, Alice,' he said. 'I think I've been mad, too, all evening. I've said cruel things to you, and they were useless as well as cruel. However, that's all over. You're a wonderful woman, Alice. You've got me right back where I was before you went away. As I was during your illness and before it. Perfectly sane.' He jumped lightly to his feet and gave her a loud, almost a smacking kiss on the cheek. 'Well, I'll go and undress now. The time's over for talk.'

'I'm glad you're sensible again,' she said, 'and if I've irritated you by sticking to my point about Walter, do forgive me. But, you see, I am so fond of Madge.'

'And just how fond I am of Madge,' he answered, 'is one of the things that you will probably never know.'

The dressing-room door closed softly behind him. She sighed with relief that the scene was over, and went on with her hair, putting down her brush and using her comb. But she had to admit that she felt shattered by this curious breakdown of Jimmy's, this appearance of frenzy and un-reason in a character that had seemed till now wholly free from them. When a coal fell from the fire, she started; and when behind the swaying red taffeta curtains there was a tap on one of the windows, she swung round and said aloud, 'What's that?', and again there opened around her an image of a lost paradise, of forgone security and peace, the sense of that blue cold noon on the clean heath. Then she remembered that the ivy had not yet been pruned this year, and that its dark arms often stretched as far as the window-panes, and she turned about again. But she felt uneasy and tearful, and was glad when Jimmy came in again, slim and well-made in the dark blue silk dressing-gown she had given him for Christmas, which he would wear only seldom, because he said it was too dandified for ordinary occasions.

He came and stood beside her, and she stopped combing her hair while she studied his reflexion, and she uttered a faint exclamation of dismay.

'Anything the matter?' said Jimmy.

'No. Only when I was in the New Forest with that young man this morning, I looked at him and thought he was very good-looking, but that he hadn't something in his face which you have, and which I specially love. . . .'

'Yes?'

'And now I see what it is. It's your mouth.'

'Well?'

'And yet your mouth's cruel. Your lips are full, but you hold them so that they're thin – it's a cruel mouth.'

'Is it?' He bent down close to the glass. 'It may be. It's hard to tell about oneself. I think I hate it when I have to be cruel, but maybe I don't. Probably one never gets into a position when one's forced to do something unless one really wants to do it.'

'Jimmy . . .' she threw her comb down on the dressing-table. 'I wish you wouldn't go on being so horrible and hateful and queer. I know I seem not to have any nerves, but I have, really. I'm frightened of lots of things. I have those nightmares, you know.'

'What are your nightmares about?' he asked. 'You've never told me what they actually were about.'

'Why, I am standing in a room – now I come to think of it, it's this room – and something awful comes nearer and nearer to me, circling round me, drawing in on me, and I know that in the end it's going to destroy me utterly.'

'And you can't stop it?'

'No. The funny thing is – now, that's something else I never remembered before after I'd woken up – I could perfectly well stop this awful horror coming at me. Only for some reason I can't. I have to go on doing the very thing that brings it nearer.'

Jimmy turned away from the mirror. 'God, what a life this is,' he said, 'full of presciences that don't do us any good, full of self-consciousness that tortures us by telling us just what sort of hole we're in but never how to get out of it. It's nothing to cling on to, really.'

'Jimmy, you're being odd again,' she said. 'Please don't. I can't stand it, my first night home.' There ran before her mind's eye pictures of everything which had happened to her during this day which had risen so early to its peak, which was falling, in spite of all she could do, to such a dark, perplexing decline, and the memory of her first, slow, satisfied inspection of her home made her exclaim: 'Oh, Jimmy, I found two things in your room that interested me.'

He was at one of the windows now, staring out into the night between the red curtains, but now he strolled back to her. 'What were they?'

'Well, you know that big photograph of me in my wedding dress? Just think, it's been torn nearly the whole way across!'

'No!'

'Yes, really. Whoever did it tried to cover it up by gumming the edges together, but now the gum's got old and it's cracked, and the tear shows again. I thought at first it was a hair under the glass. It must have been that dreadfully clumsy housemaid we once had, called Lilian, Hall.'

'I wonder if it was?'

'It would be Lilian, she ruined everything she touched. Then the other thing was the tube of white powder in your pocket.'

'You found that too?'

'Yes. What is it?'

He dug down into his dressing-gown pocket and showed it to her on the palm of his hand.

'Yes, that's the thing,' she said. 'It looks like one of old Dr Godstone's phials.'

'That's just what it is,' he said. 'Once in his dispensary I picked it up, years ago, and he told me what it was. Then long after when he died and I was going through his effects I saw it and remembered the name on the label, and I slipped it in my pocket, though I never thought I'd need it then. Yet I suppose I must have known I would, really, or I would never have taken it.'

'Well, there's no label on it now. What's it for?' said Alice.

'It's just something that sends people to sleep.'

'But if you want anything of that sort, why don't you go down to Leo and get him to give you whatever's most thoroughly up to date? You know what old Dr Godstone was. This is probably something that was used in the Ark.'

'Oh, don't be too harsh on the old man. There's nothing wrong with this. It works quite all right if you give it in the right dose. If you give too little it's no good; and if you give too much that's bad, too. But if you give the right dose, there's no more trouble.'

'Well, I suppose that's all right, provided you know the right dose.'

'I do now,' he said. He sighed deeply and stood for a second or two rolling it backwards and forwards on his palm, as though he would not be sorry to drop it; but he kept his eyes on it all the time. 'I only found that out ten days ago. Saturday before last I felt restless all the morning ...'

'Oh, darling, I ought never to have left you,' said Alice, 'but I wrote you every Monday, Wednesday, and Friday, so you must have had a letter from me that morning.'

'I had,' said Jimmy. 'Well, in the afternoon I got out the car and drove right across England to Bathwick. I'd never been there before in my life, I don't know anybody there. When I found myself driving past the Public Library I stopped and walked in, just as if I was a good Bathwick ratepayer, and consulted a book on drugs. And I got the proper dose.'

'Well, it seems a casual way of taking medicine,' said Alice, 'but I suppose you'll be careful. Come in, Ethel.'

But it was Cook who came in with a glass and a steaming jug on a tray. She put it down on the dressing-table with a clatter, and her body was solid as masonry with grimness.

'Seeing as how there was unpleasantness about the new brand of chocolate,' she said, ignoring Alice's absent smile, 'I came up myself to explain that this is the old brand which I got through sending my sister's girl special down to the stores.'

'Good gracious, is Minnie back from her place in London? I'm afraid they'll never keep her anywhere you know, she's so untidy . . .'

'She's home on her holidays, while the family's gone to Italy,' said Cook with quiet triumph and shut the door with a bang.

'What's all that about?' asked Jimmy. He was still rolling the phial of powder backwards and forwards across his palm, and looking at it as if it were a jewel.

'Oh, a fuss about nothing. She's a rude woman, and she'll have to go. It's only that she bought another brand of chocolate malted milk,' said Alice, filling her glass from the jug, 'and I like this. The sort she got was mawkish stuff, I could taste the malted milk through the chocolate, and I hate that. This is very strong, you can't taste anything but the chocolate.'

'So if you hadn't made a row with Cook, you'd be

drinking something with a milder flavour to-night?' said Jimmy. 'By God, that's funny.'

'Why?' asked Alice, and raised the glass to her lips. But she set it down again, because Jimmy was holding up his finger and jerking his head towards the door, 'What's the matter?'

'Why has Cook gone down the passage to the spare rooms instead of going upstairs to her bedroom?'

'Has she?'

'Yes, I heard her.'

'What an extraordinary thing. But these women,' she tiptoed to the door, opened it softly, and stood for a minute on the darkened landing, peering down the passage and listening. But she heard nothing save the creaks and stirrings that are the voice of an old house at night, and presently she heard Cook's ponderous tread across the ceiling above her. She went back into the bedroom and said, 'Jimmy, you're dreaming,' and sat down at her dressing-table and drank her chocolate.

Jimmy did not answer her, and she turned and looked at him over the rim of her glass. He was standing on the rug in front of the fire, his hands shoved so deeply into the pockets of his dressing-gown that his shoulders were hunched up, and his tallness looked rangy and wolfish. He was watching her with eyes that stared like a fever patient's, and his teeth pulled in his lower lip and let it go, again and again, as if he were enduring agony.

'But you look so ill,' she said, and set down her glass.

'Drink up that chocolate!' he told her, and she obeyed, then turned to him, her brows knit in annoyance, her lips parted, waiting for an explanation. But he said nothing, only came towards her and took the empty glass out of her hand with so curt a movement that she cried out in protest. It was a movement of a quality utterly unexpected in him, quite unlike any gestures she had ever seen him make throughout all the years they had been together. So might a burglar have snatched a ring from her finger. She stared at his back as he hurried out of the room, and put her hands to her head, trying to puzzle it out, when she heard the bathroom taps running.

'But what are you doing?' she asked as he came in with the clean glass in his hand and put it down, on the tray beside her, and poured into it what chocolate was left in the jug. 'What are you doing?' she repeated, as he poured the chocolate back again out of the glass into the jug.

Her own voice sounded far away in her ears, but his voice sounded farther away as he answered, 'Just taking precautions that probably won't be successful, but I really don't care much about that.'

She wanted to ask him to repeat what he had said, and say it more intelligibly, but then she thought she would rather tell him that she felt very ill. Sweat had come out on her forehead, snakes seemed to be sliding through her bowels, she wished she could either sit in a chair with a back to it or lie down, she was afraid she was going to slip down on the floor. She found it, however, difficult to speak. But Jimmy had seen for himself what was happening. She felt his hands slip under her armpits, and knew that he was carrying her over to the bed. With a great effort, for her lids were now very heavy, she opened her eyes and tried to see his face, and though everything shimmered glassy and wavered about her, she was sure that he was looking sorry for her, and as he laid her down and drew the blankets over her, she caught the words, heard indistinctly as through the surf of a tremendous sea, 'Poor little Alice'. She rolled over, cooling her damp forehead against the fresh linen pillow-slip, and moaning, because she knew that it meant something, if she could but collect her wits and think what it was, that now the taste of chocolate had gone, her mouth was full of a haunting bitterness. But she was too tired, she could only mutter that she wanted some water.

THE ABIDING VISION

THE ABIDING VISION

WHEN Sam Hartley took his wife Lulah to the window of their new apartment to look at the white cliffs of Park Avenue she broke down and cried. It was not that she was appalled by the magnificence that was henceforward to surround her, for she had been someone in Chicago for quite a few years now. But before she had been someone in Chicago she had been someone in Omaha, and before that she had been nobody at all in Butte, Montana, and the journey had taken a long time and a great deal of faith. So she laid her wet face against his cheek, and he comforted her. The roughness of her skin made him think of that winter in Denver when they were both just a couple of kids, and he was sick and could not hold down a job, and she had baked cakes and made candies to keep him in between whiles of nursing him. There travelled through his mind a quiet procession of all the things she had done for him, and he put his hand behind her head and turned her kind, lined face so that it pressed right into his cheek. It was no wonder she was tired. They had both gone through a lot. He was quite tired himself. He sighed deeply; and there flashed before his inner eye, as real and pricking as if he saw it with the eye of his body, a face unlined with care, smooth and shining flesh undepleted by self-sacrifice.

Absently he said, 'Why, Lulah! Why, Lulah, honey!' and he led her by the hand to the big sofa facing the panel of tapestry he had bought for the new place. He had had a New York decorator furnish the apartment for her as a surprise while she was still in the Chicago hospital recovering from her bad spell, and all its wonders were unknown to her. Cradling her shoulders in his arm and rocking her, he pointed out the queer beasts that peered through the bushes at the back of the panel, the white dog that lay on the ermine hem of the lady's gown. It was the kind of thing she liked. 'That's the fun of it,' he thought, 'we're still like a couple of kids.'

But they were not kids. Lulah was forty-four. He was forty-five, and he had another birthday coming in August. He would be putting on weight soon if he were not careful. And lately, if he chanced to wake up in the early hours of the morning, he had become conscious of an appalling desolation that could only be morbid. He thought, gloomily and without any upward spring of the spirit, that he must start doing setting-up exercises. Maybe in the summer he would go to that sanatorium up the Hudson somewhere, and drink milk and take up his boxing again. He continued his caressing mutter, 'Isn't it cute, mother? I thought you'd like it,' and bent to kiss her ear, but a night engulfed him.

The telephone on the table whirred for them. 'It's not for me, yet,' said Lulah. He knew what the slight complacence in her tone, its knowingness, meant. To-day nobody in New York knew that Mrs Sam Hartley had taken an apartment on Park Avenue. In a week's time that telephone would be ringing now and again. People who used to live in Chicago and had moved to New York, New Yorkers who had dined with them in Chicago, would have been approached by Lulah, not as a newcomer seeking to strike root, but as a reserved personality conferring a benefit, murmuring invitations to theatre parties with no perceptible anxiety that they should be accepted. In a year's time the telephone would be ringing all the time into the ear of a neat social secretary, not underworked. Lulah had been fighting that campaign all her adult life.

A voice said to Sam out of the distance that it was Jim Leavensoe, and that Bill Crammers had come up from Washington, and that they were going on a party that very night. They had seats for the Follies, and maybe afterwards they would collect some chorus girls and take them dancing, and would he come along with them?

'Sure I will,' said Sam, 'sure I will. I'll be up at your place by seven.' He said good-bye and put down the receiver, and strolled back to the sofa, looking over his shoulder at the shining altitudes of Park Avenue. Now he felt young and relieved. He thought of his early morning desolations and remembered what they were; it had seemed to him that the business he had done all his life, the foundation of the Mount Couzens Corporation and its eleven subsidiaries, had no reality at all. He and Jim Leavensoe and Julius Geylor had ridden a long way one day when they were young to see a mountain, and then they had written a lot of letters, with the result that the flanks of the mountain and the flats in its shadow were harrowed up and cancered with tall chimneys and puffing, ejaculating factories, and then they had written a lot more letters and had got rich. In the early hours it seemed to him the connexion between the mountain and the letters was too thin, and that someday somebody would notice it, and that he had come into the racket too late to be able to defend himself. Now such thoughts seemed to him an absurd delirium engendered by a sickness he meant to treat drastically. Confidently he settled down by Lulah and made plans for what they would do when they were settled in, until it was time for her to go to bed. She was not quite right yet, she had to rest evenings; that was why he was able to go out on the party.

He liked each of the three girls they took to Texas Guinan as much as the others. They were all young as to-morrow, their eyes were long lakes of lustrous substance right across their faces, their lips were so bright and wet that the lipstick they constantly applied looked dull and opaque, their bodies kicked inside their scanty clothes as if nakedness was their normal wear. They all threw their heads back when they sluiced their throats with Scotch and ginger-ale, showing round high-lights just above their gowns on their rising breasts, and they all looked round the club with wide, circling glances that took everybody in and made no discriminations; they would just as soon have been with any other men in the room as with their own party, they would just as soon have been with their own party as with any other men in the room. They seemed entirely free, they were always speaking about walking out on people and parties and shows, and they made a man feel free. Sam would not have known which to take as his girl, if it had not been that Jim liked only brunettes, and so had to have the one called Gloria, and Bill had got together with the one called Greta because they both came from Indiana. So he had to take the fair one with a touch of ginger in the deep waves of her hair, that they called Lily.

He muttered to her, 'God, you're beautiful. God, you're lovely! You're the sweetest girl I've seen in this town.'

She answered crisply, 'My, you've got a good line.'

As the cabaret show came on, and the nearly quite naked and excessively young girls pressed in on them, singing, 'She knew her onions,' in the electric drill voices of school-children, he took Lily's hand. It lay in his like a fine piece of ivory carving. She made no resistance, even when he lifted it and pressed it backwards and forwards against his nibbling mouth, but she made no response. A good many young women liked his heavy grizzled handsomeness, but it was not clear whether she was among them. It was evident from her expression, which was smiling but non-committal, that she felt that she had not got enough to go on yet. When he was taking her home he passed his great hand over her knees, and found that she would allow him nearly all liberties but the ultimate ones. Yet even then her little slim body was sitting cool and stiff in the middle of her clothes, retaining full possession of itself. He liked her a lot. Whatever was going to be would be just what it was, there would be no big pretence that it was something delicate and sentimental. The kid had sense.

When they got to the apartment where Lily stayed, she asked him up for a last highball. From the cushions on her sofa she watched him while he drank it slowly, looking round the room over the edge of his glass. It was a cheap place, and the furniture was messy, but here and there were objects that must have come from the wreck of a more expensive house: a Chinese porcelain vase, a coverlet of Genoese velvet, a huge radio. He grinned at her, stuck out his little finger at the radio, swallowed, and lowered his empty glass.

'Did you fetch away the refrigerator too?' he asked. 'Or did you leave 'em that?'

She grinned back. 'I left 'em that,' she said.

He asked her abruptly how old she was. She answered that she was nineteen, but he did not believe her. She looked more like twenty-one or twenty-two. In any case, her past probably included everything but tears. With those, he was sure, she had never had anything to do. She was so magnificently free from emotion that he felt liberated to the point of soaring, that he groped about for grave thoughts as ballast.

Sam put down his glass on a table, smiled and nodded at her, and said, 'You're just as cute as could be.' For the purposes of experiment he advanced on her, but just as he had expected, she repulsed him with arms that swung as free as a colt's.

'Hey, you!' she said, 'What's the hurry?' But she flung back her head so that he should see her throat and bosom, and looked down her small, straight nose, so that he should see the incredible length of her lashes, and turned around so that he should see how her long waist rose out of her hips. Yet her fists were still clenched.

Sam laughed. He knew that she was sending him away because it showed that a man was serious, that a woman could really hope to get something out of him, if he came back a second time to dispute a first denial. Also, it would give her time to make inquiries and find out whether he really had the dough.

He said, 'I'll call you to-morrow, sweetheart.' As he

went through the door she laid a hand on his arm with a gesture he adored; it expressed so plainly good humour combined with extreme indifference. She did not care a brass nickel whether he came back to her or not, there could have been no movement less imploring. But in either case she would be well disposed towards him; there would be no resentment.

When Sam got back to his apartment he went into his library and sat down in his big stuffed arm-chair and pulled off his boots so that he should not wake Lulah as he went into their room. When he had finished he sat back and smiled at the ceiling, and muttered, 'A grand wench! A grand wench!' He breathed deeply, as if mountain airs were flowing round him.

After he had closed the bedroom door behind him he looked over to the bed, and fear struck him stone-still. Lulah had read herself to sleep, and had not switched off the reading lamp. She was lying on her back and the circle of light fell straight on her face, making it white as chalk. The sheet was crumpled as if her crossed hands lay on her breast. He listened, but he could hear nothing. The air in the room seemed quite dead. He bit his lip, knowing he must restrain himself, for since Lulah's illness this terror had come in more than once without any real cause; and he tip-toed over to the bed. But over there it was just as still, and she seemed even paler. He clutched his throat and was about to groan, when Lulah stirred, sighed, and raised her lids. She saw him, smiled, and tried to say something, but rolled over and nuzzled deeper into sleep. Sam gulped back the spit that had filled his mouth, and bent low over her wonderful face, the map of their years together. Gently he brought down his lips to her brow and murmured, 'Good-night, mother,' and waited until she had smiled and murmured to him from the depths of her sleep.

Then he went back and began to undress in the far corner of the room, before the long mirrors. When he got down to his vest and pants he straightened up before his own reflexion and passed his hands over his chest and stomach and flanks. He had been panicking, he was not putting on weight, it was only that he had sagged in his skin, that he had let his muscles fall slack. Sharply he pivoted his trunk to the left, keeping his hips still, his stomach flat, and dropped the right hand down in front of the left foot. He could get the whole palm of his hand flat on the floor. He repeated the exercise several times, making it quicker and quicker, though always silent, so as not to wake Lulah; and he felt more and more exhilarated. He could have started the night all over again.

It took Sam a fortnight in time, and the expenditure of many dollars at a Fifth Avenue jewellers, to become as intimate with Lily as he had intended. There was a splendid lack of mealy-mouthedness about the whole incident, so that he was able to discuss the progress of his wooing quite frankly with Jim and Bill. They told him he was a fool to take so much trouble, that they could get him fifty just as good as Lily and twice as easy. But he shook his head and laughed, and said that it was Lily he wanted. He liked the hardness of her body under the fluffiness of her evening frocks, the looseness of her kimonos. He liked the contrast between the fragility of her appearance and the toughness of her nerves. She would sit at the window of her apartment, as delicate as a spray of cattleya, and by not one tremor would she recognize that on the corner of the next block they were building a new apartment house, and the noise of the riveting and drilling was enough to shatter a six-foot policeman. It pleased him, too, that not for one moment was she embarrassed by the issue that lay between them. She gave him to understand, not crudely but quite definitely, that if she yielded to him she would expect very shortly afterwards to move into another apartment; and that, if he did not accept her conditions, there was some-body else who would. With a matter-of-fact recognition that on this latter point she might not be believed, she con-trived an over-lapping of appointments, so that Sam should one evening meet in the hallway outside her room a man who was very much like himself, in the late forties, handsome and heavy, but who had perhaps been in New York longer. Sam looked at him curiously, but Lily would not tell him who it was.

When at last the arrangements were completed, and the surrender took place, Sam knew he had had the right idea.

Lily was hard-boiled but she did something to him. As he combed his hair before her mirror he felt like a god, and there were no strings to it. She was as pleased as he had been, she was pacing the room behind him now, flushed and softer-looking than he had ever seen her; but it was the embrace that had pleased her, not him. If it had been any other man that had given it to her she would have been just as pleased. There was not an atom in her, so far as he could see, of the foolishness which would persuade her that there was something special between them, and it was obvious that she had a great deal of experience which would convince her to the contrary. This meant that any time he wanted to leave her, it would be just a matter of arrangement, the same as it had been getting her. It meant, too, that she would probably walk out on him some day, and that was good too, as he supposed he would soon get tired of her.

Lily came and stood beside him, smiling proudly at their reflexions. He smiled back, but as he fixed his tie his eyes fell on a newspaper, one of the tabloids, that lay on the dressing-table. Across the front page sprawled the huddled bodies of a banker and his best friend's wife, found poisoned in a hotel bedroom.

Sam shook his head, murmuring, 'Sentimentalists get punished, sentimentalists get punished.' He slipped his arm round Lily and made a hurried farewell. There were folks to dinner, and he knew it made Lulah nervous if he were late.

He gave Lily a new apartment, and was amused by her vigorous but sensible avarice. It had to be in a fairly good district on Central Park West, and it was her taste to have it decorated in the modern style with lambskin rugs, aluminium and looking-glass tables, square stuffed chairs covered with soft tweeds, and a broad, low bed, which things were apparently as costly as the oldest and most precious furniture. Before he gave her what she wanted he referred the sum, as he did all his personal expenditure, to the thought of Lulah. Was it so large a sum that it would take away from Lulah any of the comfort and dignity which were her due? Was it so large that it struck at the foundations of the solid fortune they had built up together? Considering the state of the Mount Couzens outfit, it was not. It was pretty high, but not so high as that. It was just stiff enough to make a man think twice before he left a woman in whom he had sunk so much money. Being sure that all these considerations had been in Lily's mind when she calculated the sum, he wrote out the cheque and laughed.

'You goddam little gold digger,' he said, as he gave her the cheque, and smacked her behind.

'You lay off that,' said Lily, folding the slip of paper away in her bag with serene finger-tips.

As time went on Sam used to pause every now and then to take stock of his life, and he was amazed to find, as year followed year, that he was still keeping Lily. The Mount Couzens Corporation had fourteen subsidiaries and some of these were important holding companies themselves; it had put out its arm and hugged to its bosom a sweet lot of properties. And Lulah had conquered New York. When she went to the right restaurants on Park Avenue she was not only just like all the other women in their ironically simple sumptuousness, she had them all beaten but the very best, and they were no better than she was, they had only been there longer. The fullness of her beauty had gone from her, it had passed even from Sam's recollection; her old photographs surprised him. But now her visible benevolence and fortitude and gentleness made people look after her in the street, hatch schemes for meeting her, to talk about her as a discovery, just as much as her famous figure and complexion had ever done. Young women who were having babies liked to have her with them, older women who were going to the doctor to see about that pain liked to have her come with them. More and more men said to him, 'My wife's just crazy about your wife, Sam,' and they were people who mattered. All his life he had felt as if he were living on a ledge on a mountain-side, but now the ledge seemed so broad that there was no danger of falling off it. In fact, one, two, three, four years had passed, and Lily was still in the apartment on Central Park West.

This was partly because he was too busy these days to have time for the excursions that might have brought him to a new girl. But chiefly it was because he had no reason to grow dissatisfied with Lily. She was steadily increasing in beauty, working on herself incessantly to that end, always experimenting with new creams and powders and rouges, and different ways of doing her hair and pencilling her eyebrows, and in their private hours she retained her power to make him feel young again and without doubts. For the rest, she was even-tempered and sensible. When he took her on a party with any of his friends who liked that sort of thing she did him credit, for she got full value for the immense sums she spent on clothes, she was pleasant with the men without letting them get too fresh, she was friendly with the other girls, and though she could drink a considerable amount of Scotch she never got drunk. To his surprise she was a good housekeeper. Her apartment was neat as a new pin, and the food was good. It was true that her avarice operated continuously, collecting from him jewels and furs over and above her regular allowance at regular periods, but as at the beginning it was always as nicely calculated in relation to his means as if she had a highly-paid statistician working for her.

As Sam told his friends, she was a good kid. If he had a doubt about her, it was whether she strictly obeyed his injunction that she should be faithful to him. Once he came to the apartment earlier than his habit, and he found a stranger strolling round the living-room with a highball in his hand, a young fellow with chestnut hair curlier than is worn by men in the Social Register, tight, brightish clothes that showed his strong hams, and the bouncing, tireless walk of a hoofer. There was something fixed in the smiles he and Lily turned towards the opening door.

'This is Mr Leo Lehmann, who was in my last show with me,' said Lily smoothly.

The young man said his grinning good-byes without haste. He might have been counting a couple of hundred to give himself the right pace for doing it.

When Lily came back it was in Sam's mind to tell her that that looked a cheap kind of fellow. But he found himself forming a notion that if he did not sit quite still he would find her using the terrible voice in which he had heard her tell the coloured maid that some pairs of her stockings were missing; and she would be using it to explain to him that New York was full of men just like him, with the same needs and the same money. He sat quite still, running his finger through the strand of hair on his left temple that had gone prematurely silver. In any case, even if she sometimes side-stepped, she was such a wise kid that no harm could come of it.

In any case there was no use worrying about it, because he could not check up on her. He could only see her rarely, twice or thrice a week, and not so often after the show. Sometimes in winter he would arrange for her to be down at Palm Beach when he was, and maybe some accommodating bachelor friend would ask them on a yacht, and in summer Jim Leavensoe would sometimes ask them up to his place on Long Island. That was about all there was to it. For the rest, his enjoyment of her company was strictly limited by the demands of business and his liking to be with Lulah. He made a point of staying with her most evenings because he did not want her to know about Lily. It was possible, he thought, that for years she had guessed how often he had got himself a girl when he had to spend the night away from her in a strange town, but he did not want her to know he had a steady. But though staying with her in the evenings served the purpose of throwing dust in her eyes, that was not the real reason why he did it. He stayed in with Lulah because he liked it.

Sam never tired of helping her to entertain their guests, or going out with her to other people's homes. He enjoyed the whole of such evenings, beginning with the way she would come in after she was ready and watch his valet finish dressing him. She always looked so grand, with the ageless fineness of her beautifully shaped head and long throat, and her soberly splendid clothes. Not for one instant did she give it away that she had spent most of her first twenty years in cotton overalls, and that he was twenty-two before he got a second suit. But she was not high-hat or mean, she only kept quiet about these things because it was kind of embarrassing to carry on when people knew about them, just as it is when one's old folks tell tales about how cute one was as a baby. She would sit back in the big Italian chair, and say to the valet, 'Joaquin, do you think those new piqué shirts are as well cut as the old ones? I wouldn't say they were.' It gave him a cosy feeling to have them both talking about him and his possessions in cool, shrewd tones. But sometimes she talked to the valet about his daughter, who was a clever girl and was going to college. Lulah's father had been a schoolmaster, she would have gone to college herself if her mother had not been sick. She thought all women ought to be educated. Sometimes she would go on talking to the valet about his daughter till they were almost late.

They used to go out of the room together, laughing, starting the evening right. Then all evening Sam used to like to look away from the people he was talking to, every now and then, and watch Lulah. She was always being so gracious, and it was honest. She really meant it or she would not be doing it. Sometimes he caught sight of her when she was speaking to nobody, after she had dismissed someone and before she had greeted someone else, and then for a minute her head would be bowed, and her mouth would pull down at the corners, like a sick woman's. Then his heart would contract with a painful sense of obligation and tenderness.

On one of the placid evenings they occasionally used to spend at home, listening to the radio and playing bezique or backgammon, he took his cigar out of his mouth, after he had watched her for some time as she knitted and smiled up at the invisible presence of Eddie Cantor, and he said, 'You know, you like this social racket just the way you would cold poison.'

Her needles fell still, she covered her mouth. But she shook her head. 'I wouldn't say that. We get to know some mighty nice people.'

'You aren't scared the way you were when we first got into the thing at Omaha,' he pursued. 'But you don't like it. You never will.'

She began knitting again. 'It's something we're in together,' she said. And flashing a young smile at him, she added, 'Mind, I haven't done so badly out of it myself.' She held up her latest diamond ring to him, and slipped it back on her finger. 'And I've got you, Sam Hartley, for what you're worth.'

Their life went on and on, up and up. One knew what to expect of each new day; more of what there had been yesterday. Sam was surprised at his own corporations as their stocks soared and soared and soared. 'The public's just a lot of suckers,' he once said to Jim Leavensoe, 'and I don't like it.'

Sam was a tall man, but Jim was half a head taller. The impact of his great hand on Sam's shoulder-blades was shattering.

'Aw, boloney,' said his rumbling Western voice. 'They're going to be on the up and up for ever. Oh, we'll stop somewhere, but not till we're pretty high. We're on a permanent plateau of prosperity. There's never been anything like it before. It's America.'

'I'd rather be in a good conservative business,' said Sam. 'Have your money sure and make no show about it. Like...'

His voice faded, and Jim showed no signs of asking him to finish his sentence, but turned away. They neither of them liked to admit that though they had travelled far, they had never come near the holy cities of finance, whose treasure is beyond the reach of thieves, because there is so much of it.

Presently, however, there came a day when he was no longer worried because that conversation had never been finished, when the whole of it seemed comically irrelevant. He learned on an October afternoon that his corporations could surprise him by doing other things than soar. They could sink as if they were lined with lead. In spring the price of Mount Couzens Corporation stock had been about fifty-four and a half, which was fair enough, and a bit too fair. Through the summer it mounted to a hundred and thirty. Nobody thought of fairness any more. September came, and a tremor ran through the market lists. 'Aw, but we'll be grand again in a couple of weeks' time,' said Sam, but as the days went on he felt as he did when he was a child and had his first ride in an elevator. But that elevator had gone up; now the movement was down. There came a Tuesday morning when he clapped his hands over his ears and roared to his stenographer, 'I don't want to know any more!' and then sat staring at a telephone. He thought of a vast emerald he had put on Lily's finger last April, and snarled, as a dying man might in thinking of the lifeblood he had been tricked into shedding in some battle contrived by treachery. He thought of a diamond bracelet he had slipped on Lulah's arm at the same time, but with infinite thankfulness, though with a little shame, for he had wanted always to give things to Lulah and never to take them back. When he called her she answered in a nervous but unperturbed voice, saying, 'Well, you haven't been easy in your mind all this fall, have you?' And when he told her that this crash was worse than anything he had ever expected she chirped, 'Aw, but it always is. Don't we have this every fifteen years? We'd be quite healthy with a lot less than we have. And it can't be worse than that winter we had in Denver.' She laughed suddenly in the blackness of the telephone, like a girl remembering a game. Immensely restored, he went back to his work, professing to his inferiors a sardonic and unafraid amusement. But later he found a moment on his hands and he called up Lily. There was no answer, and he remembered bitterly that rats forsake a sinking ship.

At length he said to Leavensoe, 'Well, we aren't doing anything sitting here talking. Not one of us knows what's going to happen. Maybe that's our luck.' He went out into the dark streets and remembered bitterly that this was Tuesday, and it was his habit to visit Lily on Tuesday evenings. In rage he reflected that she would probably be waiting for him now, swathed in one of those negligées that dripped soft ostrich fronds round her slender ankles, over her white hands and their vermilion nails, and at the thought of her body and the embraces which they had often shared, which she would no doubt expect him to renew that evening, he felt as if his mouth were being crammed full with sickly sweetmeats. 'God, I'm going to tell that broad where she gets off,' he muttered, and grumbled into his coat collar all the way in the automobile to Central Park West.

But Lily was wearing a hard little black suit with a lingerie blouse, and instead of putting her arms round him she waved him to an arm-chair with her long cigarette-holder and poured him out a good strong highball. She asked him questions about the day's prodigious doings, and sat on a footstool by his chair, nodding at the answers. She was grim and amused about it all, the way he had pretended to be with his subordinates.

'Well, baby, now you know the way us girls feel when a show's a flop,' she said finally, when he got up to go.

'Yes, I guess that's all it is,' he said, his arm about her

waist. 'We've all got to take our medicine sometime.' He felt steady and comforted, he could go home to Lulah feeling that he would not collapse too heavily on her fragility.

With her hand on the front door she stretched up, close pressed against his height, and gave him a cool, casual kiss. 'Gee, it's tough on you,' she said kindly.

Sam went out into the darkness saying, 'She's a grand girl, she's a grand girl.' During the following months he grew to count Lily as well as Lulah as among the few things he could still be sure of in the changing world. The price of Mount Couzens Corporation and its subsidiaries, which he and Jim Leavensoe had used to drawl out to their friends, sitting crumpled in their chairs because they were too proud to sit straight, became sour jokes. They tried to be funny about it themselves, and knew why Jews tell Jewish stories and how they feel when they are telling them. The financial complexity of the outfit, which he had never understood, which it had not been his business to understand, since his part had always been to sell and prophesy expansion with all the conviction of his bullish physical strength, now alarmed him. He had never been quite sure, so that he could have explained it to a class of college boys, why it had all been fixed up so that Mount Couzens Construction Company held a twenty per cent interest in Mount Couzens Building Inc., and Mount Couzens Building Inc. held a ten per cent interest in Mount Couzens Development Corporation, while Mount Couzens Development Corporation held shares in the Mount Couzens Construction Company, and the Leavensoe-Hartley Process Corporate held shares in all the others. Leavensoe and Crammers did the understanding of all that, and they still said, 'Aw, it's sound business method, I'm telling you. Don't they all do it?' But now it meant that a solid mass of property shrank on every side at once, and went on and on shrinking so that it seemed only a matter of time before its name would be no more than a notice-board marked 'danger' on the edge of an empty quarry.

Sam Hartley was not a very rich man any longer. The bloom of his reputation as a power had gone. He knew that if there was not a quick recovery in Wall Street the substance of it would be gone as well. There was left to him very little but Mount Couzens itself: the real mountain that he and Jim Leavensoe and Julius Geylor had ridden a long way to see when they were young. That had proved as distinct from the paper schemes that had borne its name as he had always feared; but now the distinction made him rejoice.

'People will always need ore and the things you get from ore,' he used to say, as he sat with Lulah in the evenings. 'We'll always have an income.'

She used to nod back, calmly and shrewdly. 'You can't move Mount Couzens.'

'And anyway we'll snap out of this any moment,' he would say. 'I shouldn't be surprised if this very next month we'll see an improvement.'

They would pass on and talk of pleasanter things.

He took to going back to Mount Couzens more often than he had done for years. Lulah no longer came with him; during the last few months she had lost much of her old vitality. He missed her a lot, when she came along she always sweetened everyone they met, and now the people out there were really in need of sweetening. Julius Geylor had from the beginning taken care of the works end of the corporation's business. He had stayed right by the mountain, which was to him like the child he must cherish, like the father he must not disgrace. He had always been scared of what was being done by the boys that had gone East, and the crash seemed to him to have confirmed all his suspicions. They talked late at nights, Sam saying over and over again, 'I tell you, Julius, you've never understood the money end of this concern. If you did, you wouldn't pan us this way, you'd know we just had to act the way we did. Everybody else was doing it. Look how we've all come down together. And I'm telling you we'll snap out of it, we'll snap out of it any day now.' After that he used to go up to his bedroom and write long letters to Lulah, saying how grand the old place looked, and how swell Julius was, but how he couldn't cotton on to things like he used to. He also started writing notes to Lily, with whom he had never before communicated except in curt telegrams telling her exactly when he wanted her to wait in for him. Once he even sent her some new photographs of the factories that Julius's daughters had taken, though he thought it pretty silly of him, because it was not likely that she would ever look at them. But to his surprise she had them on her dressing-table when he got back.

There came a time when he was out at Mount Couzens and wrote only to Lily, and telegraphed to Lulah. He had left New York knowing that what he had said all the previous year was only partly true. People might always need ore and the things that are made from ore, but they cannot always pay for them. Their sales were shrinking to nothing and the dividends would be away down this time. There would even be a question of passing a dividend altogether before very long. But he kept on saying it. 'We'll snap out of it, we'll snap out of it any time now,' but when he reached Mount Couzens he said it no longer, because Julius Geylor screamed at him in exasperation. It was he who had to order the hands to be turned off, it was he who had to drive his automobile down the streets where they all stood and looked at him, it was he who had to tell them to let out one furnace and then another, thus depriving the night of flames that to him and all the town were as familiar as the stars.

It came to Sam, sitting that night in his bedroom with his notepaper in front of him, that maybe they were not always going to have an income, or at least anything like the income to which they had been accustomed for years, and that it was not certain that anybody was going to snap out of anything. He found himself unable to write to Lulah. It had hurt him to see that lately, particularly during the last six months, she had reduced her expenditure in many ways. They had a parlourmaid now instead of a butler; the cook had to work now without a kitchen-maid; Lulah had given up her automobile. It seemed to him a sufficiently shameful deprivation of her rights that he was no longer able to buy her immense diamonds and prodigious furs every now and then. He felt disgraced by the prospect that she should suffer any more visible diminution of her dignity, and he thought with a flush of guilt that Lily cost him some thousands of dollars a year. She did not cost him as much as she had done. Some time before, quite a while back, not long after the crash, she had suggested that he should give her less, as she was going to lay off buying things. But he had no right to spend anything on her at all if it meant that Lulah had to go without.

He took his pen and wrote to Lily that things were terrible, and that in these times we had all got to be hardheaded, and put sentiment to the wall if it interfered with the real things in life, and that when he was back in New York they must talk things over. After he had stamped and closed the envelope he got up and took a long drink of Scotch, feeling as shaken as if he had just concluded an interview with some angry person. He felt sick all the way back to New York in the train, ate too much by day, and by night drank Scotch to make himself sleep. Other men had told him how hard it was to give some girls the air. They swore, they screamed, they waved guns. At any rate Lily would not try blackmail. She knew too well how things were with him.

When Sam got back to New York he let forty-eight hours pass before he went to see Lily. In the hall he found the Italian chair heaped with a man's overcoat and hat and gloves. He stood staring at them, choking, seeing fantastic pictures of Lily showing a quick and cold adaptability that was more than he had meant to demand in his letter. 'By God,' he said to himself, 'I'll show them.' He was tearing off his overcoat when the door from the living-room opened and

Lily came out, dressed in street-clothes and wearing a small round cap inclined over her left ear. In her hands she carried a pencil and a piece of paper.

'Hello, daddy!' she said, and tilted up her face for a kiss. It was cold, as if she had been walking briskly among the fall frosts in the Park. 'Oh, boy, we have been lucky.'

'Lucky?' he said. 'Lucky?'

'Listen. A young married couple, got married suddenly when their families weren't looking, and they ain't got nowhere to live, and he don't like hotels. They came into this block yesterday morning and asked the elevator man if there was somewhere they could stay. He said half the house, but they liked my bathroom. Remember, I told you that interior decorator had done a cute job on my bathroom. Well, they just could have eaten me when I told them the lease had a year to run. I'm moving out to-morrow.' On the threshold of the living-room she kissed her finger-tips and waved them to him, but held back to say, 'Sneak into my bedroom for a bit. I've a kike in here that's buying some of the things that the married couple don't want and we can't use in the noo place.'

He stood looking at the closed door. Behind it he heard her voice shrilling and harrying a deeper one, and he knew she was taking pleasure in the contest.

'God, she's got a lot of feeling,' he muttered. 'After all I've done for her . . . She doesn't care a hoot.'

He went into the living-room because he felt so miserable and lonesome that he had to have company even though it was the company that had made him feel that way. He wasn't going to sit by himself in a room. Grumpily he jerked a greeting at the Jewboy, and huddled down in an arm-chair.

'Aw, quit kidding,' said Lily. She and the Jewboy were standing side by side looking down at the largest rug.

'I ain't kidding,' said the Jewboy. 'I'm just being sensible.' There was a silence, and he added stoutly, 'You got to have sense these days.'

'I know, I got it,' replied Lily coldly. 'That's why I just stand here and laugh when you talk about three hundred dollars for the rug. A thousand dollars I paid for that rug.'

The Jewboy whistled. 'Gee, how you ladies get done,' he said. 'A thousand dollars. I wish I had been the guy who got a thousand of your dollars for that rug.' He laughed softly as if picturing an ideal existence, innocent of all but ease and luxury, but barred to him by his severer standards.

'Aw, you make me tired,' said Lily. 'Nobody ever did me over nothing. Do you think I bought that rug without walking all over town to see if it was the right price they asked me? And I got a friend in the business. I said to him, "Shall I buy this rug?" And he says, "Yes."' There was a long silence and she asked, 'Well, will you let it go?'

'Everybody's wanting to sell me things,' said the Jewboy softly. 'Nobody's wanting to buy.'

'Too bad,' said Lily. 'Give me six hundred or get out of here.'

'I couldn't do it,' he said tenderly, almost inaudibly.

'See here,' said Lily wearily. 'I got my friend here, and him and me's something to talk about. If you don't want my rugs you get out, and send round to-morrow for the other things and leave the money. I'm telling you that's the way I feel. I know you like playing around like this, but I'm different.'

'I give you five hundred dollars,' said the Jewboy.

'Done,' said Lily. She looked at the list in her hand. 'That's nine hundred and eighty dollars you owe me.'

'You wouldn't make a mistake,' said the Jewboy, and tried to catch Sam's eye so that they could laugh together.

'You'll be sending a man with the dough to-morrow at eleven,' she said, 'and he'll take the things. Now we'll all have a highball.'

She poured out the Scotch and the mineral water, and sat herself on the arm of Sam's chair. 'Here's luck,' she said.

'There ain't no luck these days,' said the Jewboy, enjoying his own luscious, racial melancholy.

She threw her head back and shrieked with laughter, digging Sam with her elbow as if to point out a joke to him. 'You'd be surprised,' she said, 'at the amount of luck there is right here in this home at this moment.'

The Jewboy swept his long lashes at her over the glass. 'I guess you'd be a lucky lady wherever you were,' he said.

'I guess she would,' said Sam, loudly and harshly. You were lucky in this world if you had no feelings, if you just went on right ahead, and didn't care for the people who had been good to you. He drummed with his clenched fist on his knees while she helped the Jewboy on with his hat and his coat, and stuck out his jaw. Well, he could take it if she wanted it that way. But he'd tell her what a tart she was.

Suddenly she was standing in the doorway, laughing like a fool, her arms way above her head so that her jacket hung loose and he could see her light sweater strained over her breasts. 'Did you hear me say there was good luck right here in this home?' she cried. 'I'll say there is, and I don't mean maybe! I never saw that rug till last night. Look, that isn't the one we've always had. I'm keeping that one for the noo place. This one I won off Jim Patterson, Nona Payne's boy friend, playing poker up at his place last night. He was lit and he gave it to me like a lamb. Gee, isn't that funny! Five hundred dollars!' She flung herself on his knee and rolled him backwards. 'Tell me that ain't a good laugh, Daddy!'

He tried to speak to her but in a flash she was up on her feet and out of the room again. 'God,' he murmured, his eyes going after her. 'She's making a game of it. It's funny to her. She don't think of me. She don't think what it means to me, to lose everything I got.' He heard, from the open door into the bedroom, sounds as if she were splashing in the bathroom beyond. 'Dolling herself up,' he thought, twitching with rage, 'dolling herself up. She don't mean to let herself go. I guess she knows where she's going when she leaves here. Well, I don't envy the other fellow. She's hard, that's what she is, hard.'

When she came to the doorway he dropped his eyes so that he would not have to see her. But she came over to him and wound her arms round his neck. 'Sore about something, Daddy?' she whispered. The soft fronds of ostrich feathers tickled his skin, he knew that she had on one of her negligées. His arms went out to her body, and she made a crooning sound, and took one of his hands, and passed it up and down her throat and over her bosom.

At last he looked at her, and smiled. She was a good kid. She couldn't help it. She had to live, like the rest of us. 'You thinking out a mighty nice way of saying good-bye to me?'

A kind of sharp and shrewish misery passed over her face. 'Daddy,' she said, 'what's this about saying good-bye?'

'I can't give my baby her sugar any longer,' he said.

She became again serene and easy. 'Guess your baby's got enough sugar to get on with,' she said. 'I hocked some of the rocks you give me. And we've the rent of the noo place right there, when the kike sends it down to-morrow morning. It don't cost very much, the noo place. It's little though it's awful cute. Time enough to worry about more dough next year.'

'Do you mean it, baby?' he asked. 'It's awful sweet of you.'

'No, it ain't,' she said. 'Hell, you always been on the level with me, I guess I owe you something now.' With her hard, slender arms she drew his head down till their lips met.

When he was ready to go, and was fixing his muffler before the mirror, he saw her reflexion stretch out its arms to the four corners of the room, and drop them by its side in melancholy relaxation. 'Gee, we been so happy here!' she sighed. 'It don't seem right that we should have to get out.'

He shook his head gravely, feeling for the monogram on his muffler, so that he could turn it to the front. 'It's the end of a civilization,' he said, 'it's the end of a civilization.'

But that was only a phrase he had read in the papers, he

did not believe it was true, particularly now that Lily had made him feel so good. As he drove home he felt sure that things would be much better by next spring. She was a good number, that Lily, and just full of sense. She wouldn't have stuck by him like this if she hadn't known it was going to be all right, and that presently he would be able to take care of her the way he used to do. Next spring he would take her out of this new dump and put her back where she belonged, maybe in a better apartment than the one she had just given up. He'd fix everything for her then.

But in spring it was quite a different removal that he was supervising. He was taking Lulah round their apartment, to satisfy her that everything had been taken out of it, before they went to the hotel where they were renting a suite till the fall, when things would be better. Though the day was cool, the sweat was running down his brow so that he had continually to be taking out his handkerchief to mop it out of his eyes. It was an agony to him to have to give up that apartment. When he saw the bare walls where the tapestry had hung, which looked dead compared to the others because the paint had not faded there as it had elsewhere since the last time it had been redecorated, he winced as he would if he had seen on his body the white patch of a leprosy. And he was scared about Lulah. She was not right. She had been swell about the whole show. The evening when he had just learned that there was not anything more that they could do and that they just had to close the place, and he was sitting around wondering how in heck he could tell her, she had suddenly clapped to the book she was reading and had said, 'Sam, I'd be easier in my mind if we got out of here.' All through the subsequent days she had not uttered one single word of complaint, but had busied herself with the practical problems of their removal, smiling placidly. But during the last day or two her smile had become unnaturally fixed. Now, as they were walking through the empty rooms in the dusk, her smile was as wide, as bright, as changeless, as if she were a wax head in a beauty parlour window. And she seemed, too, to be walking funnily, stumping along with her feet wide apart and clutching his arm, as if something had happened to her balance. Once, when he took his arm away, so that he could get hold of his handkerchief more easily, she swivelled round on her hips so that her head and chest struck the wall, just as if she were a revolving door that he had let swing.

'I know, honey, how you must be feeling,' Sam whispered, when they were waiting for the automobile on the pavement.

Lulah answered in an oddly little, brittle tone. 'It's all right. I haven't left anything up there. I wouldn't want to leave any of my things up there.'

All the six blocks between them and their hotel she sat rigidly upright and went on smiling. It was in his mind to tell her to relax, but he was afraid. When the lights were against them and other automobiles surrounded them he saw people staring in at her in wonder. In the hotel lobby he turned to her and almost cried out in protest, her grimace was glittering so strangely. But he stayed silent because her face was bluish, her lips were blue.

In their sitting-room Sam pushed Lulah into an arm-chair and went over to call their family doctor. As he said, 'I wish you'd come right over now, MacLaughlin,' she fell out of the chair like a sack of meal. He finished the call and then went to pick her up, his blood turning to water because she, who had till two days ago been the most graceful of women, had suddenly become chunky and clumsy to handle. Also, she was not conscious. Her eyes were open all the time and as he laid her on the bed she made the insane remark, ' Pa, I want to go to college. I want to go to the State University.'

At half-past eleven the hospital nurse had moved in and they told him he must go. They could not say quite what was the matter with Lulah. It seemed her heart had been in bad shape for a long time, though she had never said anything to him about it. But that did not quite account for this attack. It looked almost as if she had had some kind of stroke, though she was young for it. Maybe it was just collapse due to worry. But they could not tell him anything more that night, he had better go away and try to get some sleep.

When he got to Lily's place she had just got back from the show and was heating up some canned beans on the stove. She stared at him with eyes still blackly perverse with the night's mascara.

'You lit, honey?' she inquired.

He mumbled, 'My wife's sick,' and leaned against the dresser.

'Do you like her?' she asked. 'You ain't never said.' She stared hard at him and murmured, 'I'll say you do!'

He began to sob. She took no notice, but turned the heated beans into a dish, and took a couple of plates off the rack and an extra fork and spoon out of the drawer. 'I bet you ain't had no dinner,' she said, and led the way into the living-room.

He said, 'I couldn't eat,' but followed her.

'Sure, you can eat,' said Lily. 'We can all eat except when we're sick, and you ain't sick. It's your wife that's sick. Don't you try and steal the show. I guess if I wanted to do your wife a good turn I'd call her up right now and tell her I was a cook or something and I was giving you your dinner.'

He gulped. 'That's like her. She's always made me eat. Even these last months when I've been so worried.'

'Well, hell, you got to keep your strength. And you got a big frame, Sam. Just eat 'em up, boy. If I'd known I'd have got you a steak. But these ain't so bad.'

After a few mouthfuls he put down his fork and buried his head in his hands. 'Ah, God, she's so sick, Lily.'

'What's the trouble? Are they going to operate her?'

'No. It isn't that. It's something queer. They can't tell what it is.' He shook with sobs again.

'Maybe it's just worry, Sam. There's been an awful lot

lately to worry people who are fond of you. And you're such a kid. It's like seeing a kid getting hurt when it's playing. You bet your life she's been worrying. She'll snap out of it when things get better.'

'Lily, she don't know me.'

'I didn't know my own Momma for three days when I had the dip-theria. That don't mean nothing. She'll snap out of that.'

'But, Lily, she ain't herself. She smiles and smiles, and she says things that ain't sense, like "I want to go to college".'

'When I had the dip-theria I said I got to have a dill-pickle and a new black dress. And I was a kid and couldn't wear a black dress. And I can't eat a dill-pickle, never could, it comes back on me. I tell you, those sort of things don't mean nothing. I was as healthy as a steer in two months' time.'

Sam ate a little more, then laid down his fork again. 'Lily, you don't know what Lulah is to me. My God, she's so beautiful.' Suddenly he remembered her as she used to be when she was a young girl.

'Sure she is,' said Lily. 'I seen her picture in the books where I get my hair fixed. And she ain't just beautiful. We're all of us beautiful, but she looked very refined.'

'Oh, sure she is,' said Sam. 'There wasn't anybody we didn't have to the house before the crash came, and she didn't have to be scared of any of them.'

'That's how she looks,' said Lily.

'And she's just as lovely as she's beautiful. Oh, God, Lily, she's been good to me.'

'But, honey, that's just why I want you to eat up those beans. You don't want her to get worried about you losing your health when she's got to get well herself. Just finish what you've got on your plate.'

Later she gave him a hot milky drink and a couple of aspirins, and for the first time he spent the whole night in her apartment. In the morning she woke him early and cooked him sausages and eggs, which he ate in a bath-robe, while she brushed his suit at the open window.

'Well, I was a cheerful lover for you last night,' Sam said.

'If you'd have been cheerful I would have thought you such a louse that you don't know what I would have done to you,' Lily answered.

'I guess you're a pretty sweet person, really,' he said.

'Oh, I know what's decent,' she answered. 'I'm glad it's a sunny morning. Why don't you walk back to the hotel? And don't carry on like a kid if your wife ain't out on the front porch ready to go shopping. I guess she's worried so's she'll be sick for a bit yet. You got to be patient.'

Sam was very patient. Day after day he said to the doctor or the nurse, 'She's looking a little better to-day, don't you think?' and they said, 'Sure she is, Mr Hartley'. But all the time Lulah continued to smile. Her smile was no longer a fixed grimace, it was now the most tender conceivable record of permanent amiability. Her dear mouth was softly curved to show that she was pleased and nothing was penetrating to spoil her pleasure, day in, day out. She was firmly sealed in some mysterious state of bliss, in some private heaven. Did Sam say in her ear, 'Lulah! Lulah! How are you feeling?' there passed over her face a slow and mild convulsion of sweetness, as if, far off in her unnamed refuge, she had faintly heard a sound that recalled to her the past and its love and service. Did the doctor or the nurse say to her, 'Give me your wrist, Mrs Hartley, I want to feel your pulse,' her arm would slowly be moved, as if some frail ghost of courtesy were lifting it. But to more complicated claims on her attention she made no response. If they were persistent her smile hardened till her face seemed of some different substance than flesh. It was as if a child turned to a wax doll under one's eyes.

Only sometimes did that smile disappear. Perhaps once in every two days Lulah's lips straightened and her face lay undefended on the pillow, pale and tired. Then her lids lifted, and her eyes stared up at the ceiling. For some minutes her pupils would roll round and round, and then her head would shake. Breathing heavily, she would try to sit up. By this time Sam and the nurse would be on each side of her, and they would lift her up so that she could look round the room. But she never seemed to see what she wanted. Then she would say, 'Hush!' and listen. What she heard was only the tide of traffic, but it caused her violent distress. She jerked her head about like a frightened horse, and her lips smacked together in attempts at speech. Once she did speak. She croaked like a tired raven, 'Change for New York and all points East!' But usually she found no words, but moaned, as one who laments the spilling of the last water-skin on the desert sand, as one to whom fatigues and efforts have brought nothing but one last, supreme, and fruitless fatigue and effort.

'Has she been in any trouble?' asked the doctor, when they called him along to see her in one of these spells.

'Doctor, you know how it is on Wall Street to-day. I wouldn't tell anybody, but you've been our doctor ever since we came to New York. I'm a ruined man.'

'I would have thought she could have taken care of that. Well, move her to a room on the courtyard. Then she won't hear the traffic.'

But in that other room, quieter and darker, she still had those spells when her smile faded and her eyes opened, and there it took longer for her to remember whatever it was that made her moan. For perhaps a quarter of an hour she would swing her panting weight between Sam and the nurse till her grief was let loose, and she moaned about this curious unidentifiable loss. It took much longer than before for her to pass the crisis and lie back on the pillows, defended again by that bright, childish smile.

'Don't send her to a sanatorium, Mr Hartley. She may snap out of this any minute now.'

'I wouldn't send her to a sanatorium anyway.'

'But she can't stay here. It isn't the right atmosphere. Haven't you got a country house, Mr. Hartley?'

'I sold it three years ago.'

'That's a pity, Mr Hartley. She'd do best in her own home, with her own things about her, and two good nurses to look after her.'

'If that's what she needs she'll have it.'

Staggered at himself, at the inspiration that filled him when he heard of her need, he figured it out in his office. If he stripped himself of the last vestige of security, he could rent a house in the country and put in two nurses and two servants. He knew of the very house, one that Joe Lennox had on the Sound and did not want to sell because he had hopes that the United States would turn the corner any day now. Thank God he had not sold the furniture but had put it into storage. Even so he would have to break into his capital. His income was to nothing now.

'But she's got to have everything she wants to make her well,' he said at supper to Lily.

'Why, sure she has,' said Lily. 'And what you going to do? Commute all the time?'

'I guess so.'

'You can't do that every night. You're working too late.'

It was so. Every minority stockholder in the Mount Couzens Corporations, it seemed to him, had been tipped off by some devil to bring a nuisance suit. Dealing with those, and beating up the market and grooming the accounts in case any of this talk about inquiries came true, kept him at the office till midnight. But he had to say, 'Guess I'll have to think twice about taking even a couple of rooms and bath anywheres at all. I'll just go to a hotel the nights I have to stay, one of these two dollar down town places.'

She said sharply, 'Daddy, you can't do that. You've forgotten how to live cheap. You wouldn't like it. You can't go eating strange food and starting off in the morning on a lousy cup of coffee and toast you could sole your boots with. And they won't fix your clothes right. You better come right here when you're in New York.'

Sam muttered, 'Honey, I can't do this.'

'Why can't you?' she asked. 'I guess I can cook your breakfast as well as any cheap joint, and I can make your clothes look good, the way I've made mine look good this long time.'

He swallowed. 'It ain't right. Oh, God, Lily, I feel so ashamed not taking care of you. I haven't given you a cent for years.'

'Who wants cents?' she said, and turned the emerald ring on her finger. 'When I want dollars I'll hock this.'

'But it's all wrong,' he said, and hid his face on his forearm.

Above him he heard her speaking. 'Guess you wanted to be a great big tycoon, and have me on the end of a string as a little Scottie or something. You've got to give up, and let me do what I can for you. God, I'm proud to do it.'

He realized with a twinge of irritation that if he spent nearly every night with her she would be bound to notice that he wore false teeth. All through their life together he had tried to keep that a secret from her. But her lips fell on the nape of his neck, and he found himself saying, 'Lily, you're sweet. And don't think I don't recognize it. But it's a surprise. Back when we were together first you weren't sweet like this.'

'Boy, we had plenty of that money then,' said Lily, beginning to clear away the supper dishes. 'We hadn't got in any jam then. I'd have looked cuckoo if I'd have gone after you like a hospital nurse.'

After that Sam spent most nights with Lily. In the morning she rose from their bed so silently that she never woke him, and when she called him his bath would be nearly full, and his clothes were lying newly pressed, with his shoes like mirrors under the chair. By the time he was just ready for breakfast she had finished making the coffee and the toast and the eggs, and they were as good and hot as they could be. He felt it was no sacrifice at all not to be staying at even quite a good hotel, and he liked starting the day with her sitting in front of him. Her figure looked good in the simple, slinky gowns she always wore then; when he praised them she told him they were the negligées she used to wear in the old days, with the ostrich feather cut off. When she saw him out, lifting her lips for a kiss and saying, 'Well, you lousy bastard, here's luck till you're back here again,' he did not feel like a god, as he used to do. Once or twice he remembered that regretfully. But all the same he felt safe, and not lonesome. When he got down to the office, and there was turned one more page of this monstrous book that his business life had become, he was able to keep in his skin. He knew that he had a place to go where there was someone with sense, so that he could eat and sleep and wake up chipper. It made all the difference.

It made him able to go through with his visits to the place down on the Sound. They got him down, though he never shirked them. He always was there week-ends, and he went out in the evening once or twice a week, driving back late to Lily's place. Always when he got there he put his hand in a hornet's nest. Either the nurses were quarrelling with each other or with the servants. He had three changes of nurses, two of servants. Whatever changes he made he was appalled by the expenses of an unsupervised household. He looked at the books and felt the heavy figures like lead in his stomach. There would be a time when he would have no more money left, and it could not be very far ahead. When that realization came home to him he used to switch off thinking and stare out through the mosquito screens at the Sound. But he did not do that for long. He had never set eyes on the sea till he was a middle-aged man, and he had never come to like it. It seemed to him a spoiled version of the element that he had loved in the clear mountain lakes, fated here to be dirty and unconfined and violent. Quite soon, he used to go upstairs to the room where Lulah lay.

Even, now, or perhaps now more than ever, Sam was transported by her goodness. It had not been merely the sum of what she said and did, for now that she was silent and motionless it existed with the same sweet, unforced force as ever. When he went in and saw her lying quite still, with closed lids and unchanging smile, he knew that he was looking at a supremely good woman, just as certainly as he would have known, had there been a branch of may lying in her place on the bed, that he was looking at fragrant blossom. He always went to her ear and called to her softly, 'Lulah! Lulah! It's your Sam wanting you,' but she never answered. She heard. That he knew because her smile became more entrancing, more beneficent. But though he took her hand it did not turn over in his and lie palm upwards, in her giving gesture, and her breathing was so regular that it was as if she were saying, 'I know you are there but I will not come back, I know you are there but I will not come back.' He got up, and went over to an arm-chair, and sat with his head in his hands and looked at her. The sheets rose and fell with her indifferent breath. Lulah was living, and her dear heart was beating in her, but she was as far away from him as though she were dead. Sometimes the tears ran down his face.

It disconcerted Sam when she had one of her spells when she stopped smiling and sat up, because they now took a form which, though it caused her less distress, marked her more definitely as not being right. Her smile would fade, her face would lie on the pillow pale and exhausted. But when her eyes opened they were glinting with purpose, and she croaked joyously, avidly, 'Book. Book. School-book.' They had learned that she meant exactly what she said. They propped her up on cushions and put before her on a sloping bed-desk a school-book, any school-book, open anywhere, and she lay for hours staring at the print, though she never tried to turn the page. Then her eyes would shut, her chin would fall forward on her breast, she would utter a moan of complaint which would, however, last only a moment. As soon as they had taken away the cushions and she was back on the pillow she would reassume her smile, as she might have drawn a coverlet over herself for warmth or decency. After these spells he felt weak, as if he had had to watch some public humiliation inflicted on her.

Yet as the months went by, he had to own that he felt an almost acuter misery when he sat beside her in her quieter hours, so long that the edge wore off his wonder that she should be so. For then something about her appearance seemed to make nonsense of their whole life together. She was there on the bed, indifferent to his love, his sorrow; and when her skin had been lined and worn, her hair grey and lifeless in the grooves of her marcel, her smile a fixed grimace, this desertion was tolerable, because it could so easily be seen that she was old and had had a mental collapse. But now there was nothing at all strained about her smile, it was as easy and natural as when she had stood beside him welcoming guests to their house. So exactly was it the expression which had been hers on social occasions that his memory of what till then had seemed their dearest common triumphs became confused and marred. He found himself thinking that at their dinners he had sat at the head of his table facing an automation, that he had mounted the stairs of great houses with a dead woman at his side. And he could no longer comfort himself by saying that this smiling stranger was quite different from the girl that he had married, for now in appearance she was nearly the same. She had recovered, with only the faintest difference, the famous complexion of her youth; and about her brows and on her bosom her hair fell in soft curls, so glossy that it was as if it had turned not grey, but ashen blonde. There was no longer any deep furrow between her brows. She might have been the schoolgirl he had courted back in Butte; and because of that he passed through twilight nightmare states when it seemed to him that the schoolgirl he had courted in Butte had always been cold and careless as a ghost in his arms, had breathed like a deep sleeper when he bent over her for comfort, had let her hand hang in his grip.

It was no wonder that sometimes Sam left her when he need not, and went down to sit by the log-fire in the living-room. But there one or other of the nurses would get hold of him, to complain of the misdemeanours of the servants, or the lonesomeness of the house. Some of them tried to flirt with him, one avidly. He thought austerely of Lulah and Lily, and built a screen of silence between them. He tried walking up and down the garden outside, but threats of trouble seemed to come out of the woods, and there was the hateful sea. Often he would look up at the soft radiance in Lulah's window and long to throw up a handful of gravel against the glass and call to her to come down; but he could imagine what the nurses would make of that. Nevertheless he felt a strong impulse to do it; and shuddered to find himself feeling it, as if he were swimming and found himself in the grip of the rapids above a fall. He would go in again and sit by the log-fire while the nurse jabbered about the way the owls sounded in the woods at night and the refusal of the cook to serve her favourite cereal, waiting till it was time to drive home to Lily's place. It was no use starting too early in case she was not back from the show.

Presently, however, Sam did not have to keep that consideration in mind. One morning at breakfast, during the early fall, she had picked up a stud of his and, remarking that its centre-stone was loose, had said she would take it to the jewellers in the course of the morning. It struck him that always before at that season of the year she had been busy with rehearsals, and he asked, 'When are you getting ready for the new show?'

Suddenly stiff-lipped, she said, 'What new show?'

'Why at Leitner's, I guess,' answered Sam. 'You've always been with Al, haven't you?'

'I ain't going to be with Al any more,' said Lily, in a level voice. 'He's given me the air.'

'Jesus, what's he done that for? Did he get mad with you over something?'

'I guess not,' said Lily. 'He was swell to me, and his wife asked me up to their place, which they don't ever do to the girls, only the principals. But they didn't want me around any more. And I guess they was right. No other manager seems to want me around either. They can get battleships full of kids of nineteen and twenty. What'd they want with me any more?'

'They're clean crazy,' said Sam; but looking at her he saw that that mysterious thing which happens only to women had happened to her under his eyes, without him noticing it. She was growing old. The process had just begun, but she was no longer bloomy and luscious. No doubt her presence in a chorus would make a manager feel like a hostess who sees in her rooms just one vase of flowers which, though far from actually faded, are not absolutely fresh. However he stuck to it gallantly. 'You look just a kid.'

Lily shook her head. 'You needn't have such fancy manners,' she said. 'I'm old and I know it. I told you a lie that first time you came up to my apartment. I wasn't nineteen. I was twenty-two. And we've been together nine years. I'm thirty-one, daddy. It's old for my business.'

'Oh, can that line of talk. You're young and you're beautiful,' he said. But he looked at her curiously. 'Maybe you're letting yourself go a bit,' he said. 'Your hair don't shine the way it used to. Maybe you don't brush it enough.'

'Brush it your foot,' she said, laughing. 'It was a Wop called Giulio on Madison Avenue used to make it shine that way.'

'Why don't he do it any more?'

'I haven't been to him for eighteen months,' said Lily.

'Well, why not?' asked Sam, spooning up the sugar from the bottom of his cup. Lily said nothing, but sat there smiling and turning the emerald ring on her finger. 'Guess it's time I was going down town,' he said, getting up. 'Well, good-bye, sweetness. And you take a hold of yourself. There's no sense in letting things slide.'

So his life swung between three existences; the office, Lily's apartment, and the house on the Sound. He succeeded in schooling himself to find this life endurable. He put away from himself the thought that in a year or two he must run out of money. After all, as Jim Leavensoe still said with unabated conviction, the country might snap out of this depression any minute now. The work in the office, once he had conquered his panic at its completely unprofitable nature, satisfied in part the side of him which had always been happy. He liked trampling down the nuisance suits, ripping out the tripes of criticism, dramatizing himself as the Westerner who brought his own pure reserves to settle the petty conflicts of the East. He began to inquire as never before into the intricacies of his own corporations, and though he never felt himself complete master of the complicated history he stood by as much as he grasped and spoke defiantly in its defence. It was his job to keep on boosting Mount Couzens till the world came right, and he got on with the job. When he got back to Lily's place it was all fine, a man could rest. And down in the house on the Sound he received sometimes, if he had kept his nerves good, if he obeyed Lily and did not get too tired, such revelations of the dear power of Lulah's being that he went back to New York a transfigured man. When he went into the twilit bedroom it was as if there had been a garden of roses blooming there.

But in these days man has only to find his balance for someone to get after him and knock him off his perch. He was getting to think that he could carry on indefinitely when there suddenly ran through the country talk of inquiries. For a time he congratulated himself grimly because, never having got near the goal he had set himself, he was not sufficiently important to be worth powder and shot. 'Well,' he said to Jim over a highball one day, 'here's to our good luck in not being any of those god damn Wall Street tycoons that used to treat us like mud off the bottom of the Hudson River.' Jim waved a glass back to it. 'Yeah, I'd rather be safe the way we are,' he said. But some months afterwards they knew that they were going to have it the worst of both ways. They had not been first-class men, but they were going to be harried as if they were. Someone influential had evidently been ruined by Mount Couzens stock or someone influential and full of intellectual curiosity had noticed that lots of people had been ruined that way, and wanted to know how the crank machine had worked. 'These damned Radicals! These college professors! These Communists!' he cried, and turned to Jim Leavensoe. 'But they can't do a thing to us. Can they, Jim? We've always been well inside the law, haven't we, Jim?' Jim answered, 'Sure we have,' but his eyes went obliquely past Sam, to the window. Some days passed, and there came out in a morning paper an article prophesying what special questions were going to be asked of the promotors of the Mount Couzens Corporations. At about eleven Jim called up to say that he was sick and would not be down to the office that day. 'Jim, you aren't worried?' asked Sam down the telephone. 'I know we've sailed as close to the wind as we can, but we're on the right side, aren't we?' 'Sure, we're on the right side.' 'But you sound worried, Jim.' 'I ain't worried, I tell you, I'm sick. No, I don't want my secretary.' His telephone answered no more that day. They thought that perhaps he had gone out to his country place. But late that evening his hotel called up Sam and asked him to come down, because there had been an accident.

He kept cool when he was talking to the people over there. He kept cool all the way to Lily's place, right up to the very last moment when he got out of the elevator.

But when he saw Lily sitting there he began to cry and wrestle with his own breath as if it were a deadly enemy.

'Daddy, daddy, what's the matter?'

'Jim – Jim Leavensoe.'

'Daddy, daddy, don't carry on so – relax – see, come close to baby . . .'

'Jim – he went through the window . . .'

'Jesus, what window?'

'Twenty-first floor of his hotel – oh, Jim, Jim.'

She stood up and he sobbed at her feet, drying his eyes on her skirt. She said coldly, 'Well, he was a souse and he had too many women. I guess he got what was coming to him.'

'You bitch,' gulped Sam, 'he was my friend for thirty years.'

'You knew him for thirty years and you miss him like you do a tooth that's been pulled out. That's all.'

Sam said, 'You're hard, you're hard,' and sobbed for a while. Then he said, 'Jim wouldn't have gone through that window for nothing, Lily. I guess you and me had better take something that'll put us to sleep.'

As if she had been waiting for this she bent down and shook him with her lean hard arms. 'I thought you'd say that!' she said through her teeth. 'Get up.'

'I'm through, Lily. I'm through. We'd better take something.'

'Not yet,' she said. 'Not yet. Get up, I tell you.'

'Lily,' he said, stumbling to his feet. 'I'm too tired. I can't face any more.' He sank on to the sofa. 'Some of that stuff you got in the bathroom will do the trick. I tell you I won't go to prison. I can't face it. We'd better do it right now.'

She began to punch him all over his body with her clenched fists.

'Oh, God, lay off,' he said, sitting up. 'You're acting crazy.'

'Do you know what you've got to do?' she asked, and

227

put the telephone into his hand. 'You've got to call up Julius Geylor and tell him about this. I guess he's the best of you all.'

He put in the call and looked up in wonder at her. 'He won't be able to do anything to help us. He doesn't know anything about this end of it.'

'Maybe you can do something to help him,' she said. 'I guess there'll be a panic when the news gets there in the morning. This Geylor guy will be real pleased if you tip him off what to do.'

'I'd be pleased to do it. We were all three young to-gether, Lily, Jim and me and this fellow Geylor you haven't ever seen. I guess he'll be all shot to pieces the way I was. Oh, hello, there! Hello!'

There came some days later the summons to the feared inquiry in Washington. He received it without excitement. 'After all, it isn't as if I were a principal,' he said to Lily. He was merely a witness called in connexion with the examination of the partners in the private banking-house Bercy & Higginbotham, which had handled the Mount Couzens issues. He just had to go on the stand. 'Sure, that's all it is,' agreed Lily. It meant a good deal of work, he had constantly to be conferring with his bankers and their lawyers, he had to go over the history of the Mount Couzens operations again and again, he was coached for hours in the answers he was to make on the stand. All this he found not disagreeable. For one thing, it ate up his energy so that he got tired out and slept at night. For another, it meant that for long people who had disregarded him or treated him as a nuisance had to be brotherly again because he was part of their defence; and half of him believed like a kid all the civil things they said, and was pleased, and the other half took a cynical pleasure in noting their insincerity, and felt that it was not worth while bothering if such bastards turned their backs on one for a bit.

Sam only wished that the business took up more of his time. For when his attention was free, and he could sit back and look round, he was struck by something ominous in the atmosphere. The pace of everything and everybody seemed to be getting slower and slower, as if life were a top that was running down. When his stenographer came into the room it seemed to him that she was taking longer to cross the carpet between the door and her chair than she had ever done, and that her pencil dawdled over the paper. She might have been saying to herself, 'He's been doing less and less business lately. Presently he won't be doing any at all.' Even the elevator man, he thought, turned on him a leisurely curious glance when he came to his floor, and opened the gates for him without haste. It was the same, he believed he noticed, when he was at the house on the Sound. The day before he had to give evidence in Washington he drove down there to say good-bye to Lulah, and as he had always done, sounded his horn when he came to the fence which divided his garden from the woods, so that his butler could come out and open the gate for him. The man had never walked down the path so slowly before. It seemed to him that the lunch he ate before he ventured to go upstairs had been perfunctorily prepared, by a cook who was wondering where she would go next when the household came to an end, and that the nurses were watching him as they might have watched a patient whose sudden collapse might happen any time now. He ran his finger along the groove of the banisters and brought it up black and velvety with dust; and he knew that if he cared to scrutinize the house he would find innumerable such indications that it was being prematurely handed over to neglect by guardians who could do nothing else, so impressed were they by their knowledge that before long it must be empty and for rent.

One of the nurses had gone ahead of him to prepare Lulah for his visit, and as he entered he saw this woman straightening his wife's arm and putting it outside the coverlet with a movement which, though it was not actually cruel or even rough, was abrupt and without tenderness.

When he got to her bedside he turned on the lamp on her table and moved it so that the light searched her face. She was no longer being properly cared for. There was a faint film of dirt under her jaw and inside her ear, which was not in the least repulsive because she seemed now to be made of some impervious substance like porcelain, and it merely lay on the surface, but which was unmistakable evidence of the lack of proper care. He lifted her hand, examined it closely, and saw that it had not been manicured for several weeks. Laying it down, he went and stared out of the window. The sight of Lulah caused him no emotion whatsoever, he had hardly remarked whether she was smiling or not. He saw her now only as presenting a problem which had to be solved by action. If anything happened to him there would be a substantial block of insurance coming for Lulah. Though it had cost him his heart's blood he had kept up the premiums. He believed that of three cousins with whom Lulah had kept up a correspondence, who had come to visit them in New York, there was one whom she trusted and loved more than the others, but he could not now remember which it was. Possibly he could find some indication in the letters that they had written inquiring after her health. Those were lying around at Lily's place. He went out of the room and drove back to New York.

Lily was out shopping when he got back, for she had not expected him home so early. When she came in with the squab and the asparagus for the dinner she was going to cook him before he went off to the station, he was sitting at the desk with the letters from Lulah's cousins before him. He had not got to them at once because one of the incessant calls from Washington had been put through to him. He was frowning for no other reason than that he could find in them no indication of which cousin Lulah had preferred, and her admission of preference had been so gentle, in its desire not to make any direct aspersion of the other two, that it had escaped his memory. It was perplexity, not depression, that was troubling him for the moment. But Lily could not know that, so she put down her marketing bag on the table and bent over him, lifting his fingers to her lips with one hand and stroking his cheek with the other. It pleased him, and it pleased him too when she said, 'Well, I got to get that squab in the oven or I guess you'll beat me up.' She was a good kid, she was always on the job. It came into his mind that if ever he had to do it she would take care of the whole thing. They would drink Scotch together first, a lot of Scotch. Then she would pour the stuff into two glasses and hold his to his lips till it was finished. Then she would drink her own, neatly and quickly, and be ready to draw his head down to her bosom, so that he could close his eyes and not see the blackness coming down. Once he realized that she would hold that door open for him and close it gently after him there no longer seemed such urgency to go through it. Since he could go through it any time, there was no hurry. They ate their dinner in good spirits, and they drank some peach brandy he had once got down in New Mexico, with her sitting on his knee. In the taxi going to the station he told her several times he was glad to get this thing over, and she agreed with him it was far better. When the train pulled out he saw that she had instantly turned about and was walking away as fast as she could, her hard, sharp, wasted profile drawing an arrow-line of flight in contrary course to the train.

One of the lawyers and his secretary came to meet him at the train. They said, 'You're going to be called to-day after all,' and he realized that they were pleased at that. They had not wanted him hanging round for days with plenty of chances to talk, because they distrusted him. To them he was only Jim Leavensoe's dupe, or it might be ally. He said, 'Well, thank God, you've got no reporters round here to worry me,' and the lawyer gave a little laugh and said, 'Guess somebody tipped them off you were coming by air, and they're all down on the ground.' In this he saw confirmation of what he suspected and he walked grimly beside them to the automobile. 'Geylor's been here since last Thursday', they said; and he realized that they had trusted Geylor. This would once have wounded him and angered him, but now it did not seem to matter. At the hotel he found Geylor greyly having breakfast, and for a minute he felt ashamed, as if he had consciously betrayed this man. But there was a smile in Geylor's tired but clear eyes, and he said, 'Well, Sam, I guess we got to see this thing through together.' At that they both fell silent, for they were both thinking of Jim, who had shown himself a quitter. The sense of him filled the room. It seemed to be happening again somewhere that Jim's great body, which had held so much liquor, bestraddled so many horses, pleased so many women, was sliding down and down through the darkness alongside the high lighted tower and pounding down on the pavement in a last reckless trial of strength. There was something about Jim which Lily could not understand. Geylor and Sam began to talk quietly about Lulah and Hetty Geylor, and ate their eggs. Then the lawyer came to tell him that he must go down to the inquiry right then.

In the automobile they kept on reminding him what he had got to say, and handed him a sheet on which there was typewritten the main points he was to aim at bringing out in his evidence. Because of the weeks of schooling he had had from them since Jim's death, this recapitulation afflicted him with an unendurable sense of staleness and stuffiness. He grunted repeatedly, 'Yeah, yeah', but he heard nothing, and he was glad to get out of the automobile, even though it meant that there ran at him a mob of people with cameras and note-books. For a minute he flinched, it was in his mind to say, 'Leave me alone. I'm through, I'm sunk, I'm old and sick, and my wife's had a stroke, and my best friend threw himself out of a twenty-first floor window.' But thinking of Jim he remembered how his friend had always liked being photographed, and used to meet those fellows' cameras with his head thrown back and a great roaring Western laugh on his face, and his hat swinging from his genial hand. He reached for his friend's manner as if he were drowning and it were a spar. As he assumed it he knew that he was making a different effect, and it struck him that Jim's expression must look grotesque on a face that had seen so much of horror as he had done lately. But as he thought that the mob, which had been standing away from him, surged closer and someone plucked at his sleeve. It was always like that, if one let oneself doubt they knew it somehow and got one down. He threw back his head, thrust out his arms and roared, 'No, I can't talk now! Listen to me when I get on the stand! Then you'll have all the news-story you want!' Smiling, he blustered them out of his way.

They took Sam into a room where there were only a few people, some of whom he knew. They talked to him and shook hands, but he felt as if he were in a hospital waiting to have an operation. The air seemed glassy and etherized. They kept on saying, 'Mr Bercy's nearly finished his testimony now', or 'They've nearly done with Mr Bercy. Are you ready?' and at last he found himself on the stand. Most of the people in the room he did not know, but some he did, and some he knew by sight. There was a youngish-looking man with spectacles, and a dinted chin and only a sparseness of mouse-coloured hair on the temples to show that he was not so young; from the unusual depth of the dint, which was indeed the only remarkable feature of his appearance, Sam remembered that this was Raymond Blunden. Sam straightened himself up. Raymond Blunden was the same sort of man as himself, who had come from the West and started on a shoestring and had always been treated like a dog by the tycoons on Wall Street; but he had had all the breaks and he had got away with it. Sam was not going to be made a monkey of in front of him. Anger stuffed him so that his first few answers were hardly audible. But after that it was as if Jim Leavensoe had left his magnificence above ground, as a Cardinal leaves his hat on his tomb, and Sam had put out his hand and taken it for himself. His voice grew deeper and more resonant, his charm warmed the questioners and then the audience. He told the story of the three young men riding out thirty years before to see a mountain, and he gave the ride the quality of a heroic deed, committed in desert air, idyllically clean. He unfolded a map of a far landscape, romantic to contemplate because it was doubly distant, lying away off in a departed youth, and in a West that was to most of his hearers either unvisited or remotely and sentimentally remembered. He felt so free in the atmosphere of large simplicity which he had created that he permitted himself little jokes, and even, later on, humility. He owned that maybe when Jim Leavensoe and he had come East they had not been so smart as they thought they were; and his eyes crinkled so humorously at the corners that no white man could take advantage of the admission. But they crinkled even more humorously when he talked of the decline in his fortunes since the crash, so that it seemed as if they were examining a man who was making a good lone fight against adversity, rather than one who had lost a whole lot of people all their money. When the luncheon interval came he stood about smiling shyly, like a cowboy who does not know what to do in the big city, though it was twenty-five years since he had lived farther West than Omaha.

They took him to eat in a room in an hotel, and they kept on saying to him, 'That was fine, Sam Hartley. You keep on going that way, and it'll be all grand. But you've got to keep your head now. You'll have Bill Knoop and Leon Levita and Lloyd Carthen heading for you now.' He was Jim now, he was eating a great meal as Jim used to do, he said just as Jim would have done, 'I guess I can fix those guys', and rocked with Jim's deep laughter. Over their cigars they rehearsed him again in certain answers, certain figures. Suddenly he pushed his chair back from the table and grumbled that they were not to worry him, that they

234

had been at him till he was completely blah. It seemed to him that his mind presented a surface like the cloth on the table, so conspicuous in its whiteness that everyone must see it coarsely shining and blank except for stains that spoke of careless use rather than design. But out in the street and in the office building, where people were looking at him, he became Jim again. While Bill Knoop, with his lantern jaws and the pockets under his eyes and his air of being pickled from within by his own bile, began to question him in the rasp of an itinerant preacher, he became mild and conciliating. He conveyed that he was in full sympathy with the people behind Bill Knoop, the simple Middle Western farmers who could not see why Easterners should get these vast sums, so much vaster than ever came into the possession of honest folks, and then spend it all on foolishness. Of course the whole game was crazy. But he and Jim and Julius had had a property to develop, and the sharks in Wall Street had fixed it so that the only way one could develop a property on a nation-wide scale was by going to New York, and once they were there they just had to sign on the dotted line. They could not stand out for the real, simple, honest American standards. The current of New York affairs was too strong for them. Some of the figures with which he had been primed during the last few hours and days came back into his mind, selected and marshalled by some genius within himself with whom he had till then been unacquainted. They enabled him to prove, with a rugged provincial innocence which Bill Knoop did not dare fight lest it seem to his supporters he was turning against their old platform, that the Mount Couzens Corporations had initiated nothing, had merely followed financial fashion.

It was not so easy with Leon Levita. He was a Wop, and maybe a kike too, if a man can be both. He was a stocky little fellow with a huge head growing sheer out of his broad shoulders, his fat face yellow like the fat on cold meat but hard as marble. He stood sideways to the audience and

opened his mouth, but for quite a bit nothing came out of
it. He just stood there as if he had been stuffed, with this
funny great hole in his face. Then suddenly there rolled
out a big, luscious lilting voice, as different from other
voices as a cinema organ is from a farm harmonium. It
seemed to have no connexion with him, it didn't shake his
chins, his black eyes kept their fixed frowning stare, there
might have been a radio turned on inside him. The sound
was grand, it was like being at the opera. Listening to him
one noticed that some things were handsome about him,
that his eyes shone, that he had good strong blue-black
hair, that he had a fine bridge to his nose and curling
nostrils, and there was a romantic drama played out in his
questions, in which he battled against malign oppressions
for the people's sake. It was no good trying to out-Wop a
Wop. All one could do was to show them up as cheap and
un-American. Sam answered his questions slowly but
crisply, and crinkled his eyes at the corners more grimly
and humorously than ever. The unfamiliar genius in him
brought out figures which proved that men of Levita's
own party had done just what his great voice was thunder-
ously denouncing in the conduct of the Mount Couzens
Corporation. In a second Sam had joined the ranks of the
cynics who had come chuckling to see the gambling
financier roasted and had dizzied them by proving that he
was really one of themselves, since here he was roasting a
figure that made them chuckle just as loud as the gambling
financier, the demagogue that fooled the people. He had
the whole room tittering by the time Levita thought he had
had enough.

It was only necessary that Lloyd Carthen should ask
two or three questions for Sam to know that that run of
luck was over. His feet and hands rapidly growing cold,
he sat with his head down, listening, figuring out what sort
of man this was; and he realized that he was sunk unless he
could think of another good line. This man was poison.
Sam had heard he had been a college professor, and he had

an air of being unfairly smart, of having stayed indoors
and read books and got the low-down on things while
decent male men would have felt an urge to go into the
open and do real jobs and be sports. He had a nondescript
but not unhandsome face, and a good upstanding body, so
that it was not easy to make a case against him. One could
not even say that he was a weakling. And he was smart, he
was smart as hell. Sam looked up and answered with
amiable candour, but his bowels were like water within
him, for he could see where the bastard's questions were
leading. 'And what was your purpose, Mr Hartley, in
forming that new corporation?' For a minute Sam's
mouth widened, and he thought of answering in Jim
Leavensoe's voice. But he saw that this man cared nothing
for magnificence. There was something else he cared
about, but it had nothing to do with Sam. While he was
answering the question in pleasant, non-committal tones,
naming the new business that they had thought that
corporation could exploit, he realized that if by magic he
could have shown this man the most gorgeous moment in the
destinies of Jim and himself, he would have been totally
unimpressed. He would not have batted an eyelid at the
apartment on Park Avenue, at the tapestry with the strange
beasts passing through the thickets, and the little white
dog lying on the ermine hem of the woman's gown, at
the painted Italian furniture. He would not have liked
the parties they had given, it would not have interested
him how much liquor Sam and Jim could drink, and how
well they played squash rackets, or what jewels they gave
their women. This man might not even have liked Lulah,
though he remembered uncomfortably she had sometimes taken a fancy to men of this type and had had them
up at the house. He would have treated Lily like dirt.
Sam answered evenly, 'No, I didn't think the overlap-
ping would be serious,' and smiled at Mr Carthen but
what he wanted to say was, 'You poor white-faced
louse of a college professor, you wouldn't know what

to do if you got among decent people, you wouldn't know what to do if you found yourself in bed with a woman.'

The unfamiliar genius in him folded its hands and was silent. It could not defend him because there was no defence. The questions came like a very slow form of machine-gun fire, and he was tied up and had to take it. Flashing a look round to spy whether other people knew as well as he did that this skunk had got him down, he saw that Bill Knoop and Levita were all ready to have another crack at him. They would have caught the idea from this devil that the way to settle him was with cold facts; and whether it was Knoop or Levita or Carthen who used that trick he had no comeback. The facts were against him. 'But what purpose could there be in all this pyramiding of companies except the gross inflation of the value of your stocks?' Sam felt cold, sliding death in his bowels. He answered, 'Well, considering how business was expanding in those days, I thought we could carry any figure,' but he knew he had stowed off ruin only for this moment, that in a minute this cold creature, consumed by passions as different from his as if he had been born on a different planet, would bring forward facts that would show this hope as the fatuous pretence of a dishonest fool. He thought again, 'But this fool wouldn't know what to do if he was in bed with a woman.' It came to him that he wanted to do something as big and simple and primitive as what a man does when he is in bed with a woman, he wanted to shake his body at all these people and break the world round him and start fresh. He forgot to listen to what the college professor was saying to him, he found himself out of his chair and standing up with his fists clenched over his head. Everybody in the room was looking at him, there were lots of mouths open and nothing coming out. For a second he paused, wondering if a great common cry was coming out of these open mouths, the way Levita's voice had come out of the hole in his face.

Then he found the moment turning sour, he was losing them, in no time they would be sweeping in on him.

He let out a great wordless roar. They wavered. It was as if invisible hands were striking them in the face. He held the moment, and then roared again. 'God damn it,' he shouted, 'you say I took risks. Of course I took risks. I found a great property in my native state. Better men might have found it, but it was me that did find it. And I knew America was a great new country and needed to develop all her resources. So I did the developing, and of course I took risks. That went on for thirty years, and nobody said I was doing anything wrong. Then the crash came, and I was stripped of everything, my wife had a stroke, and my best friend killed himself. And now you get into a snarl under my feet saying I took risks. Of course I did. And so did all the men who made America what it is to-day. We weren't the sort that plays safe.' His voice roared up through the depths of his body. 'You can put me through this third degree till we're all deaf and dumb and blind and old. You won't find out more than I own. I am an American and I took risks.' He faced Lloyd Carthen who had dropped his papers, who was looking white. Sam knew it was all right, he had found the line Carthen could not answer. Switching round to the on-lookers, he shouted, 'I'm through, I'm going now. You can send after me, you can indict me, you can send me to prison. But you can't break my spirit. You'll never stop me being proud to say I'm an American, and I took risks.' He put his head down and charged his way out of the room. He moved through a silence, and it was not until he was out on the street that the hubbub caught him up. People caught him by the arm, but he shook them off without looking to see if they were friends or enemies. He jumped into a taxi-cab and told the driver to go to the station, and his fist found the two fellows that jumped on the running-board, one just under the chin, the other on the ear.

Lily had not expected Sam till the next day, or later, but she showed no surprise when he came in at the door that night. She asked him nothing, it was only for his own relief that he said, 'I quit, Lily. I wasn't going to stand up there and have them all make a monkey of me.'

'You're right,' she said. 'Let 'em eat cake. Baby, shall we go out and have a bite to eat at the dance-place round the corner? I got nothing ready cooked in the ice-box. I was going to make me a cup of cawfee and go to bed.'

'I guess that would do me too,' he said, 'just a cup of cawfee.'

'No, no,' she said, 'that ain't right with your big frame.' She put up her hand to his chest and touched his body as if it were a third party, to which they ought to be reverent, which was only a visitor in their home. 'I guess we'll go round to the Alcazar.'

'Your own way, honey,' he said.

It was a cheap place, but it was good. They both had corn-beef hash and apple pie à la mode; he had noticed for some time past that they always ate the same things when they went out to a restaurant, just as Lulah and he had always done. The noise of the nigger dance band soothed them, and they sat on after they had finished their meal, and watched the girls and young fellows dancing.

'Funny thing,' said Lily. 'I didn't see you put your bag down when you came in.'

'I didn't bring it back,' said Sam. 'It's at the hotel at Washington where I breakfasted with Geylor. I went straight from the office building to the train.'

She seemed disconcerted, and drearily Sam realized that his circumstances were so changed that the replacement of dressing-gown and pyjamas and toilet articles now seemed a crushing addition to the wrong side of their budget. She made as if she were going to spin the emerald ring on her finger, but it had been gone for some time, though neither of them had mentioned it. She said, 'Oh, I guess they'll send it after you'.

He said, 'I guess it doesn't matter much if they don't.'

She said, 'What's that?'

He repeated, 'I guess it doesn't matter much if they don't.'

They sat for a little longer watching the dancers, and pointing out to one another some among them who were especially young and comely, with a kind of tender excitement, as if these boys and girls had been cast to enact a dangerous drama. Then Lily said, 'We got to cross that floor to get out. Dance me across, daddy'. They were clumsy on their feet, it was so long since either of them had danced, but they went twice round the floor, her head down on his chest as if she were a little drunk.

In bed that night Sam lay awake hour after hour, but not tossing or craving for sleep. He lay stretched out in a diamond-bright, diamond-hard state of consciousness, his mind working brilliantly, his memory recovering useful details that had long been lost. One was so useful that he exclaimed in satisfaction, and at that Lily asked, 'What you got, daddy?' She was as wide awake as he was. Then, suddenly as tropical night, without any intervening period of drowsiness, sleep fell on him. He was not vexed even by dreams until it was full morning.

At breakfast Sam looked round the room and said, 'Seems you've been giving the place an extra spring clean.'

'Yes, I felt like it,' said Lily.

'I'm going down to the office right away,' he said. 'I remembered something last night that's important. It was when I called out and you asked me what it was. You know I got scared about Lulah day before yesterday when I went down to see her. She didn't look to me as if those nurses were keeping her right.'

'God, the lousy bitches!' exclaimed Lily. 'What they been doing to her?'

'Oh, I don't mean they're being cruel to her,' said Sam, 'but she wasn't dainty. Her hands weren't right, and there was dirt on her neck.'

'Well, of all the filthy tricks!' said Lily. 'Those great trollops all day in that house with nothing else to do! Would you think a person could act that way?'

'I suppose it's just human nature, really,' said Sam. 'There's nobody there to see how they act. Now, she's got three cousins, Ina and Louie and Gert. They're all married out West, and Lulah thought one of them was a pretty grand person. If anything happens to me there's enough insurance to take care of Lulah, and I thought of fixing it up so that one of these three women would take care of her. But I can't remember which it was she specially liked.'

'Haven't you got any letters that would show?' asked Lily.

'I've been over all I've got, but there isn't a thing. Then last night it came back to me I'd got something in the safe down at the office, a paper Lulah wrote saying who was to have what for keepsakes if anything happened to her. I guess that'll tell us. She'll have left that ruby ring she wore all the time, the first swell thing I ever gave her, to the one she really liked.'

'I guess you're right,' said Lily. When he was ready to go she put her arms round him. 'You'll come back here, daddy, won't you?'

'Sure I'll come back, honey,' he said.

When Sam got to his office it seemed stranger than ever to him. The staff all looked at him with surprise; and, until he figured out that they must be looking at him that way because they had not expected him back from Washington for a few days, he suspected that they were surprised because he was not already dead. But he guessed they were not really supposing anything at all. If the pace of the office was slowing down it was only because these people knew that some day its affairs were bound to collapse and they would be out on the streets looking for jobs which would not be there. They had been so brought up to have faith in his kind of man that they probably believed him to have made ample provision against disaster.

He might once have taken this as cruel and unfeeling, but it now seemed to him like the innocent unawareness of dogs, who chase and play round the yard even if their master is lying dead upstairs. When he called in his stenographer to bid her take out his private papers from the safe, he saw her sharp ageing neatness with a new eye. That she was wearing a sprig of an old-fashioned flower such as one cannot buy from a florist, seemed to him a hint that opened vistas of speculation about her character, her circumstances. When she told him that it had been brought to her by her married sister, who had come up for two days' shopping from her home in New Hampshire, and faintly smiled and frowned as she said it, as if there were some story behind these facts which was from one aspect warming and amusing, and from another perplexing and embarrassing, he fell into a reverie. He wondered if many lives, if perhaps most lives, led to ends so bizarre as his house over in Connecticut, beside that hateful sea, full of those hateful nurses and servants; where his wife lay smiling, who had died before him, who was to live on after him. So deep was his absorption in this wonder that the stenographer had to ask him twice whether he wished her to call Mr Raymond Blunden for him.

'What's that? What for?' Sam asked, when the strange question had penetrated.

Mr Raymond Blunden had, it appeared, been on the line twice, asking Mr Hartley to call him back at the first possible moment. It was written down on the block before him.

'What, already?' said Sam, stupidly. But the stenographer smiled at the bars of noonday sunlight on the floor, and he realized that he had slept like a tired dog, and came to his office three or four hours after his habit. He had not looked at his watch. Of late time had grown to seem more and more unimportant to him.

This was one of the most mysterious things that had happened to him, even since the world had gone hay-wire. He could not imagine why Raymond Blunden should want to speak to him. It would be something fantastically crazy and unimportant. Maybe Blunden had been staying at the same hotel, and Geylor or one of the lawyers had asked him to take Sam's bag back to New York. But it could not be that. No one would use Blunden as a porter. 'You'd better get him for me,' he said to the stenographer; and presently there bored into his ear the quiet gimlet of Blunden's voice. He spoke with an Iowan accent that had been transplanted to Los Angeles, a flat accent that it was not easy to read, but it seemed to Sam that there was urgency and even cordiality in his request that Sam should come over to see him as soon as he could. As Sam listened he was watching the stenographer drawing circles in her note-book round the uncompleted instructions he was giving her about getting his private papers out of the safe; and it struck him as funny that a request, which would at any other time have seemed important and gratifying, should now seem merely mildly interesting, because of the far greater importance of what he planned to do before another twenty-four hours were gone. This reflexion made him answer Blunden not as if he were flattered, but as if he were a busy man whose press of affairs prevented him from feeling more than a slight degree of pleasure at any advance from the outside world. He noted the instant reaction in Blunden's tone. The invitation was repeated with definite urgency. Sam said, 'Well, if it's like that, Mr Blunden,' and paused, in wonder; and Blunden shot in 'Or shall I come over to you?' Sam said that would not be so convenient; he had an extreme disinclination to have Mr Blunden coming over to his office, and turning those shining glasses and the dinted chin this way and that, perceiving such subtleties as this slowing down of the general pace. But, he assured him, he would come right over; and indeed he finished his instructions to his stenographer and went for his hat. There was, after all, no reason why to-day should be empty. It had come into his head several times during the morning that he would like to have soft-shell crabs for supper; and it would give him a different but not less intense pleasure to find out just why Blunden wanted to see him.

When Sam came in at the door Blunden stood up as if he were being visited by a superior officer and said, 'Congratulations to you, Mr Hartley.' He turned to his stenographer and said, 'Now we're not to be disturbed for half an hour,' and said it with a crispness that showed he was really regarding this interview as important.

Sam sat down, scratching his head. Because of something in the small, square aspect of Mr Blunden as he sat behind his desk, Sam decided to come clean. Anyway, what did it matter? He said candidly, 'Just why are you congratulating me, Mr Blunden?'

'Well, naturally because of your triumph at Washington. I was there, you know.'

'I know you were,' said Sam. 'I saw you. But did that seem to you a triumph?'

'It certainly did,' said Blunden.

Sam crossed his arms and swung one knee over the other, and laughed. Blunden looked at him with a hard perplexity, and then shot out a forefinger at him. 'I know. You haven't seen this morning's newspapers.'

Sam shook his head. He had not looked at them, any more than he had looked at his watch. They were part of something that was not going to bother him after to-night.

'You thought they were going to pan you, didn't you?' said Blunden. 'Well, none of us like that. I'm as sore as a bear when the muck-rakers get after me. But you were wrong. You had a good press. Oh, the Administration papers bawled you out all right. But the anti-Administration papers have picked you for this season's hero.'

'Uhuh?' said Sam, his head on one side.

Blunden picked up a bunch of clippings from his desk. 'Want to see 'em?'

Sam turned them over in silence.

'See what they said about your eloquence?' said Blunden. 'But that's no surprise to you. You realize, don't you, that you fetched us all out of our seats in that inquiry room?'

With a dazed smile Sam put the cuttings down again.

'I suppose you've been doing that sort of thing all your life?' pursued Blunden.

Sam said absently, 'I used to be reckoned a pretty good amateur actor when I was young.' He was resentful of the irony in this success. Here he had become a headliner, a national figure of the sort he had never managed to be in his prosperity, just when he was due to go.

Blunden seemed amused at something. 'Pretty good?' he said. 'Well, you're damned good now. But that's what you've been doing all your life, isn't it, carrying people off their feet, persuading them of things?'

'I guess so,' said Sam. 'That was how we parcelled things out in our outfit. Julius Geylor looked after the plant, and Jim saw to the financing, and I kidded the folks along.'

'That's how I figured it must have been,' said Blunden. 'Well, you preached a dandy sermon yesterday, and you did it well. There isn't an anti-Administration newspaper that isn't thrilled to death at you as a representative of the free-born American individualist, who has built up our great country with his adventurous spirit, and who is getting it in the neck now. I suppose you've read a lot about the ethics of individualism?'

'Nary a word,' said Sam. He was reckless in what he said, because there was something about the man, for all that he was so colourless, which reminded him of Jim Leavensoe; and anyway it did not matter.

'What made you make that speech, then?'

'I had to get out of that room somehow,' said Sam, 'and I guess I'd heard several people say something like that.'

Blunden put out his cigarette carefully, looking at its smouldering point with an exaggerated attention which, Sam realized, was designed to conceal with what intensity he was considering some problem. Abruptly he said, 'Take home these clippings. They'll give pretty well the complete shorthand notes of your speech, and you'll see exactly what you've said. I want you to keep it in mind, because it would be a good thing for you to be able to make it over again some time, if you accept an offer I'm going to make you. Are you free to link up with our organization?'

He had to repeat the question before he could abstract Sam from his reverie. Then Sam replied, smiling vaguely, 'Well, a friend and I were thinking of doing something together, but I guess we'll wash that right out.'

'You see, Mr Hartley, it had come into the minds of me and some of my friends that maybe we could follow up your speech and make it a mighty big thing for the country. I guess that if a sound group of business men, with at least one good name among them – and I won't say that wouldn't be mine – took hold of the Mount Couzens Corporations now, they might do something with it. I guess that if they dolled up the finances, and took advantage of the rising markets, they could get something going that would make it look a damn shame that you and your bankers had ever been treated like a bunch of crooks.'

Sam nodded, and said, in a soft, rapid murmur, 'That's so. I've thought of that. It's down so low, and the stock-holders are so discouraged, that you could steal it from them for the asking, and start fresh on a reasonable basis.'

Blunden put up his hand. 'Yes, yes, but it's the political end that interests us. We've got to keep quiet about this. It's got to look good and simple. It's the justification of the big man who takes risks we're after.'

'Of course, of course,' said Sam.

'You've got the lay-out of the whole business before you, I suppose?' said Blunden.

'I guess so. But maybe you'd better get in touch with Julius Geylor while he's still at Washington.'

'I think not,' said Blunden. 'From what I saw of Julius Geylor on the stand I don't believe he's going to be nearly as useful to us as you are, Mr Hartley. We'll leave telling him till the very last moment, when we've got everything sprung. Now, Mr Hartley, before we discuss anything else, there is the question of how you're going to stand in on this matter. We would want you to be perfectly happy and comfortable.'

When Sam got out into the street an hour later he leant against the stone lintel of the door and used his hat to shade his face from the sunlight. He had never before known sunlight feel so strong. Gradually he slid away the hat so that more and more of his skin felt this glorious burning of the thing that he had thought he was going to lose, that he had miraculously recovered. He would have liked to rip his shirt open so that he could feel it on his chest, but he must not get odd if he was going back among folks. He realized that for days his bowels had been coiled hard and tight in his body, like a snake getting ready to lie up because the winter is coming, the cold and the dark; now they felt supple and easy, like a snake on a hillside in summer. Over and over again he kept on saying, 'Jesus, Jesus, Jesus,' and let his hands shake the way they wanted. Then he hailed a taxi and drove to the best delicatessen store he could think of, a kind of English place, full of imported things, very expensive, down on Madison Avenue. He pointed to jar after jar of foods he had not tasted for years, or had never tasted, to caviare, to pâté de foie gras, to preserves that shone like jewels behind their glasses, to cock's combs, to lots of different kinds of biscuits, and he had them all put in a taxi. Then he went to a florist's, and he bought a gardenia for himself, the same as if he were going to the Opera, and some roses, red and white and bronzy-pink for Lily. Later on in the afternoon he would take some flowers over to Lulah, but he would buy those on the way. Going home in the taxi he kept on saying, 'Jesus, Jesus, Jesus,' and every time he saw the sunlight on a wall or on the trees in Central Park he groaned as if he had a twinge of toothache.

When he opened the door Lily was sitting with her elbows on the table, leaning her chin on her hands, and staring down at some dollar-bills. She looked up at him, her eyes the centres of vast blue circles, and said, in a voice weak and creaking with fatigue, 'Honey, I've been thinking.'

'What were you thinking?' he asked, amused because, whatever her thought had been, it must be changed out of all knowledge by the news he was bringing her.

'I was thinking,' Lily said, 'how'd it do if I went off and took care of Mother instead of that nurse? I looked after my own Momma when she died, and the doctor said I was grand. I'd be good to her. And maybe we could go on a little longer.'

Sam found he could say nothing. He sat down facing her on the other side of the table.

Lily dropped her great eyes. 'But if you don't think it would be decent, having me to look after Mother,' she said, 'or if you're too tired and want to stop right now, I guess that goes with me.' She brushed the dollar-bills aside with her long, bluish fingers.

Sam found that he still could not speak. He could only stare and stare and stare at her, mastering her appalling haggardness, the deep lines running down from her nose to her mouth, the stringy sinews under her chin, all the frightful ruin that her service to him had worked on her. She had no face any longer, only a tortured mask that no attempt at expression could now move. But that mask had been painted by goodness itself. There was not a line on it which had not been drawn by sacrifice, and sweetness, and devotion. And now, in this last moment, she had surpassed all that divine achievement. Because of the humility that made her doubt if she, a saint, was worthy to serve another woman, because of the selflessness that made her refuse to insist on the last chance of life, if he were too tired to avail himself of it, he found he could not speak.

At last he was able to mutter, 'Get up. I'm telling you, get up.'

She got out of her chair and stood upright, her head falling on one side, tired out.

He went to her and took her in his arms. 'Baby,' he said, 'it's all over.'

'Yeah,' she said, 'I know it.'

'No, Lily, I don't mean that at all,' he told her. 'I mean our bad time is over. We aren't going to have to do it. I got a job.'

'You got a job?' she said.

'Yeah, I got a job. A big man called Blunden's going to take over the whole of our outfit. He's going to buy a big block of shares off me to get control and get me to stand in with him. And he's going to pay me a whale of a salary.'

Faintly she asked, 'You ain't kidding me?' Then she sighed deeply and seemed about to slide down through his arms to the floor. But he tightened his grip on her, and a shudder ran through her body, and she clutched at him, crying out. He saw that for her it had not been so much that she was going to die as that she was going to lose him. Keeping her huge eyes on him, she croaked, 'Sam, Sam, my Sam', and began to cry, very painfully, as if some enemy inside her were beating with fists her ribs and stomach. He hugged her closely, murmuring, 'Lily, Lily, you're a grand kid,' and reflected that as soon as he got that lump sum he would settle something handsome on her, so that she would be all right as long as she lived. Tenderly he rocked her to and fro, and in gratitude she laid her poor worn face against his cheek. The roughness of her skin made him think of what she used to be, and what she was. There tracked through his mind a record of all she had done for him during the past few years, how she had cooked and swept and mended, and had stood by ready to companion him down to death when he needed it. He put his hand behind her head and turned her kind, lined face so that it pressed right into his cheek. He felt the fatigue, the long-standing trouble in her mind, like a defect diffused through her substance, like the heat that pervades the flesh of a fever patient. His heart swelled with pity, and he muttered, 'Why, Lily, you swell kid, Lily,' speaking flatly, overcome by his own exhaustion.

They had both had a long row to hoe, a long row. He must have a rest, and get on his feet again. He sighed deeply; and there flashed before him, as real and pricking as if he were watching a naked girl dance in a cabaret, the vision of a face unlined with care, a body still smooth and shining, undepleted by self-sacrifice, restorative with youth.

If you would like to know more about Virago books, write to us at Ely House, 37 Dover Street, London W1X 4HS for a full catalogue.

Please send a stamped addressed envelope

VIRAGO
Advisory Group

Book Tokens

Give them
the pleasure of choosing
Book Tokens can be bought
and exchanged at most
bookshops.